I used t

able to make people happy
able to give punters a good time
busy and content
able to set a good example
able to help people achieve
proud and happy
caring and sympathetic
a hard worker
an achiever
carefree with money
mean with pennies
adventurous with holidays
an innovator
a teacher
inspiring
interactive
a decision maker
controlled by the clock
the Polish pot washer
a professional grass cutter
a smart dresser
with clean shoes
a capable chef
and dogs body
a car park attendant
a toilet cleaner
a grumpy inn keeper
a Father Christmas

After nigh on 55 years in the licensed trade this is how it all started and how my life continued up to 2017 when I retired after a life as a landlord in several pubs and hotels throughout the North West which I would not have achieved without Grace by my side, the help of our loyal staff/team, and members of our families who supported us both physically and financially, also the many friends we've met along the way.

I was born at Preston Royal Infirmary in 1948 and then taken home to 19 Clovelly Dr. Penwortham which was a medium sized village on the outskirts of Preston. The house was built in engineering brick and in 1934 had cost £450. Clovelly Dr was one of many similar Rd.s spurring off the A59 which ran north/south towards Liverpool and Southport, this artery would have a major impact on my later life.

Mum Ada was a nurse and Dad Harry was a journeyman. From my earliest I cannot remember much about my parents as Ada was on nights at the hospital and Dad worked long hours at the power station situated on the banks of the Ribble. When he was at home his large greenhouse was his passion, growing tomatoes and huge chrysanthemums. The base to the greenhouse was constructed from bricks which had found their way home from my dad's work in the saddle bags on his bicycle. He had built up the soil level of our back garden because the pond in the back field flooded in winter and drowned the veg and plants in Ethel and Burts garden next door but not ours. The pond on which we kids had a raft was always one inch deeper than my wellies. Our road and all the other roads and avenues which radiated from the A59 were not very long and beyond that were open fields and farm land, lots to muck about in, and explore. All the lads from our Rd. would go out into the fields after breakfast and spend all day there till tea time unless we had a run in with the gang from the next street Carleton Dr. That is of course if we weren't at school which I wasn't too keen on.

On the corner of our St. there was a grand bungalow owned by Mr and Mrs Coulthurst the local butcher and around it was a low brick wall which was great for sitting on, we sat there for hours waiting for cars to travel by when we wrote down their registration no. and make of car. That was until Mrs Coulthurst came and shooed us away. Then we'd go to Ian Mendel's house for cold toast and if we were lucky it had sugar on it. Ian's dad Joe used to take us kids swimming to the river Douglas just off the Ribble in his old black American Packard with running boards and huge tyre containers attached to the side of the car. If the river was at low tide it was more like a mud bath but it was great fun. At a moments notice Joe would pack us all into his car and take us on a visit to Fyfe's banana warehouse at Preston docks. It was very exciting; especially the centipedes in the bananas but some of our parents were not overjoyed as Joe had not told them he was taking us on a trip.

At this point I should mention my three siblings, David, Rowland, Sylvia, and some of my extended family. David 6 yrs older was the brains of the family and went on after technical college to become a qualified electrical engineer at the power station but at the age of 22 after an operation his blood cells were adversely affected which eventually led to him suffering from manic depression. He never worked again and was in and out of hospital for the rest of his life. Rowland 4 years older lived a life I admired, out on the town, well dressed and lots of girl friends. He went on to join the R A F. Sylvia was 8 years younger. She was just a baby as I grew up; I had little to do with her.

I remember several other relatives who were scattered mainly around the Preston area. Mums Mother Grandma Robinson lived in a little two up and down at the bottom of Tulketh Rd. You entered over a freshly donkey stoned door step. She wore a black smock dress and a brilliant white apron with brown snuff all down the front. An ancient black iron fire in the kitchen cum living room and a Belfast sink with a wooden draining board in the back room. On the flagged floor was a worn out rush mat. In the small back yard there was a corrugated dolly tub and a huge mangle which was in use every Monday. In the corner stood the well used brick outside loo with the scuffed lock and a door which had a rotten jagged bottom. (sic)

My Father's parents lived in a terraced house further up the Rd. in Henderson St. We very rarely visited them and I never remember them visiting us.

Auntie Annie lived at the top of Strand Rd. near Umberto's chippy and the docks. My Mum and I often visited pushing sister Sylvia in her Pedigree pram. About 3 miles there and then back, rain or shine. Auntie Annie took in lodgers to augment her income after her black American husband died. They had met when he was drafted as a G I during the war. The huge Victorian terraced house was always alive with the latest American 45's music played on an electric radiogram. We had a wind up record player at home playing 78's. The house had exotic cooking smells of faraway places, Caribbean I think because most of her lodgers were big, dark and tall. I found out the dishes were of curried tripe, boiled pigs trotters and rice and peas. It was an exciting place to be but I don't remember ever tasting the food. Auntie had a dusky granddaughter called Sheila who was married to Bill and they lived just off Hartington Rd. I used to visit but don't remember what happened to them after about 1970.

My Mum's sister Auntie Maggie lived in Slade St. off Bow Lane. Uncle Jim and Auntie Jessie lived in Leyland. We always used to go there on Boxing Day for a Christmas buffet and fabulous sherry trifle. At the time I thought Leyland smelled strange and it wasn't until many years later I realised it was because of the paint factory, Leyland Paints. They had a daughter, Dorothy who is now married to Phil and they live in Crawley.

Our road was still unadopted by the council and it was up to the residents to fill in any potholes usually with ashes from the household fires. When the weather was dry it was dusty and if wet there were puddles which us kids used to join together to drain away the murky water in riverlettes. It was great for playing marbles. I had loads of large and small coloured crystal glass alleys. Mum used to give me a telling off when I went in muddy and dirty, but it was soon forgotten.

Clovelly Dr. on our side had 7 semi-detached houses so 14 residences in total and a small plot of scrubland. At the top was Newlands Ave. which made it T shaped, this Ave's ends didn't go anywhere except to the fields on the left and to a pond on the right where we would go fishing for sticklebacks. Apart from the Gemson family, the boys being Rowli's pals we didn't have anything to do with the other residents. On the right of the St. there was a similar no. of houses but they were one house up because of the bungalow at the bottom. At no. 21 next door lived Ethel and her brother Burt. They were quite elderly and Ethel used to have a nap in the afternoons. When I was young I was encouraged to have a sleep with her whilst my mother had a rest before making tea and going on nights at Whittingham Hospital. At the house adjoining ours lived Mrs. Adams and next door was a young family with a small daughter, and then there was the Hardmans. Steve being my age and an elder good looking daughter, well Rowland thought so. About this time, where there had been an empty plot between no. 3 and no. 9 two new houses were built.

When I was in my early teens I thought Gillian at no.1 was hot. Probably my first crush but after walking past, just by chance, on several occasions it came to nothing. The family moved when she was about 13 to Winmarliegh Rd. Ashton. Half way up on the other side lived the Mendel's a family of 6 children, Mum and Dad Joe. Ian was the eldest son who we used to knock about with. The last family I remember were the Outrams who lived at no.24. Mum, Dad, son Brian and daughter Jean. Both the kids were older than us but Dad Jim who was a retired policeman kept us amused with funny faces and would frighten us when he took out his false teeth.

Time passed without any major incidents that concerned me or that I didn't know about. Because mum worked nights I started nursery school when I was 3½ at Howick, then at 5 I attended Penwortham Primary in Miss. Pickup's class, I remember the nit nurse and playing in the playground come rain or shine. School holidays stretched out forever in the warm and sunny days of July and August when we explored our local environs. All about 1sq.mile which we thought was the world. At this time our Rd. was adopted by the local council and eventually workmen came, dug big holes for drains and services, laid pavements and the Rd. had a smooth layer of tarmac. This caused disruption in the area but made the Rd. friendlier to traffic and the corona pop mans wagon didn't rattle quite so much. As kids we were allowed two or three comics, the Eagle and either the Beano or Dandy. Later on Sylvia had a girlie comic. On Saturday mornings we would go to ABC minors at the cinema were a guy called Uncle Joe would try and control a couple of hundred lively kids, he never found out who dropped the stink bombs, what? The pictures were obviously aimed at a young audience with characters like Superman and Popeye and in some of the films you could see the wires that the rockets and characters were being controlled with but great fun. There was always an exciting cowy.

Then everything changed and I suddenly grew up.

After a long hot summer suddenly a new school loomed, not just any school but Penwortham Secondary, new teachers, new students and new classrooms with a new timetable. We were the dross who hadn't passed the 11 plus and therefore were not eligible for Hutton Grammar. The school for the elite kids.

I settled into this way of life and just got on with the structured education 5 days a week with homework after school and the only too short weekends.

When I was 12 an event occurred that affected my future. Rowland had taken his evening paper round but on arriving home realised he had missed a paper for a house across the main A59 so I was dispatched with the said paper. Probably being miffed, I did not look both ways when crossing the Rd. I awoke in Preston Royal Infirmary missing my two front teeth. After a period of time I was fitted with two false teeth which over some years developed into a full set.

Family holidays were few and far between. In my early years we (Mum, Dad and us two young ones) visited the Isle of Wight and when I was 12 we holidayed at Butlins in Pwllheli North Wales. Butlins was lively and nonstop fun but the accommodation consisted of tiny cramped terraced chalets with outside showers and toilet facilities which put me off caravans and narrow boats for life.

About this time one of my friends was Alan bailey who lived at the last house in Moorhey drive on the corner of the ginnel that went to Green Dr. I mention this because they had the first ITV television. It was a slim t.v. on spindly legs with two channels, BBC and ITV. Wow! To get to his house we'd go to the top our Rd. and across the field.This was just before the developers acquired the land for development.

Within a few years acres and acres of green belt was swallowed up in the name of progress. After the workmen had gone home it was a great adventure playground. A few ceilings ended up holed because one of us missed a ceiling beam and a few measures were moved on the building plots. We thought it great fun but I'm sure there were choice words used by the builders when they came to work the next day. Very shortly after this I discovered the need for money and as pocket money was only about 2 shillings a week there was only one other way to create it honestly, work.

I did the milk round. Jumping off and on the milk float from early in the morning till lunch, getting a shilling's pay if you were lucky and nearly getting killed by other vehicles. I decided there must be something better. On fine days we'd walk down to the River Ribble and collect pop bottles which would be taken to the offie for 2d refund. I thought we could cut out all the travelling to and from the river by shimming over the offie wall and helping ourselves. The lady got suspicious when we got greedy and tried to refund a soda siphon bottle for 5shillings. The job was up. So for a bob or two from neighbours for odd jobs and on one occasion I went for coddy muck from Crookings farm for my dad's roses. I only took the wheelbarrow twice as it was two miles away and it stunk. He also got me to creosote the garden fence without wearing any sleeves. The following day my arms were covered in blisters from the creosote. No one had heard of risk assessment in those days.

Whilst talking about Dad I should mention that after the lean-to and green house which he'd already erected he went on to build a brick garage with an asbestos corrugated roof and inspection pit for his car which was a big improvement from the motorbike and sidecar. About this time dad decided to move the kitchen into the glass lean-to creating more room inside for a dining room. The lean-to was hot in the summer and freezing in winter especially first thing in the morning. Rowland took morning and evening newspapers to people's houses from the newsagents and when there was a vacancy at Waterhouses paper shop for a paper boy I jumped at it. Little realising the downsides to the job, early mornings, rain and freezing cold weather, but it paid well, 1 shilling and 6d for evening and 2 shillings for mornings. Other rates applied for Sundays (boy were they heavy) and the Saturday sports. I didn't like doing the latter because I couldn't get out early. That was a couple of years hence when we'd go to St. Mary's hall for the Saturday night dance. This job helped me to save up enough to purchase a brand new Sun bicycle. It was bright yellow with drop handle bars and Disraighly gears. My pride and joy. Part of the Penwortham round took me to Parry's farm which was down Blasaw Lane and through a wood adjacent to my school. It was fine walking through this wood to school during the day but on dark, cold winter nights there seemed to be a ghostly stranger behind every tree and bush. Some of the papers did not arrive at the farm. This situation continued till I was 15 when on a very cold and dark winter's morning my fingers froze to a metal gate in Stanley Grove and I thought; sod this for a game of soldiers.

St.Mary's hall played a prominent part in my life starting with Sunday school and later the youth club from about age 13 which took place upstairs in the old village hall. It was an old Victorian building with a huge hall and stage on the ground floor and a large room with lots of smaller rooms and nooks and crannies upstairs. The smaller rooms were mostly out of bounds to us inquisitive teenagers, but we enjoyed exploring whenever the opportunity arose. Of course there was a price to pay both for the youth club and Sunday school; we were encouraged to attend St. Mary's church every Sunday at least once. Have you been to church this week? Oh yes sir.

The 60's music was a revelation to us kids and we lived from one Sunday to the next listening to the top 20 and after January of 1964 we'd huddle round the t.v. every

Thursday to watch top of the pops. Turn that rubbish down! At this time I discovered Radio Luxembourg which I would listen to late into the night with my transistor turned up high under the bedclothes. Our lives revolved around these great events especially at weekends. 60's music was fantastic and some of the 70's and I will always remember the Rolling Stones, Beatles, Animals, and all those free love songs of 66 and 67 like Don't go to Sanfrancisco. Bob Dylan was introduced to me by Mick Morris whilst he was at Bolton Tech. The only major change that came my way was because my mum who baked 2 or 3 times a week she encouraged me to help her bake cup cakes, Victoria sandwich sponges and jam tarts. At school I was bored with wood and metalwork so I asked to join cookery classes. This had never been done before, but after much discussion it was allowed. There were pro's and con's to this. Believe it or not I have always been shy around girls but it taught me to get on with the opposite sex as I had no option. Some of my mates thought I had gone soft, others saw me as a way of getting introduced to lots of girls. This was probably my introduction to girls which then got in the way of my music lessons learning to play a Boossey and Hawkes clarinet, which in later life regretted.

At this time I should mention that at birth I was born with what appeared to be six toes on my left foot which during my younger years had no adverse affect on me but I was now advised that it may have in later life, so a decision was made to have a toe removed. This ended up a little more complicated than was first thought. As the three small toes were webbed and the middle one had no bone in it, there was no option but to remove two toes. This surgical operation was carried out at Wrightington Hospital near Wigan and necessitated a stay of one week (today it would be a day's job.) I couldn't wait to get out and when I did, much to Ada's Char - grin I was out on the town on my first night wearing winkle pickers.

I am now into the last 2 years at secondary school which had not had any great success with me. I remember Mr McKinnock who was a maths teacher at which I did not excel but he did teach me a little German. I was good at running on the track but not cross country. All cold, muddy and wet. I found that my interest in weight lifting and training got me out of the field and track events in the cold and as I achieved good results I was encouraged by the sports teacher to also train at lunchtime. It certainly did build up body muscle which in later life had two major effects on me. More later. I also used to play squash which continued into my late 20's when pressure of work got in the way. After the 5 years I achieved 1 ULCI and 3 GCE's. Cookery, English and Geography. These enabled me to go on to further education at Lancaster College (now called university) other events first.

1963. Because of Mothers work as a nurse and now as a district nurse she had made a lot of contacts and she knew everybody and everything about everyone. When I was 15 one of these people, probably after Ada had just mentioned it, a weekend 'chef's' job was available at the Plough at Freckleton. This was a real wake up call. Out in the big world with adults who expected you to get on and do. Not necessarily being a real 'chef 'as I told everyone but I was expected to turn up, on time and earn my keep. As always in licensed premises there are many stories. The chef used to concoct many dishes with rum in the ingredients such as rum baba or Caribbean chicken, the rum had to be requisitioned from the bar then most of it disappeared down his throat, he'd then use the rum essence from his store cupboard to flavour the dish. In later life when dining out I often queried head waiters about the spirit content of certain dishes. On busy occasions which meant we finished late it was too late to catch the last bus so one or two of us would sleep over on the bar seating with a blanket. Being young and not knowing these things happened I was somewhat surprised to find a hand crawling up my leg. Not knowing who was at the end of the arm I knew it shouldn't be there so I lashed out, heard an OUCH and went back to sleep. In the morning one of the waiters had gone home very early. Shortly after this a vacancy arose at the Ship Inn, still in Freckleton overlooking the Ribble estuary.

The downside to both of these establishments was the travelling time and the bus fare which amounted to 2 shillings return each day from a wage of 10 shillings each day. Just think, 1 pound for two days work minus the bus fare = 80p. However to put it in prospective a pint of beer was 1s10d about 9p in today's money.

So with £1 you could have a good night out. Much more of that later.

After leaving there I went to the Rams Head at Tarleton working in the kitchen. This didn't last long as I had a disagreement over a long distance telephone call I had not made but they had been charged for. Yes I did know how to tap out a telephone number, which you could do in those days. The call was to Scotland and yes I did know a girl in Scotland who I had met on the I.O.Man. I did not make the calls. At weekends I'd sleep over in a partioned off caravan which was kitted out with damp bed linen and cockroaches putting me off caravans etc.again for life. The Rose and Crown in Much Hoole was my next pub working as a bar waiter with Mick Morris. Bar waiting on was of the time, sometimes with bells to summon the waiter. Good tips, usually two and a half pence (1.5d).

He was 18 and I was 16 but nobody asked, so what, the pay was good and the tips we usually spent on beer. The tables in the lounge were close together which Mick and I weaved our way in and out of much to the trepidation of the customers especially as the night went on and our beer consumption increased. The bar was central and behind the lounge was the restaurant which was very popular. Lunch was 10 shillings for 3 courses and dinner 12s 6d. Remember in those days there were no micro-waves so the crust on the daily pie was crustier at the end of service and if you required pink beef you made an early reservation. There were two sisters, I think twins, Carol and Sue. I took a liking to Carol but she had a big boyfriend so I hid my glowing light under a bushel. Years later they married. A previous landlord at the pub, Albert Pierpont had been the last public hangman. Mick the other waiter was a very clever and knowledgeable guy. If you wanted to know anything about anything you asked Mick. The trouble was he'd tell you whether you did or not. Around this time I went on to work at the Fleece Inn in Penwortham again as a floor waiter with Gerry a mid forties guy. The landlords were Stan and Molly. I'm sure characters of the landlords Jack and Annie in Coronation St. had been created with them in mind. Their son who Stan adored was a County cricket player and on one occasion, Stan showing a customer his son Wilfs bowling technique bowled the customers change to him and the customer bowled it back to him. Stan was not a happy bunny. The brewery at that time was Groves and Withnall later to become Greenall Whitley. Usual pub games were played but it was the first were I had seen Bull ring being played were you had to get a bulls nose ring attached to a piece of string onto a hook screwed to the wall. Very difficult to accrue points which were awarded for different positions on the hook which had a v cut into the end of it. Great fun. Stan and Molly ran a very straight pub and the only way was theirs, or out you go. At that time the food offerings were pork pie with English mustard, pickled eggs and salt or crisps. Plain Smiths of course with the little salt twist inside the packet. Opposite the pub there was a fish shop then a chemist and next to that Coulthursts butchers, as mentioned previously.

After that I went to the Railway Inn on Butler St. next to Preston railway station. At weekends there was a quartet fronted by the landlord Wally on his double bass. A busy local town pub. After meeting Jean at the Fleece where she worked I was impressed by her fabulous legs, we moved together into a house at the bottom of Christian Rd. which in all honesty was a dump. However being young and stupid and not wishing to going back home as Ada said I should because 'no good will come of it' I married Jean at the registrars office in Guildhall St. when I was 20. The do was held at the Railway which is where I still worked part time and full time at Leyland Motors, this situation carried on for a couple of years in which time I had moved to Alcester Ave. and I will chronicle what happened later in the story when her two young children who never accepted me and me probably the same for different reasons came to a head. My last job in a pub working for somebody else around 1973 was at the Blue Anchor in Hutton owned by Billy who was helped by his lady friend Molly. I was sort of head hunted for this job because Billy wanted an experienced barman. I wanted to be a waiter because of the tips but Billy paid me double pay to be behind the bar at £3.00 per night which at the time was very good. I learnt a lot of the tricks of the trade at the Anchor. Because Hutton was approximately half way between Liverpool and Blackpool, during lights season many of the charabancs used to stop for a quick drink, sandwich and a pee. There was no food available in the pub but next door there was a huge wooden building known as the tea rooms. All those wanting food would go there, and the rest would retire to the pub for twenty minutes after which time the bus driver would usher his customers back on to the bus. Not always an easy task. Billy always with his two corgis would run round the big car park putting the buses in order for a quick getaway. This car parking experience came in handy later on. During the season we were packed out especially at weekends and on one particular busy Friday night I mentioned this to Billy and he remarked that we'd had 100 buses on their way to Blackpool and 60 on their return. I earned my double pay.

We also used to practice a regular customer preference. Billy thought that the coach people took glasses away with them, which they did if they couldn't finish their drinks in time and some damage was caused occasionally. So we added a 1d to all of their drinks. When the floor waiters shouted out their orders at the bar they would insert either lettuce or cabbage into it. This distinguished to the barman that the cabbage order had a premium price. They could hardly have shouted regular or visitor. It was in the interest of the regulars (who generally kept away during the season) to keep their mouths shut. After these sessions the place was a tip and after closing at 10 30pm we would have to clean the pub and toilets. All the chairs put up on tables with their legs wiped, rubbish removed, all the cleaner had to do was mop and Hoover in the morning. After we'd finished Molly would offer us any leftover food from the tea rooms and Billy would give us a drink which was much appreciated. The bus was my main form of transport at that time so by the time I'd finished it was a long walk home and up early for my shift at Leyland Motors. One other function I remember working at was at Blackpool Winter Gardens as a barman. How or where this job came from I can't remember but I learnt an insight into the dark side of the licensed trade. At that time gin was a popular ladies drink, they say everything comes around. Gin was flying out that night. All the glasses were standing upside down in a tray of liquid, the liquid was gin and the lemon slices were laced with gin on another tray. So on service the glass rim is soaked in gin; add a slice of lemon soaked in gin, lots of ice, and a measure from the gin bottle which is full of water and use 2 bottles of tonic for three drinks to finish off the perfect gin and tonic. The customer has the strong taste of gin from the rim of the glass and says 'wow that's strong'. Adjust the till and those in the know split the profit and shazam, double wages. I wasn't in the loop. Honest.

Let's go back to being 15/16. By 1963 still at school but working weekends (which with hindsight I wished I hadn't because it stopped me getting involved with the trips and games that my disappearing mates did then) however it gave me money in my pocket which at the time I didn't think I could manage without. The youth club became a bit juvenile and instead two or three of us would jump on a P5 bus into town. In those days we were smartly dressed, shirt, tie, suit or jacket and clean shoes. We could find several pubs to drink in including the Victoria and Station and the Bull and Royal cocktail bar in the centre of town. Both very smartand we were never once challenged about our age.

Coffee bars were a big attraction at the time both for the frothy coffee and the girls.

I remember the Cedarwood in Winckly St, the Torrela on Friargate and the Coffee Bean in Bamber Bridge.

School came to an end and three of us went off to the Isle of Man for a holiday in 1964. There was Sam Nigh, Pod Hodson and I. Never go on holiday or anywhere as a three some. The other two were best mates and I was left on the side but I soon remedied that when I teamed up with Pat. She was from Scotland, holidaying with her parents who I never met. We'd walk round Douglas and sit holding hands on the cliffs overlooking the harbour listening to Hard day's night by the Beatles and the loud fog horn when the mist was down. There was a lot of sea mist around the island. When she went home we promised to write and telephone each other which we did for some time and on two occasions I set off to visit but never got further than Lancaster. Shortly after that I teamed up with Geoff Green to plan a holiday around Europe. We had limited expenses and limited knowledge of the Continent but what the hell it sounded good. I had £50 in my pocket when we set off on this epic journey which was estimated to last about one month. We thumbed down to Dover, across the Channel by ferry arriving slightly intoxicated at Calais. Where to now? Toss a coin and off to Brussels, then after several car rides we came to Karlsruhe in Germany. It was a lovely sunny day and the day stretched out in front of us. On our travels we had met some interesting people and with a lot of pigeon English had in general managed to be understood. Standing on the roadside at the junction of the Autobahn we couldn't believe our luck when a guy in an open topped Mercedes offered us a lift. He was travelling all the way to Bregenz in Austria via Munich. The journey took several hours with a refreshment stop at a road side food stop were we had bratwurst with loads of German mustard and onions.

Travelling through such beautiful and spectacular scenery was outstanding and we soon arrived at our destination where there is a huge lake called Bregenzsee. Geoff had arranged to see some distant relatives and we went to their chalet house on a hillside surrounded by huge trees. All I can remember is being fed on yoghurt and picking blueberries which grew in abundance all around in the fields. It reminded me of the sound of music. We stayed there for a few days and I was fortunate to have a trip on the lake with a beautiful young blonde, a blue eyed maiden called Heidi. Perhaps the yoghurt and blueberries were not all I remembered. After a few days we went on our way travelling to Lichtenstein but we got no further because we didn't have the correct visas. So, about turn and return home, our route then took us through Switzerland where we went to Basil and Baden-Baden. Beautiful scenery and staggering mountain views. At some time during our return home Geoff decided to go his own way. I think because he met a girl and wanted to spend some time with her. Threesomes again. So I just had enough of the £50 left for a 2nd class rail ticket all the way back to Preston. I didn't fancy thumbing all the way across Europe on my own. That was the end of the summer holidays and so off to Lancaster College to expand my catering education. My parents had received a £50 grant for this purpose which was to go towards books, knives, chef's whites etc. How times change, today it cost us parents thousands to send our kids to Uni. I also had a rail card as each day I took the journey by train to Castle station Lancaster. The carriages were now drawn by diesel engines and were void of corridors, so god help you if you were taken short. Any hanky panky, if there were just two of you had to wait till after Garstang station. Well we were young, being educated at school and learning lessons in life.

Most of these first year students had no catering experience so I got fed up putting my hand up to answer the questions as I had previous Knowledge of from school and catering kitchens. I learnt to keep quiet and after two years progressed to Courtfield College in Blackpool for 1 year. Blackpool was to become home for a short period after that and also later on when I was a relieve manager for Bass.

Back now to being 17 in 1965.

Life revolved around college, folk clubs, working weekends in pubs and drinking in pubs anytime. Remember with a quid in your pocket you could have a damn good time. Mick had a car which enabled us to get to the Rose and Crown for work and venture to other country pubs. The fleece Inn which was nearest was out of bounds because they knew our age but there were many more that didn't seem to bother. These included The Sun, (Rowli's favourite) The Lamb Inn, Black horse which had a cocktail bar upstairs called Sully's, the Boars head and the Lamb and packet which were all situated on Friargate. Also several pubs on Lancaster Rd. but never in Yates's Wine lodge which we associated with ladies of the night, Aussie wine and sawdust strewn floors. Harry my dad and David used to visit there on their Friday night stroll around some of Preston's bars which my dad would call "a trip out to watch the chukkies dance". It took me years before I realised the meaning of this phase. By this time I regularly used Mick's car to knock about in when he wasn't using it. After six months or so I passed my driving test, first time as I reached age 17. This was probably down to my self help driving lessons. The one time I nearly got into trouble was on a very rainy day when I was visiting a nurse called Kay in Blackpool. The roads were like lakes and Mick's car floor was made of wooden planks. I ploughed into a puddle, the engine stalled and I was left high and dry. sic. A policeman approached and offered assistance for which I was very grateful and relieved when he said 'safe journey home sir'. Kay the young lady was a trainee nurse at Blackpool Victoria Hospital and lived in Cleveleys but when on duty stayed in the nurse's home which of course did not welcome gentlemen callers. The architects who designed the building hadn't banked on nurses who lived on the ground floor having swing up and down windows. On one of these visits I borrowed David's 150 cc motorbike of which I had no experience and on my return I came off at the junction of Strand Rd. and Fishergate Hill because the lights changed suddenly and I slid to a holt. At 2am there was no other traffic so I wheeled the bike home and kept stum, and never set foot on a bike again. I still have an aversion to motorbikes to this day.

I remember that there were 3 bus stations in and around Preston, one in Starch House square at the top of Orchard St., another off Lancaster Rd. which was the terminus for Ribble buses and the Fishwick bus terminal was at the bottom of Fox St. The destination for these buses was Leyland. At the corner of the entrance to the Ribble bus station was a fantastic sandwich shop called The Sandwich Shop. The fillings in the sandwiches exceeded the thick bread and there was a huge selection, only sold as one round or multiples of the said sarnnies because they were so big.

As mentioned previously I dressed smartly and had my hair cut at Kershaw's in Winckley Sq. and bought some of my clothes from Lingards on Fishergate, especially shirts and also Hellewells in Lune St. were I would buy Daks trousers. Guy Walsh was a director of the company and a friend which helped when it came to the discount. We drank together in the Fleece in later years; sorry should have said he drank in the Fleece, treble gin and tonics, yes treble. He died early, in his fifties. This life style was expensive so whilst working the pubs I also had several other jobs. Sold houses for Anthony Holdsworth in Blackburn, £5 per house, visited farms selling chickens and cages to farmers. This job came with a Vauxhall Victor which had a column change, a big boot and a full length front seat, but at one farm where I told the farmer that our American Welp chickens were superior to his Rhode Island Reds he set his dogs on me. End of job.

One of my favourite cakes was and still is a custard slice which Ada had bought from the local bakery and which I devoured. Suddenly I am whisked off to hospital for an appendix operation, then the doctors realised it wasn't my appendix at fault but I had contacted Typhoid from the Chinese dried egg used in the preparation of the cake. I then spent the best part of 2 weeks in the Infectious disease Hospital on the corner of Blackpool and Deepdale Rd. I was cosseted by the nurses and was given Iodine baths daily which was lost on me at the time. Whilst there a girl I had known for a few weeks visited me regularly but I asked her not to because her mother looked and acted like an old battle-axe. "Look at the mother". After my recovery a new world opened up. Back to Blackpool.

A vacancy arose with Lobster Pot Group which was part of the Top Rank Group in their Market St. restaurant. I was employed as an assistant manager, which meant floor walker or crowd controller dressed in tails and striped trousers. All the 5 outlets in Blackpool were extremely busy and I could be operational at any branch for which I started out on a salary of £5 per week. I found a little bedsit on Waterloo Rd. for £2.50 per week (work out the sums) and settled down to working shifts. We were allowed 2s6d for lunch which just about covered a sandwich or a dessert. However the chefs sometimes took pity on us and slipped us leftover scraps. I would return home whenever, especially if I had some washing. This was another expense I could little afford so after some weeks I plucked up courage and asked the boss for an increase.

Surprisingly he agreed to an increase to £8 per week. There's a lesson in life, if you don't ask you don't get. This situation lasted for several months but I could not see any future in it so I came back to Penwortham, living at home but having discovered the joys and some advantages of a not being under parental control this situation didn't last long either. During my life I have never been out of work, perhaps with breaks in between but something always turned up. A situation arose for a demonstrator with North West Electricity Board at their branch on Friargate. Mother knew the manager. The job was really a sales assistant with cooking experience so that I could demonstrate the latest electrical white goods and vacuum cleaners. Very tame but it had its moments. The sales, because of commission were sown up by the two seniors, Mrs. Beer and Velda (she made fabulous burnt toast at break time thickly spread with butter) One day a couple, who looked like they didn't have 2 bob two rub together viewed several appliances. The seniors disappeared and left me to deal with the customers. I enquired as to their requirements and was most surprised at the list: a washing machine (Bendix) a refrigerator, a cooker (Tricity) a freezer and a Hoover Senior upright vacuum. Assuming they would require H.P. I enquired if they would like to purchase them on the "never

never" for which I thought they would be refused, the man put his hand in his pocket and peeled off the correct amount. The seniors were somewhat miffed but the manager congratulated me on my sales technique. I also remember either being late on a few occasions or turning up rather worse for wear because on warm summer nights we'd head off to Lytham and a mixed group of us would have some fun in the sand dunes, (sand does get everywhere) arriving home early the next day, sometimes going straight to work.

Just around the corner in the new St. Johns shopping centre was Wisemans Electrical, again selling white goods, TVs, radios, gramophones and it had a record department of which 75% of the customers were young women. A new concept at the time was for the public to have the goods now and when they wanted them. The old way was to save up and wait till you had the money but there was a new innovative idea. Buy now, pay later. This concept caught the imagination of the public to the extent that they thought "why should we wait"? It's there, let's have it today. We were enthusiastically encouraged to promote the "never never" payment system and for some people that was exactly what it amounted to because they would build up so much credit that it was "never" paid off.

Although these jobs paid a decent salary I soon got bored doing shop work 9 to 5 and at the time my situation had altered because of higher overheads due to becoming a house holder with the help of the bank and a mortgage.

There was one other major change at this time. At nineteen I left home due to me becoming involved with a girl called Jean who worked at the Fleece. Mother did not approve, but being of an age when you think you know everything, did I care? Ada had a lot on her plate at this time. David was resident in Whittingham Hospital and Harry who had been ill for many years was now seriously ill and died at the age of 59. All his life he had been in the building industry, being involved in building many of the large government buildings in Preston which he'd tell me about as we passed by. However his final situation as foreman, which he'd held for many years, was at the power station on the Ribble. Apart from general building jobs he and his team were involved in relining the furnaces and this work as well as being dangerous was incredibly dusty. At the time I don't think they'd heard of risk assessment and the men would be breathing in all this dust and in the end Harry died from broncol problems. In those days no one had heard of compo.

As I've mentioned houses I will relate to the properties I've lived in:

Christian Rd. (rented)

Alcester Ave.

Birch Ave.

Rawsthorne Rd.

Honeyfields. (Investment)

Westholme Cl. (started as an investment and later became our home)

There was a break for a few years after I left Rawsthorne Rd. until Grace and I bought Honeyfields in Tarporley because previously the monies we had were invested in the licensed trade. It was important to us at that time that we had a home to fall back on just in case. The licensed trade is a very fickle business and I have always advised prospective licensee couples to be prepared and have an exit strategy.

Living now in Alcester Ave. with a mortgage my need for increased wages due to larger outgoings I decided to go into industry as the opportunity for higher income was opportune. I was employed at Leyland Motors in their south works as a welder. This situation came about through the recommendation from a pal of mine called Jim. God

13

knows what he told the PR department about me to encourage them to give me the job. I think somebody must have owed Jim a favour.

This came as a shock to the system and I soon learnt to knuckle down to as the benefits in increased pay outnumbered the boring repetitive work. It became a battle between the shop floor and the rate fixers which with the help and connivance of the union we always ended up on the right side. This meant that we always had time for extended breaks and time to read the daily paper, usually sat on the toilet. "Where have you been Smith"? "On the toilet sir'was the usual reply to the foreman if he caught you on his inspection tour after he'd read his paper. It was at his time, '72 that the miners decided they'd had enough of the bosses and called a national strike which impacted us all between '72 and '74, eventually causing the three day week Jan 1st to March 6th; this led to wage shortages and became a great trial to many. How British industry ever succeeded I'll never know. A little side line I had was selling quilted hooded jackets which I bought from Cheetam Hill in Manchester which cost me £2.50 and sold for a fiver. Good business and I was to make better profit margins after I met a guy in the Olde Cock Inn Didsbury who said he manufactured these jackets and could let me have them at a slightly cheaper price. Everything went well for several months until the supply of certain sizes started to be erratic and it was then that I discovered that this manufacturer had actually been selling us knock off goods. Our business association ceased immediately, which was a shame. I also had a little line in ladies knickers which I would advertise when I went out by putting a colourful pair in my top pocket, like a hanky. They did good business too. Two mistakes I did make was buying a load of silk nylons just when girls went over to wearing tights and I bought (very cheap) a whole load of pottery plant pots which this guy was getting rid of just as growers were moving over to pots an inch bigger. Couldn't sell them for love nor money, but eventually I sold them for very little profit and a headache. Lesson learnt.

The Leyland Motors situation lasted for 5 or 6 years working shifts which consisted of days or nights at about £40 per week (5 days) and £10 extra if you worked nights (4 nights) which played havoc with your life style. I should just mention that one day in '72 I came home one morning after doing the night shift to find Alcester Rd. gutted out, even the new carpets which I'd paid for with a win on the Grand National. ('Well to do' won that year) I never saw Jean again.

Also in '72 Preston Guild which is celebrated every 20 yrs. in Sept. with a huge festival of marching bands, tabloids on lorries which depicted the various industries, charitable organizations and the churches were all represented which go to make up the diverse Preston communities. The roads and streets are decked in bunting and flags from all over the world and whilst the march snaked its way around the town the streets are lined with all the armed forces and are thronged with just about every person who lived and have lived at one time or another in Preston. They are proud Prestonians. P.P. I didn't get to enjoy much of the celebrations because of my many work commitments which in later life I came to question.

During this time I was working at Leyland and was mostly on days whilst working at the Blue Anchor at weekends which didn't leave me much vacant time to get bored. I remember green flared trousers and shoes with chunky heels which were called lifts, oh and long curly hair in the cavalier fashion. It was whilst working at the Blue Anchor that I met Hazel and after about 9 months we were married at Penwortham Congregational church and Barry was born in 1976 whilst living at Beech Av. on a new housing estate. At about this time I was offered a job managing Happy Haddock chip shop on Plungington

Rd. just at weekends for Terry who was the lessee and he was finding it too much hard work for him. So I packed in the bar work and became a part time chippy. So much for my catering experience. Terry taught me how to make a 2oz fillet of sprag cod look like a whale and how to squeeze out the fish worms which were prevalent in cod at certain times of the year. I learned which the best potatoes to fry were and how to make batter and mushy peas. Terry's menu was not very extensive and so over a short period I expanded it with items like potato scallops, battered black pudding, sausages, haggis and mars bars. Anyhow after a few months Terry decided to retire and seeing what a good opportunity this was I decided to jump in on a full time basis. The rent was £200 per week which everyone thought was outlandish, but I knew the potential of the business. So I left Leyland Motors and became a lease holder to Happy Haddock Ltd. and I became self employed which in itself was quite scary but I soon became accustomed to the strange hours. Sunday was my day of rest which usually meant catching up with all the gardening and other household jobs that had been neglected during the week because of the demanding hours at the shop. During the summer, especially in the holidays business was very brisk and thankfully I had helpful staff who were usually ladies, so the majority of the heavy work (peeling spuds and gutting fish) fell to me. Thank god for the potato rumbler this took off the peel but did not extract the eyes. This was a long and tedious task and before it was o.k. to eat the skins. You now pay a premium for skin on fries. Having staff also had its plus side and gave me the opportunity to 'nip out' at quiet times which was about 9.30pm most nights. Luckily just around the corner no more than 20yds. away was the Plungington Tavern, I would nip round for a quick one or two standing in the off sales dept. Out of site of the other customers but not out of smell range. Some of them could smell the chip shop aroma which was embedded in my clothes and I could hear them remarking that they fancied a fish supper. Job done, this became my excuse for my nipping out for a quick one most nights. Another local haunt was the Withy Trees which was on Lytham Rd. adjoining Garstang Rd. and was a much more upmarket public house. (Closed in 2020)

Over the next 3 yrs several events happened in quick succession which would have a great effect on my future. Gave up my lease at Happy Haddock and decided to set up a f&c shop in Chorley on the corner of Bolton Rd. and Pall Mall, the area known locally as The Big Lamp. This was a very successful move but Chorley was not for me. All the women had a shopping trolley and went to either the long hair hairdressers or the short hairdressers so after a short period I moved closer to home and bought a shop in Lostock Hall which also had a hairdressing saloon on the 1st. floor. Now this soon became a very successful business and I settled down there and also became involved in the local community where I set up and became Chair of Lostock Hall Community Action Group which I had manipulated from the outset because I wanted to be in the chair. It had been suggested to me by Anne the local labour councillor that I should mention my name during the inaugural meeting as often as possible so that people would remember me and not those that they could not remember their names, it had the intended result, I was voted Chairman. Like all business there can be downsides and mine was the local youths who would congregate outside making a nuisance of themselves because of the light from the shop. Often I would write on the window advertising special offers and the next day they would have rubbed it all off, so clean the window and write it all again. Ah ha, write it backwards on the inside with white shoe marker pen. That flummoxed them. One little tip perhaps I can pass on is an incident that taught me a lesson which I have remembered to this day. A customer brought back a Holland's meat pie which she said was bad so I duly mentioned this to the delivery driver. He said give it to me and the company will test it and we'll get back to you. After several days I enquired as to their findings to be told it had been lost in transit and guess what I hadn't a leg to stand on. Case closed but Grace and I used this valuable lesson later on. Another fauxpas I committed was when two swarthy Italian guys came to the shop selling rolls of suit material at very good prices and were on their way home to Italy after a clothing exhibition in Manchester and didn't want the bother of taking the material home so would give me a very good 'disconti'. Being a mug I bought a suit length and handed over a cheque which I believed would be safe. Then I went round to see Guy at Hellewells to be told there were so many snags in the material that it wouldn't even make a perfect sleeve. Round to the bank to find that the cheque had been cashed that morning. Another lesson in life.

Still living in Birch Ave in 1976 our son Barry was born at Sharoe Green Hospital, a little bundle of joy. He had all the attributes of the Smith clan including a little extra small piece of skin on the side of his toes which was removed at that point and after a week mother and baby returned home. I was always at work or the pub and perhaps did not play my part as a doting father.

A new public house opened at the end of our Ave. called the Tom Finney. The landlord was Sid Blofeld who with his wife Pauline ran a very friendly foodie pub where I would spend too many hours having the odd one, or two with my friend Archie. Archie lived with his wife Jo just a few houses away on Birch Ave with his two sons. We spent many a happy late hour listening to our favourite music which consisted of ELO, Elton, REM and any 60's music. Some years later he and his wife Jo split and she was replaced by another lady called Jo. (Lads might think about that) About 15 yrs. ago Christmas cards were sent as usual but one didn't return and it was only the following year when another Christmas greeting was sent that we received a message from his then new partner informing us that Archie had died the previous year. His new partner was a girl he'd known from school, what a lad.

Sid and Pauline went on to manage the Black Bull in Fulwood which was and still is a premier Bass house which I would later go on to do some of my Bass management training.

In 1977 we acquired a new house, No. 7 Rawsthorne Rd. which wasn't a new house but a quaint Victorian ram-shackled semi detached cottage for the price of £7.000. The money was scraped together from the sale of Birch Ave. a small mortgage and Bob the helpful bank manager. Always keep on the right side of your bank Manager. Bob would discuss the news, the day's topics and eventually ask why you wanted a meeting. He always acceded to my request for a small loan to help the business which was not always the real purpose of the loan. The house needed a lot of refurbishment and the tangled garden which was surrounded by an overgrown high hedge also needed a makeover with a digger to rip out the brambles. Inside all the electrics and plumbing were in a disastrous state and needed replacing and the plaster was knocked off up to a metre high to install a damp course as the original cottage didn't have one. On completion and after several visits to Bob the house was a picture and probably my favourite house, but I had plans to extend the outbuildings at the rear of the property for which plans were drawn up. However these were abandoned as my life was to take a turn in a different direction in the near future. One of my greatest pleasures about living in Rawsthorne Rd. was I became great friends with Meg and Keith who lived at No.15 with their two daughters Kate and Claire who had both been adopted. Meg soon became Auntie Meg and later she and Keith became an invaluable source of help in my new life. Keith I had known from the Black Bull at the bottom of Cop Ln. which was a quaint, clicky, pork pie and pickled egg sort of small drinking pub consisting of three small rooms and bar all with low ceilings, a cloud of smoke always present. Then that was the way of this style of drinking establishment were everybody knew everybody and usually met their friends at the same time each day and then a different set of locals came in at other times of the day. This was only interrupted when a guy was transferred to another job out of the area or when someone died to whose funeral all his friends would go and get pissed up at the pub later regaling stories about the deceased's life.

The business at Lostock Hall was booming but I missed the pubs and I got itchy feet to move on and life had become monotonous. Up early, off to the shop, peel the spuds, fillet the fish etc. serve the customers, shut up shop, and go home for a couple of hours then repeat in the evening 6 days a week. So I took the bull by the horns and applied to Bass Charrington to become a pub landlord which had always been my life's ambition.

Did I think that life would be more glamorous or that the grass was greener I cannot recall but I'm glad I made the decision to venture into a new life and the experiences that ensued.

After the usual interviews we were accepted and told that when a public house became vacant we would be asked to visit. The shop was put up for sale and we readied ourselves for a prompt transition. Brewery management were a new concept and I hadn't realised that it's all to do with politics of the system and their needs, not yours so after being made several promises about this pub and that by many D/M's I finally agreed to become a relieve manager, which entailed running a pub for managers when they went on holiday. This wasn't my ideal position but with hindsight taught me a great deal and brought about a huge change in my life. I now realise that I had not been the best husband or father and Hazels indiscretions with the trainer landlord in Blackburn was probably partly caused by my neglect and we then decided to part, but she did stay with me on paper at least until I was given a pub of my own which did occur about 6 months later. The pubs I took care of were varied both in situation, quality and quantity and I managed them on my own after the aforesaid pub in Blackburn. The Bass management and the D/M's either turned a blind eye or were clueless to this situation and I was dually assigned my first pub to relieve for a week. The Jolly Sailor in Fleetwood was a small pub with an off licence department and a central bar which had a steady group of locals who would pop in for a chat and a few drinks with their pals and the off sales did a roaring trade. Well that's what the books showed. A bottle of scotch sold in the pub at 32 measures x 50p = £16 and a bottle of scotch was £8 from the offie so it was obvious that it was advantageous that most of the bottles were seen to be sold from the offie for stocktaking purposes. The only problem that could have arisen was if a smart D/M had clocked the amount of tonic sales in relation to the amount of bottles of gin. Nobody drinks tonic on its own.

Blackpool called once again and the next pub was the Saddle on Whitegate Dr. which was a small two long roomed house with a very small bar. This venue will remain in my memory for the rest of my years. When I had sold the shop I had purchased a brand new Ford Cortina estate which now came into its own as I used the large area at the rear of the car to transport the goods I needed to survive because as in the case of the Saddle the licensees had locked all the bedrooms and sitting room so I wouldn't be able to use them, but had left the toilet and very small kitchen available for my use. I suggest they must have had a bad experience with a previous relief. So out of the car came a sleeping bag, in which I slept on the landing, a microwave and other bits I needed to survive. A little mishap occurred during this week when I was washing some dishes in the sink upstairs. One of the bar girls called me down to deal with some matter and I duly obliged and after a few minutes there was a shriek from the same girl who was behind the bar. I dashed to see what had caused her to cry out and found water dripping from the ceiling filling up the inverted light shades causing the light bulbs to fizz as the water level got higher and also a bulge appeared in the ceiling paper. Realising as to what the cause could be I retraced my steps upstairs to find I had left the tap on. This of cause should not have been a problem as there was a water outlet but unknown to me the outlet had no overflow pipe connected. Downstairs to clear up the mess much to the merriment of customers present and those that weren't were soon informed. Thankfully there was no serious damage and once dry the ceiling paper contracted to its original shape. Other pubs I looked after in Blackpool were the No. 3, The Grosvenor, The Palatine, The Palladium and The Devonshire Arms just under the main train line bridge past the biscuit factory and at this pub, just by chance the landlord had given most of his full time staff the week off so that he didn't have to manage without them on his return. At the No. 3 some bright spark had booked a beach themed week whilst the resident licensee was on holiday so it fell to me and the assistant manager to put this in place. A load of bumph arrived from the sponsor, Bacardi. Deckchairs, cardboard palm trees, grass skirts and hoola necklaces and 2 tons of sand. Yes 2 tons of sand which after laying down plastic sheeting we covered the floor inside the pub with. This went down a bomb and we did record sales and I was glad that the clearing up was accomplished after I had gone. At the Palladium situated just off the Prom and close to the Tower I learnt a very valuable lesson, use doormen in order to keep order at very busy times, especially in Scotch week which occurs in the middle of the season. At the Devonshire I also learnt that where air will go, beer will go. In general most landlords will not give away their trade secrets or what is commonly known in the trade as fiddles but because they need to keep everything on a level playing field he needed to inform the relief what he got up to. This was a huge public house with a large beer trade which was delivered by tanker into either 7 or 9 barrel tanks lined with a large plastic bag which cannot be tampered with as some unscrupulous landlords have been known to either dilute beer and lager with water or slops (beer spillage from the drip trays) This of cause is not recommended but were profit margins are of the essence someone will find a way as is the case here. On my first day I was shown around and the licensee took me into his cellar where I spied 4 large meat hooks screwed into the ceiling beams. What are they for? He takes a bucket full of left over beer (slops) from the previous day and hangs it on the hook on the beam, takes the air line from the tank which he then inserts it into the beer and whoosh the bucket empties into the tank. 2 gallons of beer = 16pints x £1.00 = £16. He then remarked 'where air will go, beer will go'. In those days there was not a vigorous quantity control and as long as your monthly stock check was within certain parameters everyone was happy especially the stock controller, if there was stock over it would be shared between him and the landlord. Higher management told us to always keep the till receipts and give them to the stock taker which was done on a regular basis but because most of the tills were decrepit no one took any notice and it became a farce when 3 pubs swapped their till rolls and gave them to the stock taker and there were no repercussions. There were other serious fiddles carried out on the Bass estate as one very big seafront pub's landlord would calculate how much beer and lager he would sell over a weekend and put a gallon of water into say 8 x 18 gallon barrels on a Friday night.

=1152 pints x £1 =£1152. He only did this at weekend because weights and measures did not work at weekends. This went on and as long as you did not get caught, everyone was happy until one week when one pubs stock take found 6 x 18 barrels full of water which he'd claimed on stock. 6 x 8 x £1.00 = £48.00. A landlord was on £100 per week wages. Oops!

Time to move away from Blackpool and on to my last two relief pubs before being given my own public house to manage with my name over the door. I was sent to Fleetwood again but this time a bigger and much more demanding establishment named the Strawberry Gardens managed by a rather large, well middle aged lady called Ada (I thought there was only one Ada) who ran the pub with a rod of iron and no nonsense or else. She had her doubts about reliefs and gave me a long list of do's and don'ts; this was probably well founded because the previous relief had lost a television. How you may ask, well two t.v. engineers came into the pub and said they had been instructed by the now on holiday landlady to repair the t.v. and after a few minutes fiddling with the set they said it needed to go to their workshop (you there yet?) so out of the door it went, never to return. The period I was at the pub was over Christmas and New Year so we were extremely busy with record sales but this brought its own problems as record sales meant record drinking and there were a few drunken incidents. The worst of which occurred on New Year's Eve when a group of lads with too much drink in them started a fight. I called the local Bobbies who arrived very promptly and calmed the situation, but as they left a glass of beer shattered above the door they were exiting thru and they were gone covered in beer. At another pub further out of town on the same night the landlord was surprised and amazed that all his customers had really taken so much trouble to get in the spirit of the season by getting dressed up in Christmas gear, he found out later that night when they left to go up town that it was his Christmas decorations that they had wrapped themselves in to celebrate the rest of the night uptown. At least he didn't need to take them down on the 6th. Situations like this did occur occasionally because these types of people knew that reliefs had no real teeth and if I barred them the returning licensee would probably do nothing and welcome them back. This was my second visit to Fleetwood and in general I found the people helpful and friendly but the whole area had a whiff of the sea and fish which didn't really make me want to stay. The next venue was the Bay Horse at Formby near to Southport which I really enjoyed even though the licensee had put all but one of his staff on holiday and stopped doing food for the duration of his holiday. Perhaps he had been informed there would be two of us but of course that didn't happen as by now I was well and truly on my own although for appearances sake we acted out the part so I could become a manager. I carried on and because I didn't like to refuse the customers who requested food, I with the assistance of the remaining lady put on a simple menu which went down a storm and earned me some extra dosh. My catering and entrepreneurial skills were not wasted after all. An intriguing feature of this pub was the many multi coloured half ties pinned on the wall just below the picture rail which when I enquired why was informed that they had been cut off customers who wore them. There was a huge selection and I thought what a hoot, but when I cut off a tie from a rather large gentleman surreptitiously it did not go down well as it had been a 50th birthday present from his wife. Oops.

Whilst on relief at this time I heard about a landlord in Preston who had ejected a drunken customer and because of the inclement weather had put him into the back of his van to sleep it off. Consequently the man chocked on his own sick and died, there was a possibility that a murder charge might have been brought against Barry the landlord who was later relieved from his job. Not wishing to miss a golden opportunity I was straight on to the brewery enquiring if I could be considered for the roll as manager at the Cattle Market Hotel and when no reply was forthcoming I enquired again, three times (remember keep your name in the forefront) well as you know we were given the job and for a few weeks Hazel kept up the charade until the night of Graces 22nd birthday when my life changed forever.

Going back slightly to when I commenced as manager at the Cattle Market there are always some problems to sort out, some are of the existing knowledge of you, by the locals, true or imagined, like you've got horns sticking out of your head and some that need to be dealt with by you straight away to put your mark out and gives the locals a message as to how you're going to run the pub and them. This was certainly the case as there were two families who drank at the pub and they fought regularly so on the first day I barred the first family who came in for a drink. Job sorted and gave a clear message that there would be no messing. Locals love their pub and like to feel safe and wanted which I set out to do. By its very name you may guess that this very busy complex pub next to a working cattle market, abattoir and auction sale rooms operated by Hothersals Auctions. There were two cattle, sheep and pig markets a week with other small animal sales. More later. I set out to bring this neglected, rough pub up to a standard that would please the locals and the local business operators, to enable all to feel at ease and provide a safe environment within these four walls which I tried to do by first, dressing in a smart country style suit, white shirt, tie and clean shoes which I hoped would set a tone and also make me look a bit older than my 32 years. On entering the front double half glass doors from Brook St. you enter into a passage and on the right are the lounge bar and behind that the tap room which was mainly a men only room entered by a separate door from the St. Back to the lounge bar where on the left through a door lies a large lounge fitted with banquets and tables with chairs, rather dated, needing a makeover. All the floors downstairs where covered with hessian squares and after market days the cleaner would water them to keep the dust down. Out of this room and passing a door to the upstairs there is a corridor leading to the ladies and gents toilets which we pass by and carry on to another lounge on the way to the kitchen and back door leading on to a large cobbled courtyard where there is the pub garage (used by the pigeon club) and in other outhouses once used by the pub there are now various business's mostly connected to market or farming activities. Back into the pub, out of the lounge and passing a small, long t.v. room finally entering the pool room which was well used by the younger clientele and has many memories and anecdotes which will wait till later. Down stairs in the cellar there was a large stillaged beer section and a secure spirit room which was my domain and was kept well stocked, more so at busy times of the year i.e. Christmas.

Upstairs now via the door in the middle of the pub to the first floor passing a set of toilets and up to the private kitchen and thru to the bathroom. Back again to the hallway off which were now three bedrooms and a lounge which had originally been a concert room combined with one of the now bedrooms and which were still huge rooms with massive windows. On up some more stairs which at one point must have been either letting rooms or the landlord's private accommodation but were now unused and dusty. Presumably the toilets on the middle floor had been in use when the large concert or function room had been operational during the Victorian era. Over the next few days I became acquainted with the existing staff, some long standing either full time or part time. Keith being a little Oscar Wildish was meticulous; nothing was too much trouble as he minced around with a large selection of keys dangling from a long chain attached to his belt which I never found out their use. Within a few days I had met them all except for one, Grace who on first meeting whilst she worked behind the bar and I was drinking with some customers, I introduced myself and asked her if I 'could have her body' to which she made a rude remark similar to 'go away' and unknowingly I didn't realise that Bill her father was in the crowd I was drinking with. Thank goodness he had a sense of humour and over a short period of time we became great friends. Grace was a beautiful young woman and at that time I didn't rate my chances, thankfully that situation changed as will become apparent later.

Market days were on Tuesdays and Fridays and I soon became accustomed to the strange goings on within the farming community that descended on these days which to the farmers was the culmination of all the sweat and hard work they had endured to bring their animals to market to be auctioned and eventually slaughtered. In those days the auction house would pay out on the day and the farmers and hands would celebrate their good fortune with a drink or two or more. There were very few wives as they tended to go off to town shopping and any road it was 'men's business' but this of course led to other ladies who were what we called 'hangers on' as the men would buy them drinks for small favours, only small favours. Because the pub was adjacent to the market it was granted a market alcohol licence which gave the pub extra hours for the farmers to consume drinks. An extra hour in the mornings from 10am and an extra hour to 4pm. This was good for business but brought it own problems in the afternoons, especially on a Friday when because of the extra hour and other pubs finishing at 3pm we would be inundated with already drunk customers hoping for a later drink which caused fights and anarchy. Learning from my Blackpool days I instigated a doorman and unless you could prove you had visited the market you were not welcome, this was quite easy, all you needed was a pair of wellies with a tuft of straw sticking out. Farmers were prolific drinkers and smoked like factory chimneys so there was always a ceiling fog which at the time nobody noticed but how many of those customers later went on to suffer smoke related conditions? Their favourite tipple apart from beer was scotch and on one particular busy session just before Christmas they drank one gallon of Bells, one of Famous Grouse and one of Grants, yes three gallons in one lunchtime session. On busy days like these the farmer's wives would collect their husbands after the shopping trip but some either had no wife or the wife would leave them to get home somehow, that somehow was often me. Well I didn't want them bunking up with me and how often could you put up with 'got to get ome, got to milk the cows' not got to get ome to the wife. I'd go to the outskirts of Blackpool and as far as Poulton le Fylde often towing a trailer full of cattle from the auction and the farmer and his hands fast asleep in the back of the car after a hard day's work.

Hazel occasionally helped out behind the bar and mucked in with the other staff but we were living separate lives and sometimes I would wander up town on my own just to get out and on some of these nights out I would bump into Grace and her friend Marilyn who also worked at the pub. With hindsight perhaps these meetings were not altogether a surprise to me as I may have enquired as to what and where the girls might be that night, perhaps I was looking for company. I should mention that I found out that Grace had an older sister called Linda and I asked Grace for her sisters' phone number (not mobile number) and with hindsight I am glad and relieved that I didn't follow up the information. By now I had got involved with the locals and sometimes after time we would have 'a lock in' which usually meant a thick head in the morning. More about this later. There were a varied collection of customers, some you saw every day and others dropped in every now and then and of course there were the marketers who descended upon us two days a week. They came in an assortment of vehicles, some brand new tractors, cattle wagons and an array of battered old bangers which they parked on the market car park in any order which ended up with a melly of parked cars. On market day when the farmers descended on the pub the bar was packed and there was a general aroma of the country but the only ones to smell it were the townies, but where there's muck there's brass which was beneficial to the business. There were so many characters associated with the market and would take up another book, but one to remember is Ginger who was a general hand on the market and who knew everything about it. He would find you a joint of meat from the abattoir which because it had not been hung was sometimes rather tuff 'but it were cheap' and there was always tickle tackle about the running of the market, some of which should have been confidential. One day he came in the pub with a piece of paper under his arm and asked me if I'd be interested, in what I was to find out when he unfolded it to reveal a for sale poster for Billsborrow Hall and all the four farms belonging to the estate circa 1850 which was and is situated near Garstang. It was an impressive poster measuring 3ft x4ft and I was definatly interested but I didn't let on. 'Well it's o.k. but I'm not really interested, what do you want for it'? We settled on two pints of Toby Light, I had it framed and latter on this lithograph print proved to have been a good deal. Another customer who assumed we had an early market license everyday was Ken Iddon who would turn up most working days and expect a pint of Guinness and a spirit of his choice, usually a double. He came at this time because he'd finished his business as a wholesale fish merchant on the fish market which entailed him getting to the market by 5am and when he'd finished his work by 9.30am he'd jump into his VW van and trundle to the pub for a well earned drink whilst studying the financial times. Ken and I became great friends, his and Audrey's house was to have a monumental effect on my life within the next few months. I knew that Ken didn't necessarily go home to Audrey when he'd had his fill with us but would go to his club for a few more and by the time he reached home, perhaps a little worse for wear he'd tell Audrey that it was that days spirit that hadn't agreed with him, to which she'd reply that he should cut down on it, and so the next day he'd inform us that Audrey suggests that he should change from say whiskey to gin.

George Coulson who I had known from my Penwortham days, drinking in the Fleece and Black Bull had left his dog Tessa to be looked after for a few months while he visited his brother in Australia, well in July of '82 he turned up at the pub and he said that he and his brother had not hit it off and requested if he could stay for two weeks before he headed off to Ibiza where he intended to live. The decision to say yes proved highly humorous and problematic. George settled in and without asking borrowed grace's mini to run an errand, without insurance, permission and no licence as far as I knew and came back to demolish a few spirits plus several pints. He had always been a heavy drinker and before long I tried to limit his alcohol intake by telling the staff to limit his consumption but he charmed the staff into letting him have 'just one more'. This came to a head when on one occasion whilst standing at the bar I heard a thump, thump, thump coming down the stair steps and on opening the door to upstairs George tucked in a ball fell onto the floor, and after standing up, shaking himself off said 'oh I'd better have a drink'. On another occasion Grace called me to her to tell me that she could hear an electric razor being used in the bathroom and as there was no electric shaver socket it was somewhat confusing but the conundrum was solved when she discovered that George had been using her lady shave and better than that was when Grace was taking a bath and George nonchalantly walked into the bathroom to go to the toilet, I mean go to the toilet and when Grace protested he said 'I won't be a minute'. Some nights we would escape and go up town and have a cosy hour at Emilio's on Fishergate just opposite the Victoria and Station Hotel where we would enjoy a bottle of wine and a nibble sat at the bar chatting to Emilio or his staff which was our time away from the pub and the local gossips. Isn't it strange that a landlords private life is open to discussion and comment by all the pub locals, this you will find in all licensed premises up and down the country, after all it is their pub. When we got back after a night out it was nice to settle down on our comfy sofa for a cuddle whilst watching tele. At this point George would appear usually with a sandwich or a little supper and lodge himself between us regaling us with his day's happenings. The fortnight turned into a month and then two and he actually set off on his Ibiza trip on Boxing Day leaving us with Tessa the dog once again and because he had no use for his very nice Crombie coat he gave it to me although he was 6' 6'. This was his final destination and so we wished him bon voyage and best wishes for his future of which there will be more later.

The bar on the other side of the lounge bar was mostly for the older male clientele and was always busy except early doors when old Jack would usually be the first customer for a half and a read of the paper. In pubs if small items are not screwed down they have a habit of going missing but this next experience shocked even me. At the front of the pub there was a little yard with railing and I thought it would be ideal for a hanging basket which I duly erected and watered it every morning. After several days I went to water the hanging basket and found it missing which I thought surprising because you would have had to get over the fence. Within the hour Ginger came to me and asked if I was missing anything as it transpired that he'd seen somebody riding his bicycle down Brook St. with a hanging basket strapped to the handle bars at 6am. Well knock me over with a feather, it was old Jack and this then brought to mind all the little items that had gone missing recently like bar cloths, ashtrays, small amounts of change from the bar and most recently a snuff box which Ken had given me. No one would have expected Jack but on reflection he was alone in the bar early every morning and nobody took any notice of him so he was the ideal candidate and me not one for letting sleeping dogs lie, I tackled him when he came in that morning informing him what had happened and of course not accusing him but saying that if the said goods were returned the matter would be forgotten but if not I would call the police. So the next morning I went out with my watering can and watered the returned hanging basket but unfortunately none of the other items did appear and so the police were informed and they duly visited Jacks address where they found draws and cupboards stuffed full of items like tins of out dated food and small diy utensils. They brought me a plastic bag full of glasses which were mainly from other pubs and because of his age no charges were brought and we never saw him again.The night time and weekend trade were a total different kettle of fish altogether because most of them lived locally and saw the pub as an extension to their home, a place to meet and discuss all their joys and woes and also there was a younger element who thought they ruled the pub, which didn't happen. As I've already mention the public bar was for the older punters and Singh who was Grace's dad's best mate although Bill had a slight problem with people from over the water, I mean Asia. The lounge bar for those that liked to stand at the bar and there was a small tele room but the most important room as far as the younger clients was concerned was the pool room where they would congregate and play pool which caused me more problems than the rest of the house. There were many issues amongst them: under age drinking, girls fighting with other girls because she'd looked at her boyfriend, guys pumping their muscles to impress and just a whole range of testosterone issues. Young ones are amateurs when it came to drinking and often only a small amount of alcohol would turn a polite gentle girl into a raging banshee which necessitated a gentle touch especially when she says 'touch me and I'll have you for rape' A drunken man is easy to deal with but trying to eject a woman or girl presents many issues because if you touch them in an inappropriate area this can cause consequences, so the best way to calm the situation is to grab them by their hair and show them the door. This measure works as you've removed the problem (the girl) unless her mates have a go at you or her boyfriend decides he's been dissed. I had a pool cue speared at me and had 3 sets of spectacles broken during my 2½ year tenure at the pub so life didn't always run smoothly but in general life was good. Over a period of the first months I became pally with a few of the locals some of whom would help out if I was stuck for anything and they were always up for a party in the form of a music event or just a good knees up which meant a piss up. In May, actually the 24th a birthday party was thrown for Grace and as usual it went on well into the night with some of the guests staying over, most of them crashing out where ever, waking up with sore heads. It now became obvious to me that Grace had, after a lot of wooing, fallen for my charms and we became an item. Later that day I escorted her and Barry who was 3 at the time to the Bank Holiday fair on Preston market were we played on the hoopla, ate candy floss and had an ice cream whilst Grace and I walked hand in hand. Over the next few weeks we gradually saw one another often and one night I was invited to their house on Tulketh Rd. for supper. Graces dad Bill always had a crab sandwich at weekend, the fresh crab Grace had bought from the open air Fish market especially for him, so when I said 'oh! I love crab'; I don't think Bill was impressed when she separated it to make two crab sandwiches, and when time came for me to depart and hopefully get a goodnight kiss Bill made it clear that Grace should not linger on the doorstep, 'are you going to lock that door now'? Goodnight.

We got on like a house on fire and after a few weeks Grace and I decided to make our situation public and after that we lived together at the pub, she working at V.A.G. as the managing directors' secretary and me managing the pub with the assistance of the staff. Today it's called the team.

Well in July Grace told me she was expecting so and we decided to go on holiday to Corfu in August which we did flying Dan Air, this was an experience. For the first few days the holiday was idyllic, sun, sea and ouzo. Grace developed a temperature and was rushed to hospital, the doctors (butchers) diagnosed a miscarriage and she lost the baby whilst being treated in third world conditions which caused her great pain and distress. I didn't know how to cope and admit I was not a great comfort to her for which I am not proud of myself. After our return it took us some time to come to terms with the loss but eventually Grace forgave me and we carried on as before with Grace still at VAG and me running the pub on a salary of £110 per week, hours not specified but there were perks like free accommodation and heating. The staff wages were paid by the brewery in cash and I was supposed to keep the wages in line with the trade and although Marie was on the books as a bar maid she did do some private cleaning for me and kitchen duties which was not officially allowed, it got swallowed up in the wage allowance. Marie was married to Bernard, lived just down the Rd. in Norris St. and when not working both enjoyed a drink or two. Their house was a typical Victorian terraced property which had been extended at the rear to provide a kitchen downstairs and a bathroom upstairs for their large family and was in need of a lick of paint. Bernard worked at Dick Kerrs on the Strand and the work had certainly taken its tole on his health and appearance but through his dower demeanour there was always a brave face and help when needed. On Sundays Marie and Bernard would be first in the pub at just before 12 noon after Bernard had prepared the veg and potatoes that morning for their Sunday lunch at about 2.30pm. When they arrived home after a lunchtime session he would take out the roast, carve and serve up the veg he had put on the hob when they had come out .Well at least the veg would be well done with a scum mark around the pan by that time.

At one of the party nights Marie had one too many and after some time we wondered where she had disappeared to so we sent out a search party. She was found sitting on the toilet fast asleep, her knickers round her ankles wearing her beaver fur coat, what a sight. She was out of it and as Marie was not a small lady it took me sometime to carry and manoeuvre her to a bedroom upstairs to sleep it off. In the morning she was somewhat surprised to be in a bed at the pub, but as a true professional she soldiered on even if she looked a little green whilst cooking the lunches. Although Grace and I were only at the pub for two and a half years there were many memorable events, one being the Kids Christmas party held in December when all the local customers children were invited to an afternoon of Christmas fun. The kids came with their parents and one or two of the parents helped Grace to entertain and feed them with me acting as Father Christmas. That day had been a typical cold winters day with ice and snow showers so the fires were lit and the curtains pulled together tight to keep out the cold draughts. The party was due to curtail at 6pm but no parents arrived to collect their charges and it was only when we opened the side door that we discovered the reason. With all the noise, jubilation, fun and frolics no one had noticed that a snow storm had arrived and the snow was up to the window ledges, some three feet high so all the parents had to walk to collect their kids. The children thought it great fun and a fantastic end to a Christmas party; they looked forward to the following day hoping the snow would still be there, which it was. Two other events happened that Christmas of '81, one nothing major but it did shape my views about farmers and the other did have a huge affect on my future for which I am eternally grateful. We decided that on the last market before Christmas we would invite the regular farmers to a free Christmas roast, nothing grand but a little thank you, so expecting about 30 Marie and I set too and knocked up a simple roast with potatoes and veg but unlike other market days the farmers had decided to bring their whole families, because 'IT WAS FREE' and although this was an unexpected invasion Marie and I somehow managed to feed them all. This was the day that we sold 3 gallons of whiskey and we gained great respect from the farmers, or perhaps they thought what suckers, but that experience was not repeated. As mention previously there were several 'ladies' who would only frequent the pub on market days and two particular, one called Sweaty Betty and the other Scary Mary always dressed in long gents type macs and one day Marie noticed a piece of loo paper sticking out of the front of Betty's mac and enquired what she had under her coat, very reluctantly she opened her coat and we discovered loo paper wrapped around her body which she had stolen from the huge loo roll holders in the ladies, she must have been dizzy from going around and around in circles to accomplish the amount of loo roll she had.

Ken Iddon and Audrey who lived on Watling St. Rd. in an old Victorian house requested Grace and my company for a quick festive drink on Christmas Day morning and we duly obliged but said we could not stay long because of opening time at 12noon. Barry was with us and later was to go to his mothers who was about to marry Ken Robinson and wanted Barry to spend Christmas Day with them. We chatted, sipped our drinks and talk changed to our future plans, when out of nowhere I said 'Oh we're getting married next year' at which stage Grace gasped and said 'what did you say'? Well I suppose that was a proposal that shocked not only Grace but me as well as our friends when we arrived back at the pub we celebrated with all our family and friends. At the time I popped the question Barry was sat on Graces knee and she turned to him and said 'looks like we're getting married next year' so I took that as a YES. Because of the celebrating, Christmas lunch was put on hold and I think we had sandwiches but wow what a day and as New Year came in plans were made for the upcoming wedding. It was decided that we would have a civil wedding at Preston registrar office and a church ceremony at Broughton church followed by a wedding breakfast at Broughton Park Hotel on the 7th April. There was much to do as with most weddings and April seemed a long way off but time flew by, the church and hotel were pre booked and menu's chosen, a trip by Grace and Linda to J.R. Taylors in St. Annes to choose Grace's wedding dress complete with crinoline. The invitations sent, awaiting RSVP's. Grace also bought the two bridesmaids dresses and because Sister Sylvia was pregnant Grace bought her a smock dress which she duly returned to the shop for a refund the day after the wedding. Cheeky bitch. On the big day prior to the wedding Ken treated the males of the wedding party to a box of langoustine which we swilled down with champagne to set us up for the day.

I remember seeing Grace at the registrar's office in her wedding dress, hair tied back and thinking how beautiful she looked and to this day that image remains with me. After the civil ceremony our borrowed Mercedes wedding car picked us up and Julio was singing Yours which forever since has been our song, so, all dolled up, Grace in her white wedding dress and me in top hat and tails called at the our pub for a quick one, no, I mean a drink. The car then took us to Broughton church where all the family guests who had attended the civil ceremony and friends were waiting our arrival on this fine warm day. The vicar gave us a beautiful service to be concluded by a young chorister singing Ave Maria which brought a tear to many an eye. Then off to Broughton Park Hotel which was literarily two minutes away, we were welcomed by the manager who escorted us to the very grand function room where 85 guests, friends and family would be treated to a sumptuous wedding breakfast washed down with wine and champagne. Rowland the best man and I both made unmemorable speeches, but Bill stole the show with his monologue asking the guests to give him any spare change they had and also how he was having to resort to going to the rag and bone man with some bits of tat to help him towards the cost of the function whilst with his spectacles in one hand and holding out his other arm at full length to make a point with the biggest smile on his face. Grace had her head in her hands crinshing with embarrassment as the rest of us howled with laughter. After these celebrations we all descended on the pub where Auntie Meg had prepared and laid out a buffet to be devoured by even more guests who had been asked to attend the evening function, she had also made the wedding cake which she and Keith gave us as a wedding present. The day was a great success and later Grace, I and Barry snook of to Bartle hall which was to be our one night honeymoon. We had drunk nothing but fizz all day and as Grace will relate to you all I went to bed very early and fell asleep. What a waste. Next morning, up late, missed breakfast and so we stopped at a scruffy transport cafe for a bite to eat which didn't go down too well, no not the breakfast, me! On our arrival back at the pub we were greeted to it looking like a bombshell had hit it as no one had cleared up from the previous days party. Grace and I and Marie who was looking a bit worse for wear got down and cleaned up the mess and I think Grace's comment was something like 'is this what married life is about? She was still working full time at VAG and working on the bar and she also had become a part time mum caring for Barry when it was our time to have him usually at weekends and she would put him to bed after reading him a story every night.

In the previous year another famous wedding had taken place on the 29th July'81, that of Charles and Diana with some similarities such as both grooms were much older and both brides were beautiful, so we planned and executed a royal wedding bash in the courtyard at the rear of the pub which was decked out with colourful bunting and union flags. It being a holiday for everyone all the customers were invited to attend to be fed with chicken, burgers and sausage and chips, all at a minimum charge and a disco played all day and night which helped the alcohol consumption. Everything went smoothly except the chicken had not defrosted as thougherly as we wished so we boiled, roasted and micro waved the chicken pieces before putting them on the BBQ, to our great relief no one suffered salmonella and a great time was had by all.

In August of '82 Grace and I organised a holiday to Yugoslavia flying with Yugo tours which ended up being the start of a disastrous holiday although there was a silver lining, no gold. Archie Baillie and Jo 2 had agreed to take us to the airport and as it was an early flight they had decided to stay overnight starting the holiday early with a few pre holiday drinks which went on well into the night and early morning before they staggered off to bed and we still had a stock take to complete before the stock taker came and the relief manager took over. We didn't go to bed and had to awaken our drivers as they had fallen into a deep sleep, probably due to the copious amount of alcohol they had consumed the night before, but we duly set off and arrived at the airport in good time. Archie and Jo stayed for breakfast, watched us off from the viewing platform and on our return were surprised we had got to our destination because of the amount of smoke streaming from the engines on take off. On boarding the plane we expected to all sit together but there was some mix up with the seats which meant that there were only two seats for three of us and it ended up with Grace and Barry sitting in cabin crew seats facing the back of the plane. Near to the arrival of our flight to Dubrovnik we were informed that we were to make an emergency at Pula airport which was in fact a military airport which we gathered by all the camouflaged and bunkered military aircraft we could see. We were not on the ground long, never found out what the problem was and were soon in the air and arrived at our destination to a somewhat third world airport which lacked many of the facilities associated with modern day airports and this was to continue throughout the holiday. On arrival at the hotel we were greeted by the commandant who demanded that we follow her to our room which was basic and at dinner we declined the dessert because after fish soup, fish appetiser and roast fish for main what would the sweet course be? Pula was a simple coastal village with very few shops and at one we purchased a wood carved chess and back gammon board which we still have, although not used. Other trips by bus took us to Split and Dubrovnik which showed us some of the history of Yugoslavia, ancient and modern including large shell and bullet holes in the stone walls of the city from the Second World War and unfortunately there would be more to come very shortly in the war between the Czechs and Serbians. The Yugoslav economy was still in tatters from the war and there was very little to buy in the shops except locally made toys and at one point I asked an ice cream vendor for an ice cream and he offered us a homemade iced lolly which looked more water than taste but then offered us a Walls Mivi from under the shelf at double the price which was still cheap compared to home prices and any bus trips we did wish to make had to curtailed by 8pm because that was the last bus. We met with an older couple, Pat and Derek who lived in Croydon, we all got on well and spent many hours having a drink and chatting and on one occasion they mentioned that we should visit their favourite beach just along the coast which we did the next day. It was surprising to see a gate at the entrance to this beach and a notice on it informing us that it was a nudist beach and although it looked a beautiful stretch of sand we decided to find a clothed beach nearer to our hotel. As with all holidays they end only too soon but this vacations end could not come any sooner as there was just not enough to do or so we thought at the time. At least we arrived home with a sun tan and I think Barry had enjoyed his holiday little knowing that very soon he was going to be presented with a baby sister. Life carried on as normal for a few months, until Grace announced that we were expecting a little bundle of joy in May '83. So there were things to do in Yugoslavia.

One morning Ken didn't arrive for his early morning pint with a shot and it was later that day that I was informed that he had had a heart attack at his desk on the wholesale market and had passed away which caused me great distress and I still think about him and Audrey when I see the very fine blue glass water set that he gave us as a wedding present which I'm sure had come from his and Audrey's glass cabinet, whether she knew about it I don't know. Marie and Bernard became great friends and we would sometimes invite them to come out for lunch with us and Bill to Broughton Park Hotel which was very grand and Michael the slightly affected bars manager would spoil us and offer us the very finest wines. One lunch, the restaurant table set with crisp white linen, shiny cutlery and 4 sparkling wine glasses we perused the extensive menu, Marie seeing scallops on the menu decided these were for her but as I knew that she could not stand anything to do with the sea I pointed this out to her, she thought they were potato scallops from the chippy.

We were all given a bread roll and after the starters the waiter collected the plates and side plates but Bill hadn't finished his roll so to stop the waiter from taking his roll he put his hand over it and whenever the waiter came near his hand went to the plate, after main courses were devoured desserts and cheese came, Marie particularly enjoyed the black biscuits which contained charcoal and left her with black teeth.

Christmas and New Year came and went and Bass informed me that alterations were to be put in place such as an EPOS till system to make stock taking accurate and needed less often which of course set alarm bells ringing as it became apparent that someone upstairs had finally cottoned on to the inaccuracies that occasionally occurred. Time to go.

By about Oct or Nov of '82 Grace was well into her pregnancy, so to help Grace out we advertised and employed a young lady as an assistant and later to babysit the expected arrival.

She was rather a large lady and within weeks we discovered that she was spreading her largess around all the local lads and was becoming known as the local bike, it all came to an end as she was spending more time entertaining than working.

At the beginning of '83 Bill, Graces dad invited us to join him and the family on a 5 day coach trip they were taking to Dunnoon in Scotland. We couldn't afford to take 5 days off and Grace was now 6/7 months into her pregnancy but we promised to join them for 1 night if possible. I was to regret that promise. I had previously agreed to take Barry to London for a visit on the train with Grace and on our return drive to Dunnoon hopefully joining the family later that night. By the time we arrived at Loch Lomond at 8.30pm Grace had had enough and so had I, so we found a b&b and booked dinner for 9pm, last orders. I was famished but grace wasn't up to it so I ate alone, in the morning we continued on the last lap of the journey feeling refreshed after a night's sleep. Bill and the family were pleased to see us and we celebrated that night in true Caledonian style at the Glen Morag Hotel with a live Scottish band provided by the hotel. Our journey home the following day was at a more leisurely pace.

We had enjoyed our start in Preston but instead of being a manager I wanted to be a proper licensee taking on running a pub of my own so I contacted a pal called John who I had met when living in Birch Ave. he was at Bass's head office, so I asked him to put some feelers out. Within a few weeks I was asked to go and look at another cattle market country pub and restaurant in Cheshire called Beeston Castle. Grace was now quite large with baby but we visited the pub and decided to stay in Chester overnight at the Grosvenor Hotel which was and still is a very top class establishment which we later developed a great attachment to both in business and pleasure. On our visit to the pub both Grace and I immediately fell in love with it, asking many questions of the landlords Jose and Malcolm, finding out later that not all the answers were completely honest but they didn't know us from Adam and had allegiances to their pals. It was a big rambling building dating back to the days of the railway, about 1850 when the Crewe to Chester railway was built and Beeston station was erected opposite to the pub to service the cattle market adjacent to the pub. The station building was a casualty of the Beeching era and had since been demolished. The pub consisted of a separate games bar with pool table and dart board where other games were also played like crib and dominoes. Through the bar to the snug and then the lounge were there was a roaring open fire and then onto the restaurant which could seat 28, on to the large kitchen area off which were several preparation and storage rooms. There were two stairways to upstairs, one off the pub lounge and the other behind the bar which led upstairs to 6 bedrooms, a bathroom, a toilet, a kitchen and a small office. Another staircase at the rear of the bar led down to the beer cellar and spirit store. The L shaped bar area serviced the Games room, the snug and the lounge with waiter service to the restaurant. The outside area was huge of which I will come to later. On our return to Preston I immediately contacted John and asked for our names to be put forward for the vacancy, and in due course both Grace and I attended two interviews, one at Trentham Gardens when Grace was very close to delivering, shortly after which, actually on the day of the birth I was informed we had been successful in our application for the pub and to attend a final interview at Chester when Haley was 2 weeks old where one of the interviewees commented something about noisy kids. Going back a few days before the birth, Grace slipped whilst working in the pub, yes I did say a few days, her consultant recommended that she be admitted to the maternity unit so that they could keep a close eye on her condition, she was then induced to bring on a speedy birth which just happened to be a market day.

I was somewhat excited so I bought some flowers and borrowed a bottle of Moet from stock and dashed to Sharoe Green Maternity unit just in time to assist in Haley's birth which was hell for Grace and stressful for me but we were assisted by Mr. Manson, Graces genealogical consultant. Champagne was popped and I've never seen so many doctors in one place, but they enjoyed the fizz which was drunk out of any available glass receptacle. The Matron in charge commented to Grace about my premature optimism with the early arrival of the flowers and champagne and on that day I informed Grace that we were moving to Beeston in six weeks and we needed to plan our move, it was decided to have Haley Christened before our departure. Grace duly arrived home one week after the birth wearing a size 10 dress which I had been told to take to the hospital the day before her homeward trip where everyone was there to greet us and we then informed them of our move to pastures new. We booked the Christening at Broughton church and suddenly we gained a new friend, the vicar who would descend on the pub at any hour usually leaving with a tin of biscuits or a tin of ham or bottle of something for the church charity raffle. He arrived one lunchtime to find Grace and Marie playing crib in the pub and at the time I was not a happy bunny but later events proved that I should not have been such a prude. When we got down to the business of the Christening there were charges for the choir, charges for the heating which we didn't need in May and also for the service sheets and all paid in cash because 'there were different departments to pay'. It came out later in the Evening Post that we were not the only people who were asked to pay in cash and that church funds had been misappropriated all because his son had a drug habit.

On the Friday before the move I had to go to Chester Magistrate court to be granted a licence for the Beeston, so I duly arrived at court in the centre of the city adjacent to the Abbey where several other expectant licensees were awaiting their fate. I got chatting to one of these only other smartly dressed guys, his name Jonathan Slater and he said he was to be the new assistant manager of the Chester Grosvenor if he got his licence. At that time he was just a young man starting out on a journey that would take him to great heights and although we never became great mates his name occasionally opened a few doors. If smart dress had been a necessary requirement for the granting of the said licence we'd have been the only two to sail through but as several of the applicants looked more like they appeared to require a motor mechanics licence not an alcohol licence and had just arrived from their garage I wondered what it was all about.

Grace and I finished off the day with a stay and a meal at the Grosvenor, not quite knowing how I paid for it. Remember if you know the bosses name in a hotel or restaurant always mention to the bar staff or waiter and perhaps ask to their where abouts, it pays off in spades.

The day of the move came and with the help of family and many friends the removal was accomplished by early evening, Grace's dad Bill came in our mini with Tessa the dog and some furniture and Meg and Keith drove Grace down whilst I came in the estate car with the two cats Stinky Dinky and Zippy, with the car piled up with precious items. After the stock and f&f had been agreed the removal men off loaded our possessions into the allocated rooms which were to be sorted out at a later date, although necessary items had been kept to one side such as a kettle, bedding and Haley's cot. Moving days are always stressful and legal decisions are best left to the professionals but on this day I learnt another lesson when it came to trusting people as when it came to the two tills which were not on the f&f but could be purchased if we carried on the HP payments on a three year agreement with one year remaining. Alarm bells should have sounded as the representative from the HP Company was present with the paper work ready to sign which we duly did, paying little attention to the T&C's. Big mistake as we later discovered that it was a 5 yr. agreement with one year paid; good job we'd said no to buying the CCTV that was installed throughout the premises which we'd been asked several times if we'd take on the CCTV but we said no. Malcolm and Josie Wright the previous landlords had been at the Beeston for many years and had built up a successful business but we were determined to stamp our own mark on our new venture, but as locals don't like change they probably imagined that we had horns on our heads because speculation about this new landlord and lady would have been rife for weeks before our appearance. We opened the pub the next day which was Tuesday and helped by our brought in help and the existing staff everything went well as we prepared for the following day which was our first market day. At the end of the first day closing time bell was rung and a few of us deserved a little drink but this was only for a few when all the regulars had gone home, to my surprise one guy was left and upon asking him to leave he said that he was waiting for Sylvia the barmaid and whilst he was waiting could he have a drink which I gathered was normal practice, so OK we all had a drink and that meeting became a lifelong friendship with Stan, or 'Stan the man' as he became affectionately known. Beeston village was situated at the confluence of three major travel networks, the Shropshire Union canal, the Crewe to Chester railway and the A49 on which opposite the pub was the now demolished railway station which still had a car park at the front of it. Descending south down the hill on the A49 from the Red Fox Inn there are few houses to the right and left before passing Tarporley hockey ground and then a side Rd. to the right which takes you to Tiverton, further down and a few more houses to r&left before coming to the Canal side Cafe on the left and Chas Harding's boat yard on the right, under the railway bridge where to the right is a reclamation yard, just before one of the main entrances to Wright Manley Cattle Market where Molly's little house stood sentinel like, guarding this entrance where he did or did not allow the many cattle trucks to enter and leave without inspection. Carry on with the pub on the right and the old station opposite with a very little village shop which sold everything, run by Anne and occasionally Ray, dependant on his or the weathers mood and next came Richard Reeves wood yard making and selling wooden farm gates, then onto Dennis Leah's garden table manufacturer with a petrol station next owned by Walter Coates from whom we did buy one or two cars but not to any great satisfaction to either of us because it always came to him refunding any monies we had paid him because the cars were rubbish.

But back to the pub where the outside area consisted of car parks to either side of the pub and at the rear a large hard standing area with a large metal farm gate at one end, amounting to about 1acre, this was situated next to cattle market and was accessed by 2 other large gates at either end of the of the car park. This land was to play a huge part in our next 12 1/2 years tenure and at that time was looked after by Harry who lived in an old caravan on the rear car park. To either side of the front steps were rose gardens and then the pavement and to the right hand of the pub a beer garden with garden pub tables with integral seating. Wednesday the day of the market dawned and although a much larger market and a bigger bar snacks and meals operation it went much the same as Preston, except I noticed that these were Cheshire farmers with newer cleaner cars and tractors, dressed for the day, still drank scotch with others taking to the gin, but they all said they had no money as the markets weren't as good as they used to be or it was too wet, too dry, or too cold. Grace somehow managed to juggle being a new mum and looking after the kitchen which on busy days was very challenging and she did not realise at the time, but later regretted saying those few words, no not 'I DO' but 'I'LL DO THE CATERING'. She always put Haley to bed and at that time Auntie Meg was with us for a short time and there were some experienced staff who had to be shown new ways and I'm sure some of them just wanted to carry on as previously, but we persevered and in due course after several months the business got busier and it became too much for the older one's like Betty who left. Within a few days of our arrival Grace commented to me about a crazy D. J. that she and the staff had tuned into when working in the kitchen at lunch time, his name was Mel Scholes on Signal Radio which had only recently started to broadcast, he was outrageous, told stupid jokes which had us all rolling about with laughter, at the time we didn't know what a great friend he was to become.

When we first arrived there was always a murmuring question about the upcoming Bank Holiday market at the end of August, there were four B.H'S a year. 'What are you going to do about the B.H market; you do know about the B.H market?' By the time it arrived I was in a stressful state not quite knowing what to expect and although I'd had a meeting with Bobby and Barry the two guys who were in charge of the market I was still at a loss. On the Sunday night the day prior to the market a crowd of stall holders arrived and began to set up their stalls and when the sun set they descended on the pub mostly in the bar where they set about drinking it dry, and when it was time to close they had other ideas and although many of them had already had too much they demanded more 'just one more boss' but after our time in Preston I knew 'one more' would be many more and that wasn't going to happen so with difficulty out they went. I had put my mark on how the bar was going to be run, and they knew it although it didn't stop them trying it on in future years. Of to bed, a somewhat restless sleep and with the dawn at around 6am, the sun shone brightly in the sky and I heard the noise of scaffolding poles being knocked together I jumped out of bed and went to the bedroom window to view a town being erected of different sized stalls all over our car park areas and I laughed telling Grace to 'come and see'. Well the day went well and we made a lot of money both from the bar, baps with several fillings x 200, lunches, and the rent from the market which after some thought regarding how many stalls there were on the day I surmised that I was being sold short and later found out that this figure given to me by Malcolm had been down priced and was another lie but that was resolved after a meeting with the two boys Barry and Bob. That early evening after the crowds had died down and the market rubbish cleared by a group of lads I sat in my office counting the takings and not wanting to keep large amounts of cash (that's what people used in those days) I placed it in a bank box and later that night took it to the bank putting it into the night safe. On the way home calling at the Rising Sun for a quick one or two to celebrate a very successful day with Grace, and 'Stan the man' who came along to act as body guard, he was repaid with several drinks. This became a ritual and we were to carry on this event till we moved 12½ years later. Market days were as follows, 1st Wednesday's horses and general implements and horses, household auction on the others with odd Shire horse sales and cattle, fat stock, small animals and poultry on Fridays with turkey auctions at Christmas. Attendees to the market would park their vehicles and tractors on our car park for a small fee, 20p which was collected by Charlie who resided in the caravan parked at the rear of the pub but after a few weeks the 20p's he was giving me didn't add up to the amount of cars I had seen on the car park, so I took an interest in how many cars parked and I tackled Charlie about the discrepancy, to be told that because it was cold some days he only been out for half the time and also some of the farmers he knew or were regular customers he hadn't charged which did not inspire me to carry on with his services, because of his age and friendships he had with some of the farmers he probably found it difficult to enforce the charges and farmers being farmers they would take advantage, so I decided to do the parking myself and as we were into September now the days were often bright and warm. I kept the car parks locked until I began at 7am and ran round opening and closing the different gates according to how busy the market was, parking the vehicles in order, making nice lines so that no one was blocked in later in the day. Of course there's always one awkward one who didn't want to park where I wanted them to or who wouldn't pay, they were told in no uncertain terms what to do and if they didn't I would clamp their car, I never had a clamp but they didn't know that and it always worked. Be assertive and always collect your money, none of this 'I will pay you later'. This situation was fine in September but became challenging as the year drew to a close because of the cold weather but the markets flourished, so did the car parking because there were no discrepancies and I was looking forward to the next year and another 4 B.H's.

Auntie Marie and Bernard were still in Preston and very shortly after our move we asked them if they would like to come and stay for their holidays, 1 or 2 weeks? They jumped at the opportunity and duly arrived a few weeks later and proved to be a great help around the pub, Marie helping with Haley and Bernard doing odd jobs for me to which I would contribute a little spending money to lubricate Bernard's dry throat after all that graft. Bernard got on particularly with Bill the cowboy and his wife Amie, Bill always wearing a Stetson, checked shirt, jeans, cowboy boots and big cowboy belt but no guns, he sure was a character and always came to the C&W music nights when we started them later, sometimes complaining if the act wasn't up to his standard even though it was free.

The Beeston became not only a new venture but an adventure were we made many lifelong friends and discovered many characters, some not with us today but one of these characters who is still with us and a true friend appeared on our door step at the time when we were forced to look for a new cook after Betty's retirement.

We whispered in a few ears and placed an ad in the little local shop across the Rd. and sure enough a Scouse guy turned up and said he had heard on the grapevine that we were looking for a cook, well I told him that Grace was looking for a lady and he replied 'aren't we all' but he suggested we should give him a trial and if we didn't like him he would disappear, we did and he didn't and that was the start of our 38 year friendship with Edi working with us till our retirement and we are still friends to this day, even though he is a Scouser. After about 12 months Doreen, Graces mum came for a short break but this ended up being a long short break and she came in very handy, baby sitting, helping out when we were busy, she slept in the spare bedroom at the end of the corridor next to our private kitchen. The kitchen was a bowl of contention between Grace and I as admittedly the kitchen was on the small side and the cooker was caravan sized, but I thought it would do, grace didn't and this featured in our next move 12 years later. When we had arrived there were several staff that stayed on and proved to be great assets, letting us know where things were, how implements and machines worked and who was who which came in very handy if something needed fixing or supplying. Percy and Joan, an oldish married couple had been there since the year dot and had been ex licensees, Sylvia as mentioned previously, Jackie on the bar, Caroline and Betty in the kitchen. Both of the last two stayed for a short time but I didn't think they approved of our change of menu so we had to find replacements, Edi for one and Kate Stockton as a waitress and Sara who was still at school joined us as a trainee chef and general dogsbody, later going on to catering college In general we always insisted that all staff should be 16 or over but in Sara's case she was only 14, nearly 15, this came about because her mum looked after Haley at play school and a similar thing happened with Nigel sometime later because he was Jackie's son, he proved invaluable in later years if you were planning a journey as he could recollect every train, boat and plane time table to anywhere. Nepotism or what? In those days HMRC were not as vigilant as they are today. Over the years we would employ many staff, far too many to mention all of them but I will try to mention those that impacted our lives or business's for good or otherwise. Putting the cattle market to one side there was also what you might call general pub and restaurant trade which could be quite different in each area of the building and dependant on the time of day, day of the week and time of year. Sunday was a rest day and the restaurant clientele came dressed up, the lounge was an area for bar snacks and drinking, wine was still a lady's tipple, beer and lager for the men and in the bar younger men and their girlfriends would congregate for a pint or two, a game of pool or darts, sometimes disappearing off to another pub or pubs. There was still little fear of the law and many would drive round several establishments enjoying a few pints, especially in the summer months. In those days 'time' was called at three and customers must depart by 20 past which meant that we could enjoy the afternoon to ourselves, returning before 7 to reopen the pub, serving food till 9pm and drinks till 10.30pm. Monday, Tuesday and Thursday continued as normal trading days with an array of car traders and locals, some of them coming in most days to prop up the bar and chat to their friends. Saturday was a busy day and the restaurant was always full in the evening, market days carried on in the same old way with very little bother except when one of the dealers or farmers had one too many. I had been alerted to one particular scruffy dealer who thought he ran the market and probably the pub, who I had suspected and been informed that he did not always use the toilet when he wanted a wee so one market day I found this to be so, I grabbed hold of his coat collar, marched him to the front door and threw him into the front rose garden, Oops the rose bushes had recently been pruned. Occasionally you've got to assert your authority to show you mean business, some of the customers came from over the Welsh border, sitting in close nit groups talking their national language so none of us would understood what they were saying, so I learnt a few phrases and one day let out a few Welsh words, they never muttered in Welsh again. 'If you can't join em beat em'. From the outset we were introduced to so many locals, casual passersby and like us couples who had recently moved into the area, one of these was Brian and Sue Baister who had moved from London for Brian to take up the position as DCC in the Cheshire police force and they were living temporally in a police house in Spurstow whilst they searched for a new house. Like us they were new to the area, we connected and got on well, more revelations later. In that first year we were introduced to many people who went on to become lifelong friends and we enjoyed their time whilst we knew them, their memories live on. Artie and Maggie Wilson were a couple we soon got to know along with the bank manager Neil and his wife Janet, Alan and Michelle Harding who owned a cheese distribution business near Nantwich were big into horses and they introduced us to Hunt Balls which were a highlight of the Cheshire season.

A couple from Bolton would come to dine, usually on a Sunday afternoon with their two sons one of whom they were taking back to boarding school after a weekend break, eventually we became great friends and went to stay with them for a night out and later to their holiday home in Portugal which we and Haley really enjoyed and at a later time when money was tight it was an inexpensive break. During the day the clientele would change and after lunchtime there would be a lull but around 4 to 5 o clock a group of guys would start to arrive to discuss cars because they were all in the motor trade, the main man was Mal Rose who was a car trader, he knew the whereabouts of all the cars for sale in the area. As usual he was the first person to arrive for a drink showing off the first mobile phone which he plonked on the bar much to the admiration of all the other guys, mobile phone, it looked like an ex ammunition box, left over from the war but this soon changed and look how far technology has moved on. The others like Mike Hind, car sales, Tom Moiré, general haulier, Ian Gossmore (Gosse) a butcher from Tattenhall and many others were worth keeping sweet because they were heavy drinkers and gave the pub a busy and friendly atmosphere. One of this group was a guy called Richard James who owned the candle factory at Spurstow and was known as 'Dick Wick' who liked the gin. Sometimes the auctioneers and bosses from the market would drop in after work which added to the hubbub of the pub and occasionally car deals would be executed between the dealers and the market men. Many of this group would come to early deaths, perhaps because of the amount of the spirits they consumed; perhaps I was a drug dealer. I was introduced to an elderly gentleman called Mr. Rowli John who was an auctioneer, very smart with a bow tie, married to Mary, living in a chocolate box cottage in Haughton near to the Nags. Over the next few years Grace and I became great friends and would often visit. Rowli was very straight forward and would not suffer fools lightly, on one occasion some guy enquired what his name was and he replied John and the enquirer replied 'OK John' to which Rowli replied 'Mr. John'. On my occasional Sunday morning visits Rowli would pour me a very large brandy which I would then return half of it back to the bottle and Rowli would comment 'ungrateful little so and so' but we got on like a house on fire.

Brother Rowli had decided to join the RAF at 19 for whatever reason, (perhaps too many people were looking for him) and it made a man of him, travelling the world, Aden in the near east and Germany, then later stationed at RAF Wroughton where he settled down with Lyni and their son Mark. For me the most memorable event occurred when after 22 years he retired from the service and had a leaving do in the Sergeants mess where the drinks were cheap, I mean cheap, 10p for a spirit and 9p for a pint, that's cheap. Well the night went well until bolstered up with drink I decided to give the invited guests our illusionists show on the stage. Without boring you this consisted of Grace dressing up as Lolita, my assistant holding out objects which the audience had given her for me to guess what they were without me seeing them. It was all a con because prior, Grace and I had agreed on certain colours that she would mention before the item of concern, this was going swimmingly until probably because of the alcohol I mixed up the colours, but we got a great laugh, perhaps not for the trick, but for us. Anyhow the night carried on until we had to leave, back to the B&B. I had forgotten where we were staying for the night and I certainly couldn't drive, so I persuaded Grace to drive which wasn't a good idea really because a. She hadn't passed her test and b. was also slightly sloshed, but somehow we made it to the B&B waking up with bad heads. A cracking do.

After we'd been at the Beeston for a few months managing with some of the suppliers that we'd used in Preston I decided to look for new and different ones to look at better prices because as we grew the business our existing suppliers were too far away if we ran short and it was time to squeeze a few hands. One of the first salesmen to visit was Colin Bachelor; he represented Briton a frozen food company from Chesterton and had made an appointment for 10am, when he arrived at 10.20am I informed him that he was very lucky that I was still there as I have always believed in punctuality, his sales talk and promise of better prices impressed us and we decided to give him our business. Many years later he told me that I'd also impressed him with regards to being late for his appointment and had never been late again, we stayed with that company till we retired and retained our friendship with Colin although he did move to Booker C&C many years later giving us better deals than Briton. Well, it's only business.

Although the name of the pub ended in hotel we were not residential but all our joint families assumed we were and would descend on us most weekends so that they could prop the bar up whilst Auntie Grace fed, watered, bathed and put their kids to bed whilst attending to the pub catering, Haley and my needs, she excelled at these tasks. Apart from enjoying a quick drink in Tarporley after the B.H. we would visit all the local pubs in the village to associate ourselves with local trade and prices so that we could see if our menu and drink prices were on a par. Also we made a point of visiting all the surrounding villages eating and drinking establishments, great fun and informative and I regret now, not putting the cost of said experience down as a taxable expenditure. There were a lot of outlying interesting and beautiful hamlets around and one was the Nags Head at Haughton, a previous smithy which was known locally as the Flash because of a nearby stream and although on a minor road it was surprisingly busy, perhaps because of the nutty landlord and the late night drinking, there were many quiet country roads which late night revellers could easily disappear down except on one occasion someone forgot or couldn't see the very sharp bend on the road to Bunbury and their car ended up in the fence, if I remember it was Tom Moiré and his lady friend ' Miss Piggy'.

In August'84 we decided to take a holiday to Jersey where all of us including Doreen travelled for a week's vacation, Haley was still in a pram but we managed to visit many of the local beauty spots and attractions inc. the German military hospital which had been dug out of the cliffs by forced labour during the second W.W. and Haley's little easy way stroller was ideal for walks on the beach. On our return it was decided that we'd put on some music once a fortnight and as we both liked country and western that was our choice and plans were put in place, but with all the best plans in the world it was a gamble. However as we did not intend to charge an entry fee and the musicians were recommended as being top class all went well and proved a great success at most of the music nights. However some months on an artist turned up as a substitute and after 30 minutes I couldn't stand his act so I decided to turn him off and put him out, but the audience were all killing themselves laughing and having a great time because of this guys act and begged me not to shut him down. We did have some fabulous artists including Denny King and Jim Ryder who were well received and on special occasions we'd hire the Chorley Mashers who were a group from, guess where, yes Chorley. Whilst discussing music Grace and the girls were still listening to Signal Radio with Mel Scholes being their favourite DJ, he asked for requests and either Grace or I would ring in and ask him to play Julio in between him making funny quips like 'what do you call a cat with a tail? a sissy and, is it a tom? no I brought it with me' this kept the girls happy even during the busy lunchtime session. When Mel played our request he commented that he and Grace were Julio's two fans, not 2 of his fans, but Julio's only 2 fans. About this time I gave Grace a surprise birthday present, a VW Golf which I presented to her at Derek Firmstone's garage in Bunbury, it was wrapped in a big pink bow and when she first saw it said to me 'oh isn't that a nice surprise for someone, lucky devil'. She was gobsmacked when I told her it was hers as I gave her the keys. This was a big improvement on the car Walter Coates had sold her which we found out later was a mix and match car, two cars welded together, but we finally got our money back. Also about this time it was time to change my car and who better to ask for advice than Mal Rose who knew the where abouts of a vast selection of motors. The trouble with Mal was you only needed to mention you were interested and he bombarded me with quotes and within a few days I was the proud owner of a nearly new Mercedes. Remember when buying a car, new or pre- loved always go to the garage at the end of the month because the car salesmen, sorry person, and the garages are always chasing their sales quotas or stats so you could negotiate a better deal when these become crucial. During our time at Beeston we had a variety of cars, the ones I've already mentioned, Skoda; mark 1 Escort, Carleton, Honda Prelude the sporty one with frog eyes, two nearly new Mercs which dad Bill was very proud that his son in-law owned, no not his daughter, his son in-law. Also our friend Tom

Moiré loaned us a mark 2 E Type Jaguar to go on one of our trips to the lakes which was very decent of him as at the time our car was a Carleton. I hadn't realised what a following these cars had and at times it was embarrassing. The car was flashed at on the motorway and when I parked the car crowds of people would flock round and stroke it and ask questions I could not answer, so I tended to find out of the way places, if possible. I tell you now that I have never been interested in the machinations of cars but I enjoy driving premium motors knowing only where to fill up with petrol and how to check the windscreen water level; the rest is anathema to me. Also Art loaned me his bevel roofed Mercedes sport so that Grace and I could arrive in style at the Black Boy restaurant in Prestbury for lunch, all went well until we arrived home. Grace asked me if she could have a little spin round the car park, this she did and in doing so managed to scrape the skirt of the car causing a little damage. As the car was my responsibility I took the blame, the car was repaired and soonest mended. Good day out though.

Now that Grace and I were self employed it was always important that the business generated an income to support not only us but all the many staff and outgoings which not everybody understands or even gives a thought to, they even think that money goes into the till and straight into my back pocket which obviously isn't the case. Think about business dustbin charges, BT charges, credit card machines, wage systems, replacement machinery which always breaks down when you're busy, upgrading furniture, repairs, stationary, decorating inside and out which everyone assumed the brewery did free of charge, bank charges, they even charged for the change we needed to run the pub and a monthly charge for the business a/c, however I opened at least 10 private a/c's which accrued no charges and I used these a/c's to move money around and pay D.D.'s, but certainly not least the many charges associated with the HMRC like MGD, compulsory pension scheme for employees and employer contribution towards staff NI. Of course our VAT had already been collected from the customer and should have been sitting in the bank waiting for payment day. This should have been the case as long as temptation had not reared its ugly head and you hadn't spent it on some other important project. Income tax was also a major outgoing which also caused pain on the wallet but if you're paying large amounts of it you must have made it but when these two items needed paying together, usually at the end of January there was always gnashing of teeth and belt pulling.

As mentioned we did visit other public houses to get the lay of the land and during these visits we got to know most of the landlords and their ladies, of which most were very obliging although one up your nose lady once told Grace that she had a lot to learn but her husband Bernard Mc Queen gave us a little advice which I remembered later, he said regarding the Swan hotel that they then owned 'bedrooms are the best way of making money whilst you're asleep'. Other pubs in Tarporley village, starting at the bottom are the Foresters, run by Alice and Ron who thought the pub was more up market than it was, then the Crown a working man's pub, next the Swan in the middle of the village which had a restaurant and bedrooms and the famous Cheshire Hunt Club Rooms which were often frequented by Prince Charles and other royals in the hunting season. Then the Rising Sun, which at that time was run by the King family, and later Mac and Cynthia who were the landlords of this typical local Robbies village pub, both families ran very successful businesses. Across the road was a wine bar called Churton's, a sister to another wine bar in Pulford near the Welsh border and we must not forget the very popular Shady Oak pub just out of the village which was located on the canal and run by John Duke and Wendy his partner. Her sister Mandy and several of her young girl friends helped out which then attracted the young boys who intern attracted more young girls which made the pub lively and lucrative, good business! He and Wendy later moved into Tarporley taking on the Crown Hotel for about 2years, then moved out of the area to the Brintyrian Inn near Bala, we visited them, staying at Pale' Hall where Queen Victoria had stayed some years earlier when a railway station was specially built to accommodate her visit.

Barry now being 10 or 11 came most weekends with either Grace or I picking him up from school on Friday and dropping him off on either Sunday afternoon or Early Monday morning in time for school. He would also join in with the kids of whichever other families had descended on us but on quiet weekends because of the outlying position of the pub we decided to purchase an old Mini that he could tear around the car park in and perhaps tinker with to keep him occupied.

The hours we worked were long and tiring but I enjoyed every minute, each day a new challenge and new people to entertain and hopefully gain as customers.

We decided that if the opportunity arose for a holiday or fun we would grab it, so on the first Christmas Day we had lunch at the Wild Boar Hotel just up the Rd. with Grace's Dad Bill who as a present bought me a Havana cigar, when the waiter told him the price he said 'I only want one, not the box'. As a short break we travelled with Barry, baby Haley and Doreen to the Lakes and stayed at the Swan in Grasmere, taking short trips around the area, and although we found Grasmere a little out of it, all the amenities closed early except for the hotel bar which stayed open late with the assistant manager Mr. Twist in charge.

After the BH market we would often go shopping to Chester and fit in a meal at the Grosvenor which was top class as we remembered from our previous stays, prior to taking the Beeston and whilst we were welcome in the restaurant children were not allowed in the Arkle bar so Grace was not happy when she and Haley were excluded. We were to go on to be good customers of the a la carte restaurant at the front of the hotel and although they did have a minimum age for children Haley was made very welcome, always seated on table no. 1 and when at some later date I enquired as to the reason for this we were told that Haley was always well behaved, we ate a la carte and chose quality wines, it could also have to do with the tip I left.

Possibly because and probably because of the demanding and stressful life Grace had been thrust into her health suffered and after many trips to the Dr.s she was diagnosed with several allergies, after taking tests it was found that the main allergy was garlic which when she handled it made the skin on her hands break open into bleeding sores, so much so that I bandaged them up every night with Iktha paste and over many months they recovered but that meant that our kitchen could no longer cook dishes that contained garlic as Grace could not avoid coming into contact with it during her work.

To thank the staff we held a staff party at Broxton Hall, those present were Stan, Jackie, Harvey, Bram, Joan, Percy, Sara, Grace and I for a lavish meal, at the end of which the boys clubbed together to buy a bottle of white port, Harvey tasted it first remarking 'what's this piss? To my side Stan produced a door knob from his pocket saying 'it's solid brass' I told him to put it back. The taxis took us home and I retired to bed waking up the day after with a head, the port was piss.

From our arrival at Beeston I had employed Tim Smith, Jackie's husband as an odd job man, painting, decorating etc. because I excelled at my job and was not a natural DIY person. One day I received the news that he had passed away so in due course Stan and I attended his funeral at Tiverton church where he was to be buried. Stan who 12 months prior had been diagnosed with cancer, had been given 6 months to live said, gazing into the grave 'that should be me down there' and I replied ' if that was either of us, could we say we've missed anything'? Stan and I had had a full life with trials, tribulations and lots of fun and intended to carry on for as long as possible, unfortunately Stan was to die within the next few months and to this day is remembered and sadly missed.

The fun carried on, we'd been invited to the Hunt Ball by Alan and Michelle, this was to be held at Stoke Hall near Nantwich and it was a very grand affair with ball gowns and black tie. The event didn't start till 10pm so we worked till 9pm, got ready, went to a pre ball party at their house and arrived already slightly sloshed to be given free champagne, poured by the glass and then given the bottle with a breakfast served at 3am to those who were still standing. In all we went to about 4 of these events, always in huge houses whose owners must have been given copious amounts of the said champagne previous to them agreeing to them saying yes to letting these hooray Henry's rubbishing their houses. That morning we arrived home rather late or should I say early, Grace's mother had just arisen and said to Grace still in her ball gown 'Oh darling you're up early, would you like a cup of tea' Grace replied ' No thank you I'm going to bed'.

On Graces 30th we organised an outside party, the day went well with the Chorley Mashers featuring their style of country music which appealed to everyone and on our 5th anniversary at the pub the year later being '88 a fancy dress party was organised. This parties theme was dance and all the guests were encouraged to dress up in whatever costume they thought best suited their interpretation. Well there was an excellent array of the theme with some most extraordinary outfits, foxtrot (foxes head with a loo roll on top), roaring 20's (flapper) ball gown, sport (leotard, tights and sweat band), John's Lynn came in a slinky red dress as lady in red, lots of fun. Two not to be named male punters came dressed as ballet dancers in tutu's.

The music nights were great fun and other people like John and Sue at the Nags also hosted country and western nights on a regular basis, also Art and Maggie would put music on at their cottage if it was either of their birthdays, this was an invitation only affair often featuring Denny King and Jim Ryder, truly authentic c & w from The Grand Olde Opera.

Another group of customers who should be mentioned were the Dungeon and Dragon contestants who most weekends would descend on the derelict Peckforten Castle to enact war games between themselves and later, still in their costumes arrive on mass at the pub. Because of their attire, which would frighten most normal people, as it was supposed to frighten their opponents I would only allow them to use the games bar with which they seemed ok. Looking at them you'd think they were a load of schykos but on paying their accounts by credit card it was evident that some were eminent people. Sometime later Peckforten Castle became famous when the latest Robin Hood film featuring Kevin Costner was made there and some of the cast would drop in for a bite and a pint, later the castle which was originally a folly built in the late Victorian era was developed and turned into a very smart hotel and wedding venue.

The White Lion in Nantwich came on the market, a little pub in the town centre, amongst several other similar establishments for which we could see promise. Grace found a management couple who showed interest and were duly given the job but what we didn't know was that the previous tenants had kept the business going with late night card schools which we had no intention of carrying on so the pub became a money pit and also the manager's enthusiasm soon waned and ended up costing us up to £1.000 per week in loses. We quickly ended the lease and ran after losing £80.000 to £90.000

but thank God the Beeston was very profitable at the time and helped defer the losses. This address would come back to haunt us.

Because of these setbacks it was fortunate that our good friends Peter and Leslie offered us their villa in Portugal as an inexpensive get away which at the time they used as a holiday get away in Carvoerio and was vacant much of the year. I remember many happy days soaking up the sun with Grace and Haley who enjoyed splashing in the private pool and having a late night snack of olives, cheese, sardine pate, local bread, salami and Casal Mendes rose wine on the veranda which was festooned with pink, sweet smelling bourgonvilier flowers. We enjoyed several of these breaks. Carvoerio village being about a 1 mile walk from the villa at Arios dos Minos, passing a little shopping area with a pool and bar, very often not passing on the way back after walking down the hill into the village, and sampling a glass or two of the local wines. Thank you Leslie and Peter.

Late one night/early morning I heard a noise outside on the car park, seeing a light I went to investigate finding a policeman patrolling around the pub, he said someone had reported a disturbance but could find nothing so I invited him to come inside. I asked him if he required a drink or something to which he replied he wouldn't mind a something, meaning a large scotch, which he enjoyed and continued on his way.

B.H. markets and cattle and horse markets continued to be successful as did the pub and by now we were enjoying the rewards of all the efforts we had put into the business. One Sunday prior to a BH we visited Art and Maggie's house near the castle, that's Beeston Castle and found her making scones for her to sell on an animal charity stall the following day, she was big into animal charities. Maggie was not a tidy person and her absolutely beautiful handmade oak kitchen looked like a bomb had hit it with used baking tins, trays and mixing bowls cluttering up all the work surfaces and the sink. Picture this, trays upon trays of stacked baked scones of every recipe imaginable and she was mixing by hand a new batch of currant scones on the huge wooden kitchen table. Directly above her, from a wooden beam hung a fly catcher which was moving with the amount of flies stuck to it. Maggie said 'help your selves to a scone if you like' to which we replied that we had just had a late breakfast. No thank you. Art her husband was a plant and demolition expert which was a demanding and heavy job but sometimes when coming home for dinner after a hard day's work he'd be given beans on toast whilst the two large fluffy cats would dine on finest cod fillet or prawns, 'well they are my little darlings'. On that last August BH the weather smiled on us, it was sunshine dawn to dusk and hot all that weekend brilliant for the market, bringing hundreds, no thousands of happy shoppers looking for a bargain, of course this meant that the loos were in great demand. Everything went well until one of the staff told me that the toilets were blocked and wouldn't flush so out with the plunger; don't ask someone to do a job you can't do yourself. It wasn't just the one loo; none of them would go down until with one last plunge they all cleared. A stall holder covered in 'slurry' came to the pub door ranting and raving that all his stock (knickers etc.) was also covered in 'slurry'. The septic tank on the car park had burst its lid and exploded, perhaps it was that one final plunge. He asked who was in charge, I told him that we were only the doormen and directed him to the market where he would find either Bobby or Barry, I didn't hear any more, phew.

After staying in Grasmere for three years annually, usually in late October, once at the Swan and twice at the Wordsworth we went to the Gilpin Lodge hotel for lunch which is near Bowness on Windermere. Discovering this fabulous establishment created a holiday destination for many years to follow, till the present day. I love this Autumn time of year, the golden colours, the crisp misty mornings, snow high up on the mountains, no kids because it is out of school holidays, everywhere is accessible because there's no crowds and the roads aren't all snarled up with caravans and traffic. Bliss.

Grace and I collected money for various local charities usually based around children and on one occasion Mathew Kelly (Stars in Their Eyes) came to pull the raffle ticket out of a hat. We got chatting to him and it turned out that his wife was a teacher at a school for handicapped kids at Winsford called Hebden Green Community School so we decided that our next fund raising event would be focused on raising funds for them. We decided to go big and it was suggested that we should hold an Auction of Promises, in other words people or businesses would promise to provide, at no cost, an item or service i.e. a balloon trip or dinner for two that the public would bid for at auction. We set about advertising the event and the response was over whelming with items for people to bid for. One of our customers was, we thought a B.A. pilot, he promised an on board Santa trip which in the end fell thru and we discovered he wasn't a pilot. There were so many items that I realised we needed to erect a marquee to hold the event in with extra seating. The auction was a great success and we raised close to £2000, far more than we'd expected but then I realised that there were certain expenses which I hadn't taken into account like the hire of the Marquee which we had got at a knock down price because we were fund raising for a worthy cause. Some days later Grace and I visited the school to hand over £1500 after apologising to the headmistress that it wasn't the total amount we had raised. She remarked that any amount was marvellous and they were very grateful and after gave us a tour of the school where we were greeted by all the students and staff, we were very humbled and would go on to raise other funds for them with Mathew coming once again to knock over a pile of pennies, in total about £1000. Just mentioning pilots reminds me of a customer called Bob B...s who liked his pop and often called in for a quick one or two on his way home from his trips all over the world. He'd say he'd had a busy day and had to be up early the next day as he was taking passengers to where ever. We never flew Dan Dare but often said to one another that if we got on a flight and the pilot said his name was Bob B...s, we'd get off.

'88 was an eventful year with my 40th at the end of January when a party was organised to which all our friends, some locals and relatives had been invited, it went down a storm. The star of the show was a hypnotist who got Auntie Marie to recall her school hood days, as she rode an imaginary bicycle faster and faster in order that she could reach the toilet so that she didn't wet her knickers and Harvey sang Rick Astley's I'm never going to give you up. I did not believe in hypnotists but those two events were unbelievable and yes it did change my mind. At this party I'd decided it was time to open the champagne that Grace had bought me for Christmas. She had had some help finding this bottle by Neil Collins who was the sommelier from the Grosvenor, it wasn't just a bottle it was a Balthazar containing the equivalent of 16 bottles of Moet et Chandon champagne or 12 ltr in today's money, a big bottle. With some of it I made champagne cocktails but this was knocking the guests out cold so I reverted to straight Champers which was difficult to pour out of such a large bottle, it did last quite a long time, enjoyed by many.

Celebration and then commiseration, the following day Tessa, George's old dog that we had cared for since his departure, died at the age of 16 and Comet our other dog was very upset. Later that year we took our first holiday to Cyprus staying at the Hermitage Hotel in Larnaca, it was warm, interesting, fairly cheap and the wine was good. We were there over their Easter and on the Sunday we were invited to a BBQ at a friend's house and because it was so warm the party was held outside. Their garden overlooked the airport runway where at that time an aircraft had been hi-jacked, the crew and passengers were being held hostage, it was resolved peacefully a few days later. A car had been booked so that we could drive around the island, up into the Trudos Mountains, along the coast and through the pine forests where you could see how they extracted the pine sap that goes into the wine retsina which tastes like pine cleaner. That night after returning the car to the rental company Grace and I walked around a few local hostelries sampling the local wine, not retsina, and ended up in the hotel bar were a few locals were gathered, one said to me 'indaxi? To which I replied 'no we've been walking'. The locals all fell about laughing because indaxi means are you OK in Cypriot. Another short, sharp lesson in Greek. In later years we returned many times, mostly to Kato Paphos.

One of our customers was Bob Price who owned Cheshire Inns, a small group of pubs scattered around the local area, mostly bought from the old Greenall Whitley Group, he then built them up, and literally built them up as in a previous life he had been a builder. He and his wife Sylvia, family and other entourage would descend on us for drinks and quite often food when business was to be discussed. On occasions they would forget we had times when meals where available but Grace would try to accommodate his requests but one or two of his group also thought that the same options applied to them and had to be told that they didn't as they did not have the same clout. One of them once said 'go get the rotvieler, she'll do it' referring to Grace, she didn't and she remembered. Bob had several pubs that needed new landlords which Grace and I thought might be just up our St. so we opted to take on the Walnut Tree Inn at Alford near Chester. Grace taking on the tenancy with Harvey as manager, he had worked with us for sometime as our bars manager. Grace set to fitting out the pub and it was opened to great fanfare. Harvey had not realised how much commitment he needed to give to the running of the business and it was only after a few weeks when Grace's bank manager rang her up, informing her that the arranged bank overdraft was well over its limit that alarm bells started to ring. Harvey was doing super sales but the takings were still in the safe, had not been banked because he got up late after having parties all night in his newly refurbished flat, which by now was a tip, needing new carpets and redecorating. Sorry Harvey but out he went to be replaced by Roy & Jean who said she came from Wobberly, she talked posh and really meant Mobberly. I wonder what happened to Harvey. The writing was on the wall and we decided that this venture was not such a good idea after all and we found out that Bob Price had only bought the pub and adjacent plot of land as a speculative venture which he intended to sell once he had developed the land along with the pub and only wanted to get some sucker to keep the pub open till the building work was finalised, then he would sell the pub and houses. Our relationship went south and some years later I went to his funeral, much to the surprise of Grace, Edi and Bobs family. When I was asked why, I replied, 'just to make sure the coffin lid was screwed down'.

Also in '88 sister Sylvia came for a flying visit with her slightly inebriated partner on a very busy hot day in July when we were all rushing round trying to keep up on a market day, we probably did look flushed but her remark to us 'you wouldn't catch me doing that' did not go down well and would come back to bite her on the bum later.

Later that year in early December there was a heavy snowstorm which totally blocked the A49 and all the surrounding fields were white over. We were fully booked in the restaurant and had expected a busy lunch but my comment to grace was 'we might as well not open' but we did expecting a very quiet time. To our amazement we were busier than we'd expected which just proves a point, open whatever.

On Christmas day because Barry's mum wanted him to spend some part of Christmas day with them we decided to have lunch at Broughton Park and drop him off later which proved to be a big mistake. We duly arrived at 12.30 for lunch, sat down, put on the hat, ate lunch and had one drink because I was driving and on our departure the 3pm lunch party's guests were arriving, all dressed up in Christmas decks, had obviously had a drink or two prior to lunch, everyone was in good cheer, intent on enjoying their day. Never take a first sitting!

If trade was brisk, like on a market day or a BH I would empty the notes from the till and back up with change, one for safety and also that the change didn't run out, at the end of the day the two till draws were taken upstairs and placed on the bookcase at the top of the bar stairs to be counted the following morning. Before we retired upstairs at the end of the night I would set the alarm which was situated at the bottom of the kitchen stairs and then the entire pub downstairs was alarmed.

Early one morning the alarm bell started to ring and so I jumped out of bed and went down the Kitchen stairs to turn the alarm off, I could not open the door to the pub as I later found out that it had been blocked, I then headed back upstairs, along the corridor and down the pub stairs into the bar. Someone or two had stolen the two tills from upstairs and must have known that by blocking off the kitchen door I would be forced to waste time running around upstairs which gave them time to escape. We surmised that it must have been an inside job and that the culprit was Syvia's son, she used to clean for us and would know the lay of the land, the money was never recovered but the empty till draws turned up on waste land at the rear of the market. Just to think that whoever it was had been no further than 6 feet from where we had been sleeping.

We would always try to get to a panto at Christmas often at the Palace Theatre in Manchester and I remember that when Haley was 4 the star of the show was Russ Abbot, what a great actor. We laughed and we laughed. Of course we couldn't visit Manchester without having a meal at Wong Chu in China Town on Faulkner St. On this visit we had our usual ribs, salt and pepper squid and duck, as a first course Haley decided to try a dish of hot 'n' sour soup, this was very hot and for the rest of the day she sipped ice cubes, she did not eat this dish again.

I decided that we deserved a treat so off we went up to town where Grace and I stayed at the Savoy; my purpose was to visit the Cafe Royal Grill for lunch which was part of the Rocco Forte Empire situated just off Piccadilly Circus. On entering we were seated in a sumptuous booth and the waiter assured us that this was Oscar Wilde's favourite table, as probably were all the other tables, am I just a cynic? The aged sommelier appeared from behind a curtained cubby hole, his tastevin or silver tasting cup dangling on a chain around his neck, he came over to advise us as to which wine he would advise us to drink with our choice of meal and probably by our dress he must have thought that we were from a higher echelon bracket because his recommended wine which was in the 100's of £'s similar to what 'Oscar would have chosen', like hell. Excellent meal and our wine choice was quite acceptable. On a future visit the aged Sommelier had been reduced to a floor waiter and his previously red nose had now turned to purple. On enquiring about his decline in station he replied, looking upwards that 'the bosses upstairs thought I was taking my job too seriously'. Venturing back to our hotel a drink was called for so we called in the Coalhole on the Strand, a large Victorian pub where all the walls are tiled top to bottom and a long bar with a variety of real ales and craft lagers. Charles Dickens probably sat in a corner of the bar writing his novels in the day.

In '89 we decided I take the plunge and have the 'snip' so off to Liverpool, for a consultation, then the procedure which took minutes with a local anaesthetic, I don't know what all the fuss was about. Linda, Grace's sister had found herself a well off bachelor called Harry Day who was a big wig at British Aerospace and lived in a large house in Lytham St. Annes to which we were invited to stay and have a night out. Whilst we were there it was time to get a sample for analysis to make sure I was now firing blanks, so in a deep warm corner bath and with some assistance from Grace the said sample was deposited in the sample bottle ready for despatch to the laboratory. Like Harry, Linda could drink and on the night of our stay we heard raised voices after we had retired to bed, in the morning we returned home and only hours later a phone call confirmed that whilst driving Linda back home to Preston they had been in a car accident which had killed Harry, Linda was in a serious condition in hospital. Harry should probably not have been driving that morning as it had resulted in a head on crash with a bus, taking out his side of the car. Linda had serious injuries and would be hospitalised for weeks, in fact three months. As there were no other relatives it fell to us to look after her two children, John Henry and Daniela who we brought to live with us at Beeston. Apart from missing their mum they loved it, going to Bunbury School and fitting in with Haley and Barry when he came at weekends. Just more work for Auntie Grace. Linda finally went home, still with a leg plaster. It was a great summer and whilst she partied on a flat roof terrace at the rear of her house she fell off and ended up back in hospital and us caring for her kids again. Thank goodness for Auntie Grace.

I heard on Signal Radio that Mel Scholes and his team were about to go on their annual trip on the Shropshire Union canal broadcasting his daily show from venues along the canal which was a short distance from the pub. Tuesday was our night off as we did not cater that evening but before we headed out for the night I mentioned to Chris the bar man that Signal's team might nip in for a drink as they were broadcasting the show from the Shady Oak, a pub on the canal about 1 mile further along. On our return, at 8.30pm who should be sat in the pub but Mel and his team, about 10 in total all gagging for something to eat which Grace set to and provided. They were very grateful for her offerings and after we sat with them chatting. Mel true to form carried the conversation with quips and jokes and the night carried on with nobody taking any notice of the time because we were laughing too much. Sometime later a few of the crew had to go as their boat was moored at Barbridge some three miles away but that didn't stop the rest of us enjoying the night, however a little later Mel said that they should retire to their boat, but first he should ring the radio station to let them know where he was, which he did. Mel to radio, 'Hi its Mel' presenter 'where are you? At the Beeston Inn, no where? Behind the bar, what you doing there? Having a drink of course. Well it seems that Mel has found a perfect place to be'. The presenter then said that he would go to the news at 2am. I thought, that's great, broadcasting that Mel Scholes was drinking behind the bar at 2am. There's more. On the following sunny day we listened to the lunchtime show which was going down a treat, when in true Schole's form he mentioned the events of the previous night. He interviewed a postman asking him what time he got up for work, he replied oh about 5.30am to which Mel said 'that's about the time we were trying to find our barge on the canal after spending the night in the pub, we tried to get in 4 before we found ours'. At least I know now that none of the licensing dept. are listeners of Signal radio as I never heard from them about our late night jollies. Now that's a name to remember as that's the club in Stoke were Mel made his name as a very famous DJ. At Jollies night club. On other Signal canal trips I would go along to see Mel and often he'd ask me to appear on the show usually ending with me asking him to play his and Grace's favourite artist Julio Iglesias's song 'Yours'. Mel was a great funny man.

Marie and Bernard visited regularly, he was getting older and would often have an afternoon kip, so after taking out his false teeth he'd lie down in his undies on the opened door bedroom at the top of the bar stairs, on occasions his little winkle would slip out of his undies on show to the world which caused much amusement to the girls. Every time he went home I saw him having a melancholy moment, wiping a tear as he sat in the back of the car perhaps wishing he and Marie could stay. In '91 at the age of 66 Bernard passed away, within the first year of his retirement, all that hard working life, what was there to show for it? We attended the funeral in Preston and Marie decided to scatter his ashes on the bank of earth at the rear of the pub overlooking his favourite place, where we later planted a yew tree to commemorate Bernard's life.

After Bernard's death Marie stayed with us for some time and made some changes to her life, one of which was to have her hair cut into a bob which made her look much younger, she had not done previously because Bernard preferred long hair. She now came into an annuity and his pension which enabled her to buy more up to date dresses, which brought her to the attention of Marcus who lived over the Rd. at the garage and he owned an American Cadillac. He requested Marie's presence for lunch and a drive in his car, for days prior she was like a teenager on her first date. After lunch they both returned safe and well, Marie was not ravaged as she had imagined.

The boys in the bar wanted to collect for a charity and a fun day was suggested featuring a fancy dress football match, sure enough they and their supporters arrived at the pub for a few pints, they all went off on the back of tractor flats to play the game, with buckets for the purpose of collecting donations. Although the day was bright and dry all the players returned looking like they had been dragged through a ditch and a hedge and after a few more drinks some took most of their clothes off with Crum taking all of his off whilst dancing naked on the pool table, which caused quite a few of the girls and lady's present to get an eye full. Some of the other boys, Gary and Steve Wilson, Swin, Dids, Dodge, Ant Manley, Mark, Bloody Hell John and Molly regaled stories about a previous landlord Edi McGill who liked a drink and would fall asleep at the bar later in the night and before retiring to bed he'd give the keys to one of them saying 'put the money for any more drinks in the till and lock up when you go'. Either very honest customers or a pissed landlord. One of the most outlandishly dressed person at that charity event was Bramwell, we called him Bram. That morning he was working behind the bar and arrived dressed as a lady, lady I mean tart, flouncy blouse, slinky skirt, tights and high heels. The staff that were in the kitchen saw him first struggling out of a car and tottering across the car park, well I can tell you we were all in stitches and he caused much amusement all day long. When he finished his shift he stayed in character and partied with the remaining revellers until late into the night, then decided to walk home to Tarporley and upon reaching the High St. slouched on a bench to catch his breath, only to be approached by an officer of the law enquiring if he was O.K. To which Bram replied 'I don't always dress like this'? Bram went on to become the bars manager at Portal Hall golf club and sadly passed away in 2014, at his funeral in St. Helens church where his eulogy, read by his son remarked that his father's finest hours were at the Beeston with Grace and I.

The popular games in the bar were darts, pool, dominos played on Monday night by some of the older boys and at half time they would be given snacks baked by Haley and her mum, they were well received even if the pastry was a little grey sometimes.

Other members of staff who stand out are Belinda and Charlotte. Belinda was asked by a customer for a half of mild and a brandy, yes she did, put them in the same glass, and when a customer asked her for a double rum she told them that we didn't have rooms and last but not least someone asked her for half a corona she asked Gary the other bar person 'Gary what glass do I put half a corona in'? Her ambition was to become a pharmacist. The other young girl showed up for work in quite revealing dresses and shorts giving the boys in the bar quite a show, they enjoyed it but one day she thought it appropriate to adjust her suspenders behind the bar which was going a bit too far, so her stepfather, who we later found out had a liking to taking girlie pictures of her, escorted her home.

Tessa had died in '88 and we then replaced her with Ben who was brought home by Grace, she had bought him from a man on the market paying £50, Stan and I were flabbergasted and immediately returned the dog telling the guy that Grace had paid too much and we wanted a return of her money, we had no intention of returning the dog, but he didn't know that, so we did a deal at £35 and over a period of time we had other dogs, only two at any one time, they all lived outside in a huge old coal bunker which had been cleaned out and filled with straw. On another occasion Molly came in with a tiny puppy and said it had been left on the market, it being so cute we agreed to keep it. Some 8 weeks later a rough looking very broad Scottish farmer came to see us and enquired about his wee puppy, yes we had it, so he said he would sell it to us if we wanted to keep it, hold on I said, we've looked after it for 8 weeks, food and vet bills, I tallied that up and told him it had cost us more than he wanted for it but if he wished to pay us the balance he could go home with the wee doggy. Farewell Mr. Farmer. This dogs name was Comet; she was Haley's dog, think about it. Ben used to wander around outside, got on with everyone, but strangers were not welcome in his compound. On markets days he would enjoy walking among the stalls especially the food stalls where he would grab any bread loaf that was in reach much to the annoyance of the stall holder, he then wandered off carrying it in his mouth. You never knew what to expect to find outside the back kitchen door, a rabbits tail, he'd eaten the rest, a huge house brick or a mound of stones that he'd collected to show to you, it ruined his teeth; he was a wonderful dog and lived for 18 years.

One slow lunchtime with just a few regulars around the bar, in walked two smartly dressed big men who identified themselves as bailiffs from the county court and demanded £1000 to settle a debt relating to the rent of the White Swan in Nantwich which we had owned previously. We were adamant that no such debt was owed by us but of course they were there to do a job and had heard it all before. I showed them the rent payments, paid by DD by the bank and on checking it was obvious there had been a mistake as it was Bass Charrington who owned the pub and the adjacent shop that were at fault, so off they went, us wiping our brows and the locals with a load of gossip to talk about later.

When the markets were really busy the rear doors at the back of the pub were opened to allow easy access to the toilets, especially the ladies, otherwise there would be a line of ladies snaking out of the front door queuing in desperation and on one such day I had mentioned to the queue of ladies that as there were no men using the gents one of them should use the toilet. Stan acting as a doorman with me informed me he needed a pee, so off he went and within minutes he came back with the biggest grin. You'll never guess what I've just seen, he said, when he went into the gents there in front of him, three ladies with knickers round their ankles were peeing in the urinal. I said to Stan 'what did you do?' he replied 'There was room at the end', one lady commented that I was exposing myself, he said 'and what do you think you're doing'? At another BH Market the flushes in the gents wouldn't flush, on investigation I found about 20 wallets and purses in the water tank where the pickpocket, after removing the cash had got rid of so that he didn't have the incriminating evidence on him. The police were informed and because the pickpocket wasn't interested in the c/cards most of them were traced back to the owners. Another influence that the BH market had was that on BBC radio 2 news bulletins, a warning was given that the roads out of Chester, Nantwich and Whitchurch were heavily congested, I clapped my hands because I knew why, they were all heading to us for the market.

By '92 we had also started doing car boot sales on the car park starting at 7am which meant a 6am rise to be out by 6.30 because the booters were queuing on the A49 causing a traffic jam, these went well especially if the weather was fine but it was a long Sunday. Up early, out for 6.30am, in for opening at about 11.30am after counting the cash, busy Sunday lunch, close at 3pm, take Barry back to Preston, back to open at 7pm, do quiz at 8pm till 10.30pm and then relax with a beer or two when Grace finally immerged from the kitchen. Just to make life more difficult some bright person, probably me, had suggested we do themed food nights, Spanish, German, Irish, French and the most popular Greek nights for which I had built a Kleftiko oven on the patio at the rear of the pub which consisted of a large Greek urn buried into a soil bank with a hole drilled in the top for the smoke to escape. Lamb was the usual meat cooked very slowly on charcoal after placing a stone over the opening and sealing it with mud. Delicious.

Talking about food brings to mind kitchens and cooking utensils which you had to go and buy, not like today where anything can be delivered. The nearest catering supply shop was Banners in Congleton run by Geoff Banner and his wife. We made a day of the trip, firstly shopping for utensils and then a snack at the Lion and Swan which dates back to Tudor times with its imposing black timber beams and white infill's standing at the top of Swan Bank, leading on to west St. Inside the waitress's wore black dresses, white aprons, and white lace caps which gave it a very grand appearance even though our lunch only consisted of sandwiches and chips. On our return trip home I took a different route and within only minutes drove though a most beautiful village, a huge church with a tall steeple, a village green surrounded by quaint cottages, in no time I joined the main A34 and home to Beeston with our purchases little knowing what impact that unknown village was to have on my future.

As I write this missive a phone call came 2 days ago with such bad news that a very old time customer had passed away and that his funeral was in two days which we intended to attend, not necessarily out of great friendship but out of respect for him and his family whom we had got to know over the last 36 years. His name was Neville Jack, a big quiet man who worked on the railways at first as an engineer and later in the offices near to where he and his wife Hazel lived in Crewe, the heart of the railways since its conception. Nev as I remarked was a quiet gentleman and appeared to let his wife make the decisions, and it's around her that most of the memories are remembered. We had not been at Beeston long when it was noticed that this couple had become regular early evening Sunday regulars who turned out to be Hazel and Neville as I called him then being looked after by chef Edi and the staff. As they travelled from Crewe every week without fail we thought something must be good, this continued until our departure in '95. More later.

Edi chef was now working on Irish sea ferries which entailed him working two weeks on board and two weeks at home (which meant he actually only worked 5 months a year, 6 months on, 6 months off – 1 months holiday = 5 months) so when he was at home we could go on holiday, ya hoooo. We worked hard and played hard so when the situation arose off we would go, either just the family or occasionally we'd take either Grace's mum Doreen or Haley's school pal Amy. Torquay was visited, staying at the Grand where we met Rod Hull and Emu, I didn't get ravaged. Later France where in Bayeux I contracted salmonella from eating contaminated oysters. In Malta I couldn't decide whether it was a building site with half built houses or a car park for old disused cars, then Rhodes which was OK but I got ripped off on the currency exchange on a day trip to Turkey which was filthy. Agadir followed where because Grace's passport didn't have enough expiry months on it she was signed over to me by the passport authorities to be responsible for her and a good job because whilst I was swimming in the hotel pool I got out of my depth and Grace had to rescue me from drowning by pulling me out by my hair, another eventful holiday was to Calpe in northern Spain where we had been loaned a villa by Ian and Thelma King, this was fantastic until two nights in when on our return from a night out we found that we'd had a break in. The window bars had been sawn and forced open, probably a small child put through who ransacked the property, not taking much but we didn't feel safe after this intrusion. We packed up and vacated, moving down the coast to Benidorm where a friend of Bob Price owned a hotel and was glad to put us up, at a price. It was a s....t hole so after two nights we made our excuses and decamped to Sidi San Juan in a grand Hotel. However because I thought we were in for a cheap holiday I had not brought enough cash and my credit card limit was getting precariously near its limit. I was forced to ring Neil a customer at Beeston and also a bank manager who after a little chat agreed to get my c/c limit extended, situation resolved.

Later in the year, end of October or early November we took our annual trip to the Lakes, staying at Gilpin Lodge where as usual we had a great time even though this year the weather was exceptionally wet and caused much flooding around the area, but one wit said 'don't worry about the water we've got several big lakes to sweep it into'. Some years previous we had found a company in Huddersfield supplying Christmas decorations so we decided to visit on our return home taking us on a different route to our normal journey south down the M6. Our new route took us via Hawes, Aysgarth, Grassington, the market town of Skipton, Kieghley, Halifax where we had a fine lunch at the Old Hall and finally arriving at K. D. Designs in Huddersfield. The business was housed in an old large mill just off the city centre, was over several floors in which were stored countless displays of all types of Christmas and myriad decorations. Barry was not present on this trip because it had been decided by me that he should be brought up by his mother and her present husband rather than shunted from pillar to post every week, so there was only Grace, Haley and I on this trip and we had arrived at a most auspicious occasion as the owner asked us if we would like to take a trip around his warehouse on his magical train. He told us that in two days time the train was to be dismantled and taken to Milton Keynes Shopping Centre where it would spend Christmas in their Christmas Wonderland. What a trip we had being transported around all the Christmas displays, giant trees with pixie heads popping out of the foliage as we passed by and huge Disney figures singing carols, one playing a guitar, this lasted for about ½ hr and at the end all of us had the biggest smiles you can imagine, as if we'd been to Disneyland. Their dec's were all on the large side which suited our pubs large rooms as I wanted customers to feel like they were at home, all warm and cosy, but because our rooms were larger than theirs at home the tinsel, bells, glitter balls and huge Christmas tree needed to look extravagant. After we'd spent up our homeward journey continued on thru Manchester, finally arriving home with all our Christmas goodies which would be put up within weeks ready for the festive season.

'92 was also another PP moment with Preston Guild being celebrated in September but as in previous years when mills and trades were massive contributors to the carnival and because of the decline of these in recent years the parades were on a much smaller scale, but we decided to visit staying over at Linda's. After an interesting day out, a meal, a few drinks we retired to bed, Haley with Danni and Grace and I in the front bedroom and so to sleep. Linda must have carried on having an odd one or two more because at some ungodly time in the morning she came into our bedroom slightly worse for wear and attempted to get into bed with us at my side, we realised this was not a good place to be, so we packed and left, where to go? Not home as we still had 2 days holiday, so at 2 in the morning (there's a song title there) we rang Peter and Leslie and asked if we could come to them in Bolton, which we did. What good friends.

In '93 Peter and Leslie also gave us help at our 10th anniversary at the pub, I say help they were actually roped in to wash up when the glasses ran out and the stack of dirty glasses was more like a mountain. To the afternoon BBQ party we had had 200 RSVP'S and were expecting perhaps 250 but in the end 400 turned up to a fantastic party with music by the Chorley Mashers, playing outside on the patio and a BBQ of burgers and hotdogs all cooked by Grace and Sara, their arms at the end of the day were red raw with the heat of the BBQ. Perhaps the gig was so popular and crowded because the day was warm and sunny and the farming community had realised it was free. You work it out. Talking about farmers I'm reminded of the market days when trading standards officers would open up the petrol caps of the parked cattle wagons looking for pink diesel that should only be used in vehicles on the farm which was much cheaper and of course led to temptation, some having secret tanks to try and trick the excise men.

We had enjoyed Cyprus so much that we decided to make another visit to the Imperial in Paphos on the beach just a little out of the centre, because of this we would hire a taxi and soon got to know one particular driver called Lagis, we asked him to take us to the places where he and his family would go, so dressed in shirt, tie and jacket and Grace smartly dressed we would be taken to all sorts of interesting places off the beaten track, one time up into the mountains to stop at an old farm cottage on the side of the road with a ramshackle veranda to front on which were a table and chairs. An old lady greeted Lagis and us in Greek, went into the cottage returning with local wine for Grace, beers for us boys, coke for Haley, olives, bread, hard cheese and ziveneer (more later.) What a fabulous day sitting in the sun, having refreshments and when I came to pay it was the equivalent of £3, I gave her a £5, she was over the moon. Lagis invited us to a family wedding in a little village church which was very ornate decorated with many religious figures and icons. The bride's attendants who were so overdressed in what appeared to be brides dresses similar to the bride fussed over the bride, mopping her brow because of the heat and keeping her make up in order. The wedding breakfast was held in a huge 3 glass sided village hall where up to 3000, yes 3000 guests attended, not necessarily invited as it was assumed that everyone from the bride and grooms villages would attend. They stood on a raised platform and on arrival they greeted all their guests who intern pinned money onto the brides dress, in the hall where as many as possible of the glass windows were thrown open. trestle tables were laid out at which benches had been placed for the guests to sit and eat. The meal consisted of many local delicacies such as

Kleftiko, Stifado, bread, mousaka and a strange corn, chicken and barley dish which was ladled out of plastic household buckets which everyone raved about, not me. However the local wine, beer and soft drinks were provided free, there was a small charge for spirits. What a great holiday.

Back home, one lunch I had a visit from a very red nosed Dixie Trainer staggering from many drinks earlier that morning, he was a local no good, I asked him what I could do for him as our pub wasn't a place for him, he asked me if I wanted to buy some wine, cheap. I asked what variety, he said, red I think, I asked how much? He said oh I don't know, say 50p I said that's cheap, he said alright a pound then. Knowing there was definately a problem with this wine I asked him to bring me a bottle to show me that night. Off he went and I was straight on the phone to the local police asking if anybody was missing any wine, they said to give them a ring if he turned up which he didn't but the force rang me later to say that they had found Dixie and his mate fast asleep in a hedgerow with a haul of Denis Lilley's finest vintage port that they'd stolen from his wine cellar, hence the red nose and very flushed appearance, red wine huh.

Also in this year the IRA exploded a bomb in Warrington town centre causing havoc and murdering Tim Parry and Jonathan Ball, The head of the team was ACC Brian and some nights he and his team would retire to the pub for a well deserved tea or something wrapping up that days very distressing information that they had detected during the investigation and on their final day Brian asked if we would allow them to use the privacy of the restaurant to wrap up their findings. Beeston was a haunt of quite a few Bobbies and higher ranks because they knew they wouldn't be bothered by any scroats they may have apprehended previously.

One afternoon Haley came to us saying that Auntie Marie needed some help, she and Bernard were staying over for a few days and after enjoying a few drinks at lunchtime had managed to fall into the bath, not horizontally but across it, she was wedged in and we heard her saying 'get up Marie, eh get up Marie', she was helped out and went for a little lie down.

Because of John's job at the chemical firm Grace Deerborn as their European Director he and Lynn were moved to Paris and we were invited to go for a visit to their residence on the outskirts in Croisey ser Seine. Our aim was to visit Maxims de Paris' on 3 Rue Royal which is reputed to be one of the finest restaurants in the world, founded in 1893 by Maxime Gaillard when it was a small bistro and later developed in the Belle Epoch decor styled restaurant in 1900 for the Great Exhibition that you see today and is now owned by Pierre Cardin. On our visit we were seated side by side on plush banquets which went all around the very grand room. The tables were placed so close together with just the slightest gap between that if you wished to get out two waiters came to pull the table out and do the same on your return. The menu was very grand French cuisine, Grace and I both chose roasted pheasant which the waiter dissected and served at the table finishing off with the ju thickened over a garidon. The pheasant had been cooked perfectly but was still full of pellets which we pinged out onto the silver salver. We could not choose what to eat for dessert so the waiter recommended that he ask the chef to prepare a Grand Marnier soufflé for us. It was the most perfect dessert I had ever tasted and we devoured every last morsel it was only to be beaten by floating islands some years later. On the table when we arrived was a bottle of Louis Rodeir Crystal rośe which at 3000 Francs by today's standards was a steal and if you decided not to drink it you asked the waiter to take it away, which I didn't, well it was a posh night out. Later we danced down the Champs-Elysees and visited a review bar where two Bacardi and Cokes cost 750 Francs which we drank quickly whilst viewing a group of nude statuest men and women. I paid and we left sharpish before jumping into a taxi to take us back to John and Lyn's where probably because of the night's alcohol I fell out of bed and smashed a bedside lantern which is often remarked about, even to this day.

In '94 super markets and big shops were allowed to open with restricted hours and at first it didn't seem to affect the BH markets but by the August I could see that the markets didn't seem quite so busy and the car boots were also quieter which meant that Grace's trips to Valerie Taylors and Feathers were not as frequent and trips to the Grosvenor less often, time for a new strategy. This was the year that we met Kevin and Edie Skipworth who came to Bunbury to represent the Australian Government on the quatercentenary of Bunbury School which is where Haley attended. The relationship between Bunbury and Australia is because Col. Bunbury from Bunbury founded Bunbury in South Weston Australia near Perth. They came to the restaurant for lunch with Barbara and Ernest Crawley which was a great success and over the next few months and years we got to know one another better and became great friends even to this day as Kevin has risen up the pole to become Adjutant General of SW Australia we have been privileged to have been invited to attend many Australian functions. Unfortunately Kev is now retired but is still very active at home and we don't see them as often as we would like but there is always Skype.

Another change I had noticed was that farmers instead of coming to market were sending dealers who didn't frequent the pub after they had bid for the animals they required which meant of course that the farmers were staying at home and not spending time and money in the pub. By now alarm bells are ringing.

During our time at Beeston we had been fortunate to find the accountancy services of Steve Mercer who lived with his wife Sue in the old church at Haughton near the Nags Head which was by now owned by Sue and John Lloyd, lively customers of ours on music nights and friends of Art and Maggie. John and Sue later went on to own the Farmers Arms at Huxley and later the Dysart arms in Bunbury, which was a very popular pub opposite the church One thing I should mention about John is that he did not like kids and only tolerated Haley because she was our daughter. Over the next few months Grace became lethargic and tired and after many Dr.'s appointments at which some said 'take it easy 'or 'have a holiday' finally Dr. Nigel O'Callaghan diagnosed an over active thyroid and sent her for treatment at Bupa Thingwall Hospital on the Wirral under a Mr. Jones and after several months of treatment she appeared to regain her old self.

Purely as a marketing exercise I thought that having a Christmas in July would be a good idea, why? Well, groups and clubs looking for party venues in December start their quest midyear so having Christmas and New Year menus available gave us a head start (how many restaurants to this day are still struggling to have menus ready in October?) So by the middle of July I would have decked out the pub and restaurant in Christmas dec's and a live Christmas tree decked out with lights and baubles. One customer asked 'where do you get a Christmas tree in July'? Uh.

Non regulars, called passing trade who visited us would enter the pub and stop dead, look at each other in amazement and of course ask why, so being me I told them the truth, I haven't taken them down from last year, or I've put them up a little earlier or the real truth is because on the middle Sunday in July Santa comes for his Christmas lunch which he doesn't get to enjoy on Christmas day because he's too tired. To this function customers would come dressed in winter clothes with their children who received a present from Santa secretly played by me. I thought I'd got away with it until Haley, about 9 at the time said she'd recognised me because of my bracelet peeping out from my sleeve. Christmas and New Year brings to mind the occasions when Peter and Leslie and the boys hired a canal boat and moored it on the Shropshire Union canal 200 yards from the pub where we'd go to parties which were great fun, sometimes the fun was a bit naughty, no I can't remember who untied the boat from the bank causing Stan to do the splits when trying to get off the boat, only being saved by me. We spent many days out and holidays with this fun couple, one trip was to see Julio Iglesias at Birmingham International Concert centre where we also stayed the night and had arranged to see Mel Scholes who apart from Grace was Julio's other fan. sic. We had some great times with Peter and Leslie.

Another exciting time around Christmas was going to the panto at the Palace Theatre in Manchester again starring Russ Abbot who was a great showman and also on these visits we'd once again go for a Chinese meal at Wong Chu restaurant in china town which should have been spelt cafe. The atmosphere in the dining room was frantic with all the smells of the orient, crispy whole ducks hanging in the window with a chef chopping them up to order, placed on a plate and sauce being ladled over, then off to a table. Lots of Chinese writing and symbols adorned the walls and when I enquired what they signified I was informed that these were Chinese dish's for the Chinese, so we requested could we have real Chinese food, from then the world of Chinese cuisine opened up to us. Ho fun, chum fun, cold crispy belly pork with soy sauce, jelly fish, chicken feet and the delights of the steam trolley that was only available till 4pm. Haley's favourite were ribs, any sort, BBQ, OK, salt and pepper, she soon picked up the nick name of Haley Bones and she was very courageous as on the one occasion when she ordered hot and sour soup, she has not repeated that order.

Just a little more about Russ Abbot who Grace and I went to visit him in a show at The London Palladium, great show, laughed my side out, what happened after taught me another lesson. It's not what you are but who people perceived you are. Grace and I were in need of food and as we were in London we wanted something special, so we looked at several restaurants and finally plumped for Langhams on Regent St., at the time owned by Michael Caine. We entered and were greeted by a young lady who asked if we had a reservation (booking up north) we said regretfully no, she replied that sorry they were fully booked but for the future could she take our address details. All I said was Beeston Castle, wow, I've never seen anyone move so fast. This way sir and madam, please this way, we were seated in the middle of the restaurant on a raised diaz and treated like lord and lady muck. From then on whilst at Beeston, I said Beeston Castle, I'm not saying it opened any doors but .....

In late summer of '94 we had been invited by Remy Martin to Burghley Horse Trials because of our Remy cognac sales over the previous year. We stayed at the Whipper Inn in Stamford which was adjacent to the town market and only 2-3 miles from Burghley House around which the horse event was staged. There was a free lunch and a bar laid on in an opened topped double decker bus where I bumped into this tall bearded guy dressed in a long hunting mac who turned out to be Prince Michael of Kent, I apologised and moved on. One of the events laid on was an artist drawing people at the event, so we had him sketch a caricature pen and ink of Haley which was very life like.

'95 dawned and was unknowingly to be a mementos year. Because of my grave doubts about the future of the pub and the stresses and strains of the job Grace and I decided it was time to sell, so without telling anybody we put the pub up for sale trying desperately to keep it secret. I've seen it all happen before; you're selling and moving, leaving the customers, unsettling their happy bubble, not knowing what the future holds for them, so why should they carry on supporting you, which leads to loss of trade. After a few weeks there was a low rumour simmering and one or two asked was it true, of course I said no, we did get several enquiries from the agent and finally a serious offer which we decided to accept, they viewed, and dates set for completion in March. Obviously they needed to arrange finance, so two bank managers came to visit, then another two and two weeks before completion the purchasers backed out due to lack of funds or as they put it, it was overpriced.

Start again, but fortunately another couple had shown interest and now we were back on the market and we met a party of three who all would be involved in the running of the business. They said they had some experience, little did we know how little, at this stage they were very keen and we managed to keep the potential sale a secret from as many as possible for reasons mentioned, even the staff but Arti said one day 'I know you're leaving look at the state of the lounge carpet, you'd have changed that if you intended to stay' By June Rowli John had got wind of our move and fell out with me good and proper, not because I hadn't told him but because we were moving and leaving. He and Mary had been great friends over the years and one little story comes to mind when he told me that the following week he'd have to be at home to clean his brasses and the hundreds of horse, cow, pig and chicken brasses that he'd been presented with for judging animals at county shows over many years. He said he and Mary set too and polished them every year, regardless.

Well the sale date was set for the Tuesday 19th of July, the removal firm was organised and all that was required was for Rosie a Scottish red headed slight lady, her partner and her brother to acquire the necessary alcohol licence from Chester Magistrates court. We were still being very close to the chest about the sale, perhaps many surmised without knowing the facts, so what. We still had nowhere to live and no real future plans but what the hell. People didn't believe this, you must know what you're doing, yes going on holiday. On the Friday prior to the move the following Tuesday Grace, I, Rosie and her co/conspirators duly arrived at court for them to be granted a licence which should have been a breeze but the magistrates asked what actual experience any of the applicants had had in the licence trade. Rosie's son had been a junior manager for some hotel chain for six months and the other two none. It was only at this point that it dawned on us that no licence meant no sale. When the licence was granted Grace and I held each other's hands and shook them vigorously whilst sat at the back of the court. It was now only 10.15am but we had to celebrate so we trooped into Chester town centre and arrived at the Grosvenor, into the bar and requested a bottle of champagne. The head waiter came over and said that the hotel could not serve alcohol to non residents till 11.00am but Mr. Smith we'll see what can be done, two bottles of Taittinger arrived and later we were off home to give everyone the good/ bad news. Sara the head chef was on holiday so we rang her mum Jean and asked her to get Sara to contact us; we're finishing on Sunday and moving on Tuesday, no rush then. This new crew didn't have the foggiest idea so all staff jobs were safe as they needed them, some like Edi and Sara stayed for a while, some didn't mainly because the new team hadn't the faintest idea how to treat them and as they hadn't intended doing much work, as they thought we didn't, the business soon went into the ground.

A lot of people's perception of a landlords and lady's life is, crawl out of bed half an hour before opening, sit drinking at the bar all day with your cronies, all monies into back pocket and just lounge about telling the staff what to do. If you can do it good luck but what a waste.

As we had no home address apart from the house in Honeyfields which was rented out, the dogs were found a temporary new home on Didd's farm were they could romp around the fields for the duration of our holiday whilst living in a huge dog house, the arrangement was open ended and much appreciated. The arranged removers arrived on the Monday as it was to take two days to pack and take most of our goods to storage whilst we fathomed out our future, but some of the everyday essentials were to be stored in a barn at the Dysart. Thank goodness for our good friends John and Sue. On the Sunday we had a small farewell party, I say small, all our friends, lots of customers and family who'd come to help us move, they also helped diminish the stock. Up early to finish the packing, take stock ourselves to hopefully tally with the official stock taker, f&f to be agreed and bandit monies to be shared, then wait for the bank transfer to be confirmed and the sale completed. Out of the back kitchen door we go not forgetting to unplug and take the radio which was playing 'don't think twice' by Celine Dion, a small tear in my eye and trepidation in my heart.

Haley had finished at Bishop Heber School for summer on the Friday, our plans were to take a holiday in Cyprus which we had enjoyed on our previous visits but that was three days in the future so with no home to go to we stayed at the Wild Boar for three nights until Edi took us to Birmingham Airport to board our plane were we thanked him not only for the transport but his hard work and friendship. We didn't get rid of Edi that easy. We had not made any room reservations for our stay, but if asked I'd have said the Imperial which I'd remembered, so first we hunted out an apartment which Grace and I wrote off as a doss hole and instead decided to find a hotel and dam the expense. The Hotel Amathus was just across the Rd. on the beach, near to town and with a fantastic pool complex. We walked up to reception and the receptionist said 'welcome Mr & Mrs. Smith' which took us back somewhat. I enquired how he knew our name and he told us that he used to work at the Imperial and had remembered us, must have made an impression. A very advantageous room rate was agreed for a superior room overlooking the beach with a small private pool for an unspecified time, Haley was thrilled. We enjoyed all the amenities especially the huge pool were one sunny hot day a customer who reminded us of Rodney (fools and horses) dripping in faux gold chains and bracelets, he was talking so loud to his phone letting everyone hear his conversation, whilst splashing about in the pool he dropped his phone into the water, ooops, we all smiled as did Vanessa Phelps looking very volumpious in her undersized bathing costume. Across the Rd. from the hotel was a small cocktail bar called Johnny's Jazz where we'd enjoy a beer for me and Bacardi and Coke for Grace, Haley enjoying a coke without the rum, the music was great. Another bar where we first saw karaoke was Bubbles bar, we thought what great singers, sounded so like the original artists, but later we discovered a monitor set in the stage floor to which they were actually miming along too with a little input from their own voices. We would dine at several places, sometimes getting Lagis to drive us out of town to out of the way places, one night we were recommended to dine at the Annabelle Hotel on the harbour. The Annabelle is a very prestigious hotel and as much as I do not remember what we ate. I do remember that as we dined at a table in the restaurant, outside on the sand under the restaurant scuttled hundreds of cockroaches and occasionally a rat ran by, which was not a pleasant experience and when we mentioned the roaches to the staff, we got 'oh yes we get them everywhere'. Did not return. The one problem with Greek food is that it is the same in every cafe and restaurant and the menus could have been printed by the thousand and a different name printed on a batch for each establishment. Only have a Mezze if you are really, really hungry as the food just keeps on coming and the Greek salads are divine, but not at every meal and don't drink retsina. Lagis the taxi driver took us to Yaraskibo up in the hills were his friend had a restaurant/cafe; he dropped us off and he went to visit relatives. The open aired large house was entered up some stairs leading to an outside veranda and on the wall in big letters was printed 'Fully Air Conditioned', there was no menu, you got what they had and they had plenty even taking into account that at that time Grace was not into meat. Lots of local wine and ziveneer, Haley on pop or perhaps a drop of wine. The week flowed into another week and another, but we were not idle, the idea came to us that perhaps we could live out there and we looked around a couple of properties that were on the market, one being The Red lion holiday complex, a hotel and bars with an open air courtyard, on the market for about £1 million, but the drawback was, a Greek had to be involved to the tune of 51%, no way, would you trust a Greek with your family jewels? The money, well anything is possible if you dream high enough, but it was not to be. Another day we went to meet Lagis's brother Jesus who was in charge of the turtle population at a site in the harbour and who later gave us a thrilling motor boat ride on the sea in his speed boat, his wife owned a rest/cafe which we visited and were entertained in true Greek style. After four weeks it was time to return home, not knowing where to but we had to think about Haley's schooling, time for more friends to step in. John and Sue had a daughter called Jackie who was a hostess for Japan Airlines based in Japan and her house in Haslington was vacant, ideal for a short term let, so this became our temporary accommodation on our return, giving us time to decide our next step.

I had thought that we would take several months off but seeing our bank balance diminish at a great rate, ex's going out, nothing coming in and enjoying ourselves, perhaps it was time to find some work.

So with money in the bank what are our options, I'd never make a fighter pilot, perhaps a pop singer, no, or a lawyer, I don't think so, but I know a lot about pubs which leads us to sussing out a few breweries. I approached Green King, Robinsons and Adnams, one up north, the other down south and the other on the far east coast. Surprisingly quickly we were asked to attend interviews, well after all Grace and I had vast experience in the trade, our C.V.'s must have impressed them, no we'd got money in the bank and were available. Is that me being cynical again or just a reality? We soon settled down in Jackie's tiny modern two bed roomed house in Haslington and set about finding a hotel we fancied that had potential. We started with the furthest afield, making an appointment to see an area manager at Adnams brewery in Southwold, what a journey.

I under estimated the distance and only just made it in time arriving on Brew day which gave the whole area the heady sweet smell of hops. The interview went well and we were asked to view several of the houses they had available at the time, some looked really pretty thatched and in gorgeous rural areas, a lot painted pink but most of them in out of the way places which with hindsight have now probably gone out of business. We decided probably not. Our next port of call was Green King in Bury St. Edmonds, again a long drive to Suffolk, the interview went well and several houses were on offer, so we visited 3, the one in Great Dunmow looked great, thatched roof, on a small river in a beautiful small village with a walled mansion house and 'promised' alterations by the Brewery. There was one more Brewery to explore, Robinsons of Stockport which I was dubious about for several reasons, one the beer wasn't my favourite and the state of some of the pubs was dire but an appointment was made to see David Chadwick. Getting to Stockport was extremely difficult and I'd under estimated the timing due to the amount of traffic at 9am and there were traffic lights on every road junction. On our arrival we were escorted to D. Chadwick's office for a talk about our future intensions, expectations and finances if they were to offer us a pub. A short brewery tour followed. D.C. was mesmerised by Grace who at the time had a short spiky hair cut in the fashion of Sue Pollard a star in the show Hi De Hi, and I'm sure this was the reason that same day we were asked to view 3 pubs which were either on the market or about to come on the market, just to give us some idea as to what might be available to us, but we should not imagine that we would be offered these houses. The first we visited was an estate local on the outskirts of Manchester which we passed by on our return home and the other two we visited for a secret look at over the next few days. Firstly the Harrington Arms at Bossley which used to be a Yates Wine Lodge, quite unusual as its location in the middle of the country on a main A Rd. does not fit the stereotypical town centre Yates's, I believe it had something to do with the adjoining pasture where cattle was raised for their food outlets. I was going to say their restaurants but I don't put Yates's Wine bars in that category as they were more spit, sawdust and Aussie wine venues. Next was a revelation as we approached the next destination. I had a déjà vow moment because I had a feeling we'd been here before. We'd got a little lost and after finding Astbury Lane Ends in Congleton we were directed to the village of Astbury which is where our next pub was situated, known locally as the Edge but was really the Egerton arms Hotel. I knew we'd been here before when we'd last visited Banners cook shop and I remembered the beautiful village in which it was situated, I fell under its spell instantly. We entered via the patio entrance incognito remembering we were only secretly viewing and had been informed that we hadn't a cat in hell's chance. We sat at a small table near the bar, good viewing point, and had a small snack whilst taking in a much as possible, the bar had several regular drinkers who were making contact with the two barmaids, most of the other tables were occupied with customers and most of them eating which was an encouraging sign. The decoration was in need of a little attention but that could soon be rectified with a lick of paint and lots of TLC. Little did we know? We thought that our secret visit had been achieved successfully but were told later that it had not fooled anybody, but what the hell; as soon as we got home I rang David Chadwick to inform him that Grace and I would take the Egerton. He reiterated that there other interested parties and would not commit himself but did arrange for us to go for a tour of the hotel within the next few days. This we did and I was still convinced it was the pub for us; it became apparent that it needed a little more than a lick of paint and a little TLC. The lady in charge was Mrs Margaret Lightfoot the wife of the absent landlord Ron, who was at that time was living in Anglesey, we later found out why and also discovered what a smart lady (I don't mean in the dress sense) she was. Within days after further discussions with Robinsons D.C rang us about 10am and offered us the pub, then, not an hour later a DM from Green King rang me and said that after he'd got the bosses at the brewery to agree to do the alterations we had insisted on he was now able to offer us the tenancy. Oops! After a quick discuss with Grace I had to inform him that he was an hour too late and that we had already made an agreement with Robinsons. Just like buses, you wait for ages then two come along, which one do you take, the first one.

Mrs Lightfoot was desperate to go, we wanted to settle, we were available, had the money and within six weeks we were in. On our return from holiday we needed to find Haley a new school and as we'd been promised the Egerton the obvious, nearest school would be Heathfield High in Congleton, although it meant a 15 minute drive from Haslington, it was round the corner from Astbury and as by now the negotiations for the pub were nigh on complete we took the gamble and Haley joined at the start of the Autumn term in September. At this point John Lloyd informed us that Jackie had decided to put the house we were renting from her on the market so we needed to move soon. During this waiting period we made the most of the free time and made visits here and there, one day going to Preston to visit Auntie Meg and Keith who were now living off Fulwood Hall Lane in a maisonette just around the corner from where Audrey and Ken used to live, on our return journey we came to Lostock Hall where sister Sylvia and her partner had surprisingly taken the Victoria Hotel just before the two railway bridges in the centre of the village. It was a lovely hot summer's day and when we entered we were greeted by Sylvia's partner who didn't know us from Adam, not because he didn't recognise us but because he was drunk, we enquired as to Sylvia's whereabouts, we found her in the tiny kitchen, sweating over a hot steamy fryer, Grace said 'you'll not catch me doing that'. Sylvia made a rude gesture, perhaps remembering her previous comment some years previous. Two other stories come to mind about my sister,

1. When she was younger, say 16/17 she got around, one night, still living at home a gentleman/man/boy brought her home in his car and he wished to have a goodnight kiss, as you do. Unknowing to them Ada had waited up for her, to make her or them a cup of chocolate, but as the night went on (2am) she became concerned, she went out to ask them in, on opening the car door was surprised to see flesh, it was his a..e, she slapped it. I'll leave you to imagine the consequences. 2. When we were much younger, me in my teens, Sylvia 8 or 9 had a big white fluffy bunny that was kept in a cage in the back garden, it was her pride and joy, well one day in December it went missing, Sylvia always blamed me for letting it go which I have always fervently denied and it was not until I was into my 30's did I discover the truth. That Christmas the white fluffy bunny had been our Christmas lunch.

Everything was going smoothly, all our plans fitting into place, the only fly in the ointment was Mrs, Lightfoot who had new demands every week, we kept our cool and finally moved in on 21st September just 6 weeks after our first viewing. Remember I said 'lick of paint and some TLC' well I was wrong, the place was filthy.

We had inherited a few of the existing staff, some stayed and some soon exited either by their own design or by ours. Two that come to mind are firstly Robert the so called chef who on the first day was asked what his style of cooking was, he replied that his signature dish was Rogan josh which we thought, great, until we found a packet of Rogan Josh mix in the cupboard and when asked to make a burger put the pate in the fryer, then in a pan and finally under the grill which took about 40 minutes, so he was then required to knuckle down and scrub the disgusting kitchen like the rest of us to be told, he didn't do any cleaning, he left. Secondly was Geraldine who worked the bar with Pam, they had obviously been doing the job for a long time, the bar was their domain and we were not going to interfere, but sorry changes needed making, like not washing the ashtrays in the glass washer at the end of the night, which had been their custom since year dot. Geraldine was a hot headed Scot and was not going to stand any interference from us, so there was only one outcome, she had to go. I am not one for pussying about, so after the first week I went round to her house in Alsager with a week in lieu of wages, P45 and told her not to bother coming to work the following week, job done. Oh no, she took us to tribunal and was awarded £800, the best money I ever spent. More about staff later.

The Hotel was located in the beautiful village of Astbury adjacent to the church and the dead centre of the village (cemetery) which lay just off the A49. There were two entrances, one off the A49 and the other off Peel lane which runs through the village on to Mosley and High town which are on the outskirts of Congleton. The building from 16c lay in about an acre of land comprising of a large car park, paddock and a wooded area with an overgrown pond which the Lightfoots had used as a rubbish tip, disgusting. As you enter through the front door there are rooms to right and left with a private staircase to the upper floors, on to the bar in front, right to the ladies and gents toilets and through to a store, ironing room and laundry. Back to the bar, follow on to the right passing more seating and down a corridor to the restaurant which also has a separate bar. Back out of the restaurant with more wide stairs to upper bedrooms, but keeping on the ground floor turn right into a long galley kitchen with the usual catering equipment (most of it on its last legs) on up a step into a food prep area with sink and assorted fridges and freezers. Down a few steps, and on the right a bottle and veg store, back left and down stairs to the beer cellar, the engine room of the pub with gorgeous smells of hops and beer. Back again to the wide stairs, up we go to six letting bedrooms, 5 doubles, one single which share two bathrooms, two toilets and one shower, they needed a lot of attention. On our first night a guest was booked to stay and Grace had the unenvious job of showing him to room 4, the bed had woollen green blankets, she apologised and said that we had literally moved in that day, he stayed but we never saw him again. Along the corridor to the private stairs from the ground floor turn left into our private accommodation which consists of lounge, dining room, bathroom with carpet up the side of the bath, kitchen which had an aspect of the path leading to the back public entrance. This is where Mrs Lightfoot used to sit to see who came and went and who was likely to buy her a drink. The kitchen only had a sink and draining board, then on into a room under the eaves where Robert used to sleep, this room was very hot because through a sliding door were the central heating water boilers with loads of storage space where in summer the heat was intolerable. The first major expense that I'd had to agree to was a new kitchen and the second a modern fitted bathroom, only on these terms had Grace said yes to the move. The kitchen which was at our own expense was fitted by a firm called Complete Kitchens from Congleton who did a good job until some of the finishing touches were missed, but after a few words the job was completed to our satisfaction. Tony our handy man of many years fitted the corner bath and tiled the walls in lovely blue and white tiles, not always quite straight; the bathroom initially had canary yellow carpet with dark blue towels to match the tiles, eventually the carpet was changed, more later. The second week Grace and I hosted a party to welcome existing customers and hopefully encourage new ones, we soon discovered that some of the regulars thought that they already ran the pub with the collusion of one or two members of staff, this was going to change. Most of the group who had the idea that they ruled the pub lived across the main A49 behind the Post Office in a caravan encampment or as liked they to describe it, a mobile homes park, they were all descended from travellers. Right from the beginning Grace and I did not allow them to tell us what they wanted, like they informed us that they intended to have a private party over the first New Year at the pub, under no circumstances was that going to happen. In effect they would scan customers coming into the pub and make comments as to whether they liked them or not because of the way they dressed or looked, which made new customers feel uncomfortable, so they didn't return, not good for business. The money they spent was good and this in due course meant they would often drink too much, they would then argue, washing all their dirty linen in public, this often resulted in a fight, this then gave me the opportunity to bar them and over a period their numbers diminished. They were known locally as the carpet baggers as their main profession was selling and fitting carpets. There must be money in carpets. It soon became apparent that this group needed to move on. It came to a crescendo one day when Anne the head of the clan told Grace what they were going to do, Grace took her down the corridor where it was more private and in no uncertain terms told Anne what and where to stick it, we never saw her again and along with her went others, Job done. Every now and then you've got to assert your authority.

On a very busy early evening Grace slipped on the lino that surrounded the bar and fell, it was evident that she had sustained an injury to her arm; Eileen McClackland agreed to drive Grace to Macc. Hospital and after having her arm X-rayed it was concluded that it was broken and a plaster cast was applied. You'd think that that would put Grace out of action for some time, but oh no, within days she was pulling pints, well not exactly pulling, but certainly pouring and even with her arm in plaster life, work, and death went on. Doreen had not been in the best of health for some time and passed away towards the end of the year to be buried in the family grave at Preston cemetery, the wake was held at the Claremont Hotel on Blackpool Rd.

Christmas of '95 was cold and snowy; trade had been good and the festivities during December had gone without a hitch so to celebrate we decided to have Christmas lunch at the Yellow Broome at Twemlow, a very smart and expensive restaurant out in the sticks. Unknowingly this trip was to become a family tradition for many years. On this Christmas day it had snowed overnight and the roads were lightly covered in snow so Grace suggested that our journey to Twemlow should be on the main roads, but me being me decided to take the country roads because it would be quicker, bad idea as when we were nearly at our destination I hit an icy patch on the road, the car slid to one side of the road, nearly hitting a big wall, then slid to the other side of the road coming to a stop with the off side bumper in a hedge. Grace's face was a picture, already with her arm in plaster, then a wall looming towards her then into a hedge with our 1 month old car. No one was injured and the car only had a slight scratch. Phew! The lunch was a great success, but I did get it in the neck for not using the main Rd.

Very shortly after our arrival at the Edge I heard that a By Pass was to be constructed around Congleton which would in affect take traffic off the A34 and channel it to the M6, this news concerned me but as no one had any real information about it I put it to the back of my mind.

By now we had met all the regulars and after the departure of the 'clan' more and more customers came on board hopefully finding us a pleasant place to drink and eat.

Again this pub had different groups, who occupied their certain parts of the pub at different times of the day. During the day the first customers were just a few drinkers who didn't stay long after a pint or two, then the Biddulph boys who's favourite spot was around the bar in a cosy little corner called the snug, I say boys, but most of them were well into their 50's and 60's and stood propping the bar or sitting near enough to reach their beer, talking about the day's events. Names to remember were Dr. Ian, Clive James, Frank Speak, Phil and Harry, many of them Rotary members. During the week diners would fill all the tables in the bar and some would choose to eat in the restaurant which was more refined, or so I thought. In the pub most ate either a snack or OAP but in the restaurant it was either a la carte or OAP. Later in the day and early evening that space was taken over by another group of younger boys perhaps only 50 or 60 amongst whom were Brian Lang, Phil, Steve Ripley, Bob Harrison and an older guy called Harold who didn't like the way I organised things and told me so, he went.

Later in the evening a group of village local men would take over this room for the last hour or so, and were some of the last to leave. There were many regular diners, some coming two or three times a week, others just for a drink like Maurice and Jean who sat on the comfy wall seats chatting with Frank and Petal and Phil and Bill. These comfy seats were later sat on by parish councillors after their council meetings, which I think were just an excuse to go for a drink afterwards. During the day the lounge bar was usually left open for customers to order their food and drinks but later on in the evening it would be crowded with drinkers, both men and ladies, some from the village others from surrounding farms, of whom were the Sheards, Wards, Suttons and Lomas's who between them owned most of the land around. There are reputedly 48 millionaires in Astbury and surrounding area.

Back now to the rear entrance doors where, on entering later in the afternoon you'd find a group of more boys who after finishing work were desperate for a quick pint on their way home, sometimes more than a quick pint, these could include Chris Naden, Charles our butcher, Willie Shaw, Ginger, Don Wilkinson, with 2 or 3 still left from the 'clan' who we'd allowed to stay like Tony, his wife Carol and baby daughter, Horace and big George, all with the surname Finney. Another character I must mention is 'F..king Hell Dave Whittaker and his wife Jean, he had the nickname because when he was speaking, every sentence had to include the F word, which was spoken very quietly, not loud enough to embarrass anyone but always there.

One more couple to remember from those early days were two people who were and still are very successful in business, on our first meeting I called them by their surname as is polite, the lady asked me if I would address them by their Christian names Claire and John as they just wanted to be one of the locals, we have since become great friends. Many of these customers would come in most days, sometimes twice, on Sundays I'd have the first ones in at 11am and quite a few stayed all lunch till 3pm and some came back for the night time session. What with the diners and the drinkers Sunday was an enjoyable day and also prosperous.

The dogs had been brought from the farm on our move to the pub and soon settled, they lived outside in Haley's old dolls house which was really a garden shed filled with straw and even had curtains which made it comfortable for the dogs and warm at night.

We were both a 'destination 'and 'passing trade' hotel which I wanted to turn into a 'stopping trade hotel 'and although we were on the A34 there was not a clear view of the pub from the main road, so I always made sure that the road side appearance encouraged the passersby to come have a look. People eat, drink and get an impression from their first view and people are nosy. Also they are very opinionated about what they like, what they want and what they expect, if they don't get any or all of these then you're in trouble and it's no good saying 'sorry' after the event, you've got to deliver.

One thing people don't like is an empty car park because they may rightly deduce that it's empty because the pub is lacking customers who have already visited and not liked it, but if the car park is full then the pub must be good; therefore find a reason to get cars on the car park and bums on seats. One way we did this was to encourage OAP's at lunchtime with a cheaper, smaller sized portion which they like because many older people don't have the appetites they used to have, don't like wasting food either and that's the trade that's out there at lunchtime these days, no more long business lunchtimes and workers can't drink either.

In '96 Grace and I had planned several events, the first being a Robbie Burns night dinner which had a good response from the customers, but we had one little problem, not enough chefs, so I rang Edi who had by now had his fill of the new landlords of the Beeston, he jumped at the opportunity in his laid back Scouse way, 'I may have nothing to do's that night, so I'll come over, but you'lls have to put me up'. This was the start of the second episode of our life long adventure together. With Edi back in tow our lives were made so much easier, if we wanted a holiday he would stay for the duration, looking after the hotel, staff and Haley who was now 12 going on 24, so in this year we visited Pathos in Cyprus staying at the Elysium Hotel where I managed to lose Grace's credit card in a taxi which caused us a load of aggravation. Later to Palma in Majorca where we stayed at the Hotel Melia Victoria right next door to Tito's night club and in November we made our usual trip to the Lakes staying at Gilpin Lodge a mile from Bowness. During the visit we travelled via Kirkstone pass to Sharrow Bay Hotel for lunch which is situated on Ullswater, a heck of a drive but what a beautiful place to be and of all the restaurants we have ever visited Sharrow Bay with its two owners Mr. Coulson and Mr. Slack is classed as 10 out of 10 and all the others are graded on that, no others come up to that mark in our opinion. On our return journey after lunch we travelled due west across the top of the Lakes to Keswick, then due south to Grasmere and down to Bowness; thereby missing out the hairaising trip over Kirkstone, a little longer perhaps. One afternoon I was chatting to Don Wilkinson, he was in the snug drinking on his own and as trade was quiet we had struck up a conversation about the time he had spent working in Dubai, he extolled the virtues of the place and I asked about flights and hotels that he would recommend. Well after searching through the travel pages of the paper he was reading whilst consuming a few drinks with him I had made a tentative booking for Grace and I on an Emirates flight to Dubai in two weeks time, but when Grace got home from shopping she was appalled at how much the flights had cost and after she had rearranged the flight times we got a better deal and went on our first of many trips to the Emirates, thanks to Don.

The Egerton was a total different kettle of fish to Beeston with bedrooms and a bigger restaurant. We were in a village, near to town but just far enough away to be classed as a country pub with good side exit roads later in day or even later on for those that didn't wish to use the A34. The bedrooms had their positive side as in the extra revenue but the downside was getting up at 6am to cook the breakfasts every day. The larger restaurant gave us more scope to the size and style of the groups we could accommodate.

By '97 we had settled into the routine and all was well until Grace had a resurgence of the thyroid problem, again she saw Mr. Jones at Heswall and thankfully over a short period his treatment was successful, he did say that if it occurred again it would necessitate an operation.

After enjoying our time in the Crowne Plaza hotel in Dubai we decided to visit another of their hotels in Tel Aviv where again the weather was very hot. As we lay round the pool an attendant came around with frozen face clothes and ice lollies to cool us down, nice touch. On a complimentary trip to Jerusalem, laid on by the hotel we visited the Wailing Wall, Mount of Olives, the 3 places of Jesus' birth (depended to which Christian faith you belonged) and the golden temple. On our return journey to the hotel on a newly constructed road a Yank got the driver to stop whilst he collected small stones and grit from the side of the road because Jesus may have walked there, cuckoo or what?

Haley now 14 and Grace got on like a house on fire, more like two sisters, two giddy sisters sometimes like when visiting a nearby hotel in Tela Viv, the bar had a dance floor being used by some really serious ballroom dancers, like strictly, the girls started giggleling, so much so that the barman gave them both paper hankies to dry their eyes as I tried to calm them which only added to the situation, we left.

Home now, it was back to work and at the time we were very busy with many functions, weddings, funerals, birthdays, retirements and planning Grace's 40th surprise birthday party. Grace knew there was to be a party, but what she didn't know was that I'd moved the date forward one week so it would be a surprise. After lunchtime on a bright May Sunday I told her that I wanted to go search for a new car in Crewe, this would be about 3pm, and so off we set, but half way there I told her I hadn't left the keys for the staff to lock up after lunch, (we still closed in the afternoon.) Driving slowly we returned about 3.45pm to find the car park still full of cars, more than when we had left, she remarked that the staff should have got the customers out by now. As we drove up to the back of the pub she saw a fish and chip van, a DJ playing music on the patio and all our friends mingling around waiting our return from my fake trip to get Grace away for that short period in order to spring the surprise. The ruse had been accomplished with the invaluable assistance of Edi and Sara and Haley. The DJ didn't want to play outside in case of rain, Tony Finney had a few words and he played outside, don't mess with Tony. Not only were all our friends present but also Grace's dad and my mum Ada, also Billy and Pat, Keith and Meg and Marie. From being a kid Grace had always wanted a Dalmatian dog, after the wooden tops, so Haley used her fashion skills and knocked up a Dalmatian outfit which Ben was wearing, Grace had to wait another 12 months before Dereck a real Dalmatian arrived. All the party goers were having a great time, the food was good, the music too and the drinks flowed, but Ada said she didn't want to drink anything too strong so I gave her a glass of Gris de Gris, (pronounced Gree de Gree in French) which she said was fine. A little later I found her slouched on a chair obviously worse for wear, I asked if she was OK and she said she had only drunk the alcohol free wine I had suggested, Gree de Gree, she thought I'd said alcohol free. She was helped to her room and later Bill was helped to his room by Edi, but not before he'd had a good time. We all had a good time.

Later in '97, as a birthday present I allowed Grace to talk me into taking her and Haley to Sorrento, I say persuaded me, because at the time I didn't like pizza or tomato paste and was not a fan of pasta. On our arrival at the airport I had arranged for a private car to transfer us to the hotel which should have taken about ¾ hr but I asked the driver to stop at a local roadside bar for a quick refreshment which he duly did. The sky was blue and the sun shone as we sat at a table on the pavement in front of a local bar, shop, coffee bar cum tabac where we were served by an Italian waiter with beer and wine (Haley by now was allowed wine) and local delicacies, a perfect start to the holiday. After a short period it was time to resume our journey so I asked the driver if he could arrange for the ilcunta but he told us that there would be no charge, I was surprised but he told us that the bar was owned by his brother and the refreshments were complimentary as a welcome to Sorrento. As the charge for the car was 70 euro I thought, thank you.

Our reservation was at the very prestigious Sorrento Palace which was situated at the top of the town underneath a rock face, I was happy to be in a suite at the front of the hotel overlooking the Bay of Naples with Mount Etna in the distance. The rooms were sumptuous with every modern convenience and the spacious hotel had all the amenities we required such as a large well stocked complimentary bar and dance floor with a well equipped restaurant leading to a large patio, then down to a waterfall which fed the two expansive swimming pools. Ensconced each day on the side of the waterfall was a man in very tiny bright green Speedo's, he was fit and knew it and each day he wore different brilliant coloured Speedo's, we never saw him move an inch, just draped nonchantly on the rocks, he must have been an Italian. Sorrento is a beautiful city and is centred around Tasso Sq. with two major lateral Rd.s which lead to many side streets and alleys where you will find the shops and hundreds of bars, cafes and restaurants, some spilling out on to the pavements or under flower strewn canopies from which come the aromas of Italy enticing you to enter. Lanterna restaurant was one such establishment situated just off the Corsa Italia to which we would frequently dine outside under such a canopy, the waiter picking a flower and presenting it to Grace in a very sexy Italian manner, 'Ahhh Signorina, for you'. Just makes you sick, but the food was good. Can't the Italians eat? At that restaurant we saw a family of 5 devour a six course meal, antipasti, soup, a whole salt baked fish, a chicken casserole, meat with a dish of spaghetti, fromagio, dessert and thick black coffee, not forgetting the volumes of various wines finishing with a fine Muscat. The holiday was fantastic with breath taking views especially on our first ever trip to Capri where we ventured around the maze of alleys with a cornucopia of expensive couture shops both for men and women or should I say rich film stars, I really enjoyed my first taste of a selection of raw shellfish.

Everyone remembers their location when a life changing moment occurs; well this was such a moment. Early on Sunday morning, about 7.30am I switched on the TV to see a message being flashed across the bottom of the screen, it was that lady Dianna had died after being involved in an accident in Paris in the early hours of the morning.

I immediately informed Grace and Haley to the news and I remember we were all shocked and very upset, when we ventured down for breakfast the news was all around the hotel and the waiters came to us saying that our Princess had died.

Certainly a moment to remember.

At the end of our penultimate day Grace commented that she had forgotten to buy Sara a pair of shoes she had seen the previous day, so I volunteered to go for them, this was because I had remembered that Grace had seen a watch in a jewellers shop window which I had tried to ignore, you should have seen the price. Anyhow after a little negotiation with the Senoiri I managed to come to an agreement which suited us both and I also remembered the shoes for Sara which was all that Grace knew about at that moment.

On our return journey, driven by the same driver I asked him to stop at his brother's bar for a last drink before getting to the airport, I ordered champagne, well Prosecco as we were in Italy and vola, I surprised Grace with the Hermes watch I had previously purchased the previous day. It was shaped like a lock made of gold with a leather strap and was very unique. Grace loved it and I was so pleased that I had spent my last spare cash on it. Spare cash?

On our return home we asked our Congleton taxi driver to stop in Alderly so we could visit the newly opened Est. Est. Est. (that week) which became a favourite Italian restaurant of ours in the years to come, I still didn't like pizza but I had fallen in love with pasta.

Home, back to the reality of long hours and although not necessarily hard manual graft it entailed lots of running up and down stairs, taking residents and their luggage up stairs, looking after customers in the restaurant, down to the cellar to care for the beer in barrels and lager and cider in kegs and not forgetting the outside areas which needed constant attention, especially the large area of grass which I cut at least once a week for about 4½ hours each week from February to November, yes mid November at least. Again, remember it's what people see which gives them a good or bad perception of what they might expect when they hopefully enter your premises, it's getting them to do just that that matters, neat tidy lawns and gardens puts their perceptions on a high level, after that you've just got to follow through.

Later that year we managed to have a trip to Luxor staying at the Hilton on the banks of the Nile which was quite swish, well the tourist part of it was but step back two streets and you were back two thousand years expecting to meet Jesus on a donkey. The food shops including the butchers were all open fronted with their wares on show on the side of the dusty streets and we'd often be accosted by beggars demanding mu-sar-ree or the landau drivers trying to get our custom.

Don had told me in these circumstances to say 'ana maskeena, ana maskeena' which means I am a poor man, as I and the girls were always smartly dressed and certainly could not have passed off as beggars this response to them usually created a smile and some Arabic comment, but they left us alone. Each night we were treated to music in the hotel bar, on most nights this was performed by Mohammed who was a very good singer and all round performer, he soon became our best friend and offered to show us some of the local sights such as the Egyptian museum, Karnack temples and offered to take us on a tour of the Valley of the Kings. I should just mention that at the museum Grace paid a visit to the ladies where at the entrance an Arab gentleman in dish dash stood giving each lady one piece of soft toilet tissue and when Grace came out of the loo he was stood there with his hand out awaiting a tip, he was lucky that Grace had flushed the paper down the loo. Being the cynic that I am I had started to get a funny feeling about Mohammed's intentions towards us but fortunately fate threw me a lifeline. We had heard of Nile tummy and had tried to be careful about our diet whilst on holiday, even to the extent that I enquired from the bar man to the origin of the ice they used in drinks, he assured me it came thru a filtration system. Strangely the water pipe to the icemaker was connected to the sink. Four days in, Grace and Haley came down with the trots and sickness which put paid to any further excursions and on the night prior to our departure both the girls were recovering, so I thought I'd try a brandy at the bar, a double of course and also take one to our room for Grace and another for me to accompany her, six brandy's' cost £64, that's hotel prices for you. Realising that Mohammed had been very kind to us and he was a good entertainer although you could set your watch to which song he was singing, I thought I should show some form of gratitude, I had brought with me a pair of 'gold' cufflinks that I'd been given by someone, well they looked good and I gave them to him as an appreciation, I hope he liked them and also hoped the 'gold' didn't rub off too soon. Whilst in Luxor we visited The Old Winter Palace Hotel which was only minutes away and although our hotel was 5* the Winter Place was on a different plain and we said we'd go there if we were to return, on the whole an interesting and informative holiday.

After Graces birthday her dad Bill had been subject to a break in at his home and the thieves had left him sprawled spark out on his kitchen floor all night to be found by Billy the following morning. Bill kept a little spare cash in the house and it was suspected by us that it was one of the younger members of the family with two of his mates had robbed Bill, but he would not say. From that day on Bill's health deteriorated and it was whilst we were on holiday in the Lakes Grace got a call from Billy that her dad was in hospital, but not to worry. We went back to Preston and straight away visited Bill in Sharoe Green Hospital and were shocked to see how ill he was, Bill told us he was b......d and within two days he passed away. He was and still is missed by all who knew him, a father of great strength, an artist of great strength (a Sandow Brother) and a true friend with great strength of character and old fashioned opinions. Thank you Bill for your daughter. At the funeral Bill had put a Havanna cigar, a can of beer and picture of Roy his old dog in the coffin before it was lowered into the grave on top of Doreen; Billie remarked that it had been sometime since Bill had been on top of Doreen, at which point he smacked himself on the head and said he'd forgotten to put any matches in the coffin and that Bill would never forgive him.

The improvements we'd made to rooms 1 to 3 had been a great success and we realised that everyone required en-suite facilities so work commenced on rooms 4 to 6, the costs of decorating, all the furniture, light fitting and floor covering became our responsibility. This was paid for as the work progressed over a period of 3 months which was a burden but in the end well worth it. The work should have taken 2 months but Robinsons workmen had one pace, slow. Turn up at 9am, have a ½hr brew at 10, lunch at 12 till 1, another brew of tea at 2.30, start packing up at 4 and home at 4.30, no wonder it took so long.

At home we regularly visited Chester, lunching at the Grosvenor where Neil Collins the Head Sommelier told us off for drinking the Montrachet wine too cold and as usual we enjoyed Christmas lunch at the Yellow Broome. On Christmas day prior to lunch I would start the day about 6am as usual, starting with cleaning up from the previous day, on this day no staff came to work as we thought it only right that they should spend the day with their families, another reason was that I was too tight to pay them double/treble wages, another reason was that Grace had done enough cooking thru December and deserved a day off and another reason was that, quite rightly, Grace refused to cook on Christmas day. You choose.

At 7.30am I would turn on all the outside lights to illuminate the building whilst the church bells rang very loudly to encourage worshipers to 8am communion. We had attended midnight mass the night before, often being the last to arrive when the vicar would comment 'now that all the customers from the Egerton had arrived he could start the service' which always brought a smile to our frozen faces. Back to Christmas Day when all the family had been awakened by the bells we would then open our presents with Dereck rummaging about in the wrapping paper, as excited as the humans especially Haley. Then about 10.00am we would ring our far away family members and friends wishing them all a Happy Christmas, hoping they would all have a good day and then I would descend downstairs and ready the pub for opening at 11.00am. Yes 11.00am, start at 11 and finish at 1.00pm giving the punters two hours to enjoy their Christmas free drink which we provided on Christmas Day to locals and regulars, not at any other time, so if you missed this special day you missed out on a free drink till next Christmas. If 'Joe' who usually came on his own came with his visiting family they'd all get a free drink but Grace and I had a nose for those who just came for a freebie and we made sure they paid. On one of these very busy Christmas lunches when we had a lull and Haley was helping out I commented to Grace 'Just look at how busy we are, all the locals from the village, all the farmers and their families, aren't we popular' Grace remarked 'don't be stupid, they're here for the free beer', my plumes well and truly deflated. We managed to get away by 1.45pm for our Christmas lunch, after which a pre-booked Taxi took us home at about 5pm. to enjoy the rest of the day, often having a short nap, then watching tele and as always the day would be finalised with me making smoked bacon, fried egg sandwiches made on thick white bread liberally spread with Lurpak butter, just had to be.

Boxing Day was a very, very busy day and it was only after we'd completed that did we finally put Christmas to bed. New Years Eve was an uneventful occasion and whatever we tried I could never make it a great success and in three years time the Millennium was looming for which I had great plans. More later.

The next big event was Robbie Burns Night on the 26th of January and we celebrated it in style but not on that actuall date because pipers were cheaper and easier to get a day before or after, who really cares? I managed to find Stewart known as the Rocking Jock who could pipe in the haggis at the dinner, repeat the oath, sing, act as DJ and do a bit of comedy, a good all-rounder. In real life he was the entertainment manager at the Grand in Llandudno, came fairly cheap, or so I thought and was good fun, when he was sober. He went down really well with the punters and provided us with several years of entertainment for a fee of £50, a bed for the night and what turned out to be an expensive bar bill which started out when he required a bottle of scotch to flame the haggis with a wee dram of the amber nectar, the rest of the bottle disappearing down Stewarts throat in quick succession so that on his final night he couldn't carry on and Grace and I thought we should perhaps close the show as we'd seen Stewarts drinking habits gradually get worse over the years.

Now in year 3 we'd sorted out the staff, those that liked our operation had stayed, those that didn't had left, or so we thought, which will come to light in later years.

I've always said that with a good team you can accomplish anything, so with Sara who joined us again on our first day, Edi who came to see how it was, James and Pam behind the bar nothing stood in our way to our being a great country hotel.

Well trained staff are the backbone of a successful business, not just trained by the management but good advice also flows from these established colleagues helping to make a good solid team, I'd sometimes let an experienced staff settle in a new employee on their first time in so they didn't feel overwhelmed. It's important to have knowledgeable and friendly staff, but a pub cannot operate just on them, you need customers who come in all sizes and all temperaments and hopefully you can try to satisfy their every whim. I've visited and drunk in a myriad of licensed premises and the one thing you'll notice, especially if you sit down and quietly observe the customers is that some stand out of the crowd, these are called characters, every pub has them and the Egerton was no exception. Usually they are from a time past and many have gone through hard or difficult times which have forged their character and views on life, the younger ones are just troublesome or rebellious, perhaps one day their attitudes will grow into them being a character of the future. One real character was Willie Shaw, dressed and looked like Rod Stewart with a deep sounding voice, 'all reet me little duck,' a very mischievous sense of humour and in general just good fun and loved by everyone, especially he thought by the girls who he asked at every occasion if he could show them 'a good time'. Well he said if I ask 100 girls and ones say's yes, I've scored. He would drink his pint of lager, glass in hand whilst talking to everyone in the group; not taking any notice of how much or how little was in the glass until it was empty. One very busy lunchtime someone, me, dropped some dentures in his glass which sunk to the bottom. Willie chatted away thinking that his mates were smiling at his conversation, no, they could see the dentures in the lager which Willie was gradually drinking and it was only when he'd nearly emptied the glass that the dentures started to rattle, upon which he shouted to Grace because he assumed she'd played the trick. Everyone was in stitches and thankfully Willie had a good sense of humour.

On another occasion I nicked his keys which he would just leave lying about on the bar and then drove his white van onto the village hall car park next door. As his van was very conspicuous with Willies Sun Beds written on the side, he noticed it as it passed the front of the pub, 'that's my van' he shouted. Willie we'll ring the police and report it stolen. 'Err no it'll turn up' to which we all smiled because it probably wasn't taxed or insured and he certainly didn't want to report it missing. Willies next port of call was the cricket club and as he had no wheels Grace offered to give him a lift to the club with Sara and Auntie Joan, whilst I took his van to the cricket club via another route and waited inside, propping up the bar. All Willie said was 'I told you it would turn up'.

One of Willies besties was Ginger, a big guy who always had a pint in, well he said he had hoping one of the bar staff would believe him thereby getting a free pint.

I always said he hadn't even if he had, two can play at that game. His wife carol nicknamed Treasure was a big girl full of fun and mischief, you had to be on your guard as she had a habit of squeezing your bits and pieces, just as a surprise. Another couple of the group who came most Sunday lunches were Alec and June Smith who ran the Vale Club on Canal St. As I mention Sunday lunch, it is appropriate to recall that although my licence allowed me to open from 12 noon, some of this group couldn't wait till then and would arrive any time after 11am and by 12 there would have been a large party that would carry on all afternoon till 3pm, if we were lucky. Another of this group was F'ing Hell Dave and his wife Jean, Chris Naden who put his wages in the one armed bandit, telling us all when he had a win but not how much he'd put in. Charles Vernon the butcher, Steve Ripley who drank cider by the gallon, Tony and Carol Finney who were left over's from the Clan, who we had got quite friendly with, and Brian and his brother Geoff Hibbet. Geoff worked for BAE as an aero engineer at Manchester Airport and Brian was a retired Police Inspector, so we asked him if he was acquainted with our friend ACC Baister to which he replied that yes he did know him, but we got the impression that he didn't think they were friends of ours. A year later Brian with his wife Sue and Geoff Churchman and wife, another high ranking Police Officer friend of ours came to visit us. It was an unexpected pleasant surprise and after a few handshakes, hugs and kisses Brian noticed Brian Hibbet standing to attention although retired and in civvies, I thought he was going to salute, he didn't but our standing was firmly established.

Quite a few of the men in this group had been involved in sport in their youth, mainly football and most of them had been regulars for a good many years which made us newcomers, also many of them were or had been heavy smokers which over the next few years would take its toll diminishing this group to but a few survivors, of which only Tony and Carol and Brian Hibbet remain to this day. This is a typical example of the changing customer scenario where customers drop off the end, move to other areas, find a different pub because they don't like you or the way you run your pub or the price of the beer etc. It's always evolving and you have to try and keep one step ahead of the market, encouraging new clientele, looking at new trends but most of all not throwing all the tried and tested dishes out with the bathwater because there are still a lot of oldies out there when the younger punters are at work, and older people tend not to dine at night. It's all about position, structurally and geographically and remember there are 'horses for courses' which just about sums up the situation with landlords of today but breweries are so desperate to get anyone to look after their properties that they'll take anyone if they have got the funds and in some cases even if they haven't on a 'suck it and see basis'. If you like it pay for it later.

Prior to half term in February we had thought about going on a cruise but in the end decided against it, so other holiday arrangements needed to be found quickly which I did at Three Way Travel in Congleton. A last minute holiday due to a cancellation was on offer from Kuoni to Barbados at a reasonable price, so believing that Kuoni was a top class operator we paid the money and got our travel documents with a departure date in one week. When we picked Haley up from school that afternoon we had t tell her that the cruise was off, but then let her know about the trip to Barbados, a big smile and then she was singing 'we're going to Barbados' at the top of her voice in the car, we may have joined in. Quick pack and we were off within days, landed in brilliant warm sunshine and waited for our private transport, we waited and waited and eventually an old decrepit VW camper van turned up, good start to the holiday. On arrival at our hotel we noticed a sign giving the names of the staff, Sara the cook and Grace the receptionist but they were just names because there was no one around but we finally found our rooms, sorry room after stepping over loads of huge frogs, the rooms were filthy and in need of lot of repair, electric plug sockets hanging off and the toilet wouldn't flush. It was late and Haley needed a sleep, the bar was closed but I found some water for her and after she was fast asleep Grace and I went into Hoe Town for a beer. It was dark by now but we found a rum bar which was packed and at the far end of the huge corrugated building we could hear the sweet melodies of a steel band, the whole building and bar were constructed from corrugated sheets. We asked for Bacardi and Coke, were given a half bottle of Mount Gay rum, a Ltr of Coke, a large bowl of ice and two glasses all for about a fiver, wow! We got chatting to a tall dark lady who every now and then excused herself and went off with a friend of hers, this occurred several times during the evening and it was only much later that we realised that she certainly did have a lot of male friends. Mug or what? By now we were starving, you know what it's like when you've had a drink and fortunately there was a lady selling piri piri hot chicken right outside on the St. Well you know you shouldn't eat chicken from a street seller, but what the hell, it was good and we had some more half expecting to be ill the following day, we weren't, perhaps it was the rum that had sterilised us.

In the light of day things were worse than we had seen the previous night, found the rep. and demanded that she found us a better hotel. She informed us that it was high season and all the hotels were fully booked but if we could find a room ourselves she would get us a transfer as long as we picked up the tab if it was more expensive. So on the hunt we went and soon found a rather smart hotel the Tamarind Cove next to the Sandy Lane Hotel which was the most luxurious hotel on the island, the transfer was executed and we moved into a bridal suite with private pool. Very nice and much more like. We met a taxi driver, who showed us around the island and also introduced us to homemade rum punch, lethal or what. We visited the next door Sandy Lane Hotel only by invitation for lunch, being driven there by our friendly taxi driver who said 'how did you get in here' as it was a very premiere hotel and as mentioned you had to know someone to get in, but we'd met people and pulled a few strings. Grace had one of the finest meals of her life which consisted of nothing more than very lightly battered tempura vegetables, quite exquisite. The lunch was stunning and whilst we sat and ate, a light shower came over and rained on the open air dance floor, upon which a group of cleaners came and dried the floor with clothes on their knees and did not leave until the floor gleamed. On Barbados all the beaches are public and all look just like the pictures on the adverts, white sand, blue seas and waving palm trees but at this hotel their beaches have guards patrolling to keep undesirables out.

At the end of the fabulous holiday I went to reception to settle our account expecting the bill to be £800 or £900 because of the extra room charge and a few drinks we'd had, the receptionist asked me for £135 which I duly paid, well I wasn't going to argue. On our journey to the airport I kept looking behind me expecting someone to tap me on the shoulder and say 'excuse me Mr Smith'. We arrived home and I forgot about our good luck until a few weeks later when I had a call from Three Way Travel informing me there was a letter at their offices for me from Kuoni. Well of course I thought that Kuoni had finally caught up with me and that in the letter would be the balance of the unpaid bill but surprise surprise it wasn't a bill, it was a cheque for £400, repayment to us for the balance of the first hotel which we had moved out of, I can promise you that I never cashed that cheque, believe me.

Later that year we also visited the Irish Republic where we intended to travel around the Kerry ring which would take us from Dublin to Corke in the far south and back up the east coast returning to Dublin in 5 days. Whether it was the hire car, me, the narrow roads or just the long distances between point A and B there was no chance we could achieve the intended journey in the allotted time, so we rang ahead and cancelled the hotels in Killarney and Corke but we did manage to visit quite a few bars in Limerick, Tipperary and Waterford on the east coast on the way back up to Wicklow, which is where the girls had a problem with the food. That night we had gone to dine in a restaurant which was part of a castle and recommended to us by our hotel. The meal was fine and we all enjoyed it, it was only the following penultimate day of the trip that Grace and Haley started to feel ill, but we cracked on to Dublin, by the time we got to our last hotel both girls were feeling sick and it was only in the nick of time that we made the hotel bedroom before they were both in need of medical attention. A doctor was called who then informed the Irish Health Board because he suspected salmonella which is a notifiable disease in Ireland. Samples were taken to be sent away for testing and within hours salmonella was confirmed, questions were asked and answered and after a thorough investigation it was established that the culprit were the starters that the girls had eaten the previous evening, they consisted of scrambled egg and smoked salmon, served in an egg shell, the egg shells had not been boiled after the contents had been scrambled; which allowed the salmonella cultures to grow making the girls sick, I had not eaten the eggs as a starter. Wasn't I lucky?

The Irish board of health wanted us to stay so that they, with our help could prosecute the hotel in Wicklow but after staying one extra night in Dublin we needed to catch the next day's ferry as work beckoned, so that was the end of the matter and a lucky escape for the hotel who, I was assured by the authorities would be closely monitored, so perhaps not a complete escape.

In '98 the boys in the snug who were Rotary Club members approached us and asked if they could perhaps move their weekly meetings to us instead of the Fox Inn at Timersbrook because Jim Tiffney Rt. was retiring and they needed a new venue to hold their meetings on Monday nights. Monday night, it was a no brainer, 30 plus guys eating and drinking on the quietest night of the week, making your car park look busy to the envy of every landlord in the area and giving us kudos because we'd been chosen by Rotary as their venue.

Grace had always, from a small child wanted to have a Dalmatian dog, something to do with the wooden tops of her youth, so we went to visit a farm near the Coach and Horses were there was a litter of newly born Dalmatian puppies, didn't they look cute, don't they always? We chose one which was hiding under the straw at the back of the barn, he was tiny and had brown spots which were just visible as they take a time to develop and we agreed to collect him the following week when he would be 8 weeks old after a price of £350 was agreed. On collection the little dog cried all the way home probably missing his mum. To everyone's delight he became a great favourite and after continuing to cry finally ending up on our bed at night although outside in the day with old Ben who must have thought who's this new little interloper, but they got on well. By the way Grace had called the little dog Dereck, yes Dereck after Eric Clapton and the Dominoes, think about it. After many calls to Mel Scholes on Signal Radio with requests for him to play Grace's favourite artist Julio and after his trip and experiences on the canal at Beeston we had become quite pally with him and he often mentioned Grace and the Egerton on his radio show, good advertising. The radio station ran a pub spot on Sunday lunches where they would broadcast the show from a selected pub venue which cost in the region of £1000 but on one occasion the pub for that week had pulled out, so Mel rang us up and asked if we would stand in at no cost to us, well of course we jumped at the offer and the show was broadcast between 12 noon and 2pm, it went down superbly and we got loads of free advertising. Some of the regular punters didn't like it as it was different and disturbed their regular Sunday lunch.

Most days just merged into each other, getting up at 6am, breakfasts and then checking out customers, making sure the cellar was in order, having a bath and getting dressed ready to open the pub for lunch. Greeting the first customers who were early drinkers, just having a pint or two then perhaps off somewhere else for a couple more anytime after 11am although we officially didn't open till 11.30. Then the pub and restaurant would fill with more drinkers and diners, at this time of day mostly older couples who would take advantage of the OAP menu or enjoy a snack. After lunch the pub would go quieter but there would always be customers popping in for a pint and a chat with either the long term barmaid Pam or their friends or myself, if trade was slow it gave me time to nip out to look after the grounds or cut the grass which in the spring and summer was a never ending job. It took (up to 4½ hrs per week) even up till the middle of November. Grace would have my dinner ready for about 4pm when I would go upstairs to enjoy and then return to let Pam go home at 6pm and await the evening punters. As much as trade was generally consistent and you got to know which customers you could expect at what time and on what day there was always the chance that certain outside influences could affect their expected presence which could then have an effect on your takings. Please remember that's why you're doing this job, not just to talk to customers and have a great time, you're there to take the money, make a profit and build a successful business which you can't do if you shut up shop for any minor problem! I would not and will not close the business for any reason, customers may go somewhere else and enjoy it and after you've shut twice for the flimsiest of reasons they may not come back, not good for business.

At the Edge Grace and I had decided that we would have no pub games, darts, dominoes, pool or cards because we wanted to focus on good middle of the road food at sensible prices and real ale and lagers at as sensible a price as Robinsons would permit because their prices to us were not the cheapest. Robinson's pubs were not renowned for cheap beer and perhaps that's why many Robbie's pubs throughout Cheshire and beyond had a good reputation.

Being on the outskirts of Congleton had many advantages; we had a large area of land which was broken down into a hard standing tarmaced area for car parking, an acre of paddock, a large wood with pond, a garden with 15 tables and children's play equipment which was a godsend in summer and a patio with a BBQ and another 10 outside tables. Many customers came from the town and local areas but others came from far and wide, as our reputation for food grew so did our client base and we became a popular venue for people to stay in the six bedrooms that we had started to renovate and improve.

At the start in '95 it was accepted that you didn't have a private toilet in a B&B but times were changing so we developed rooms 1 to 3 into en-suite in '98 which enabled us to increase the rates for those three rooms and showed us the way soon after to improve the

facilities in rooms 4 to 6, the work being done by Robinsons contractors, us picking up the bill, not as many thought that Robinsons were paying. Bedroom business was good, even if it did mean early mornings. Remember, you're making money while you are asleep. Other sides of the business that flourished were the weddings and funerals; in my diary I denoted funerals as 'fun' because in general they were very profitable. In most cases the first approach about a funeral booking would come from the funeral director who knew from previous bookings that we would take great care of their clients, it not only reflected on us as the venue that they had recommended us as part of their package which all their clients who would mull over their experiences after the event and remember this in the future for further inevitable bereavements. As our restaurant was not huge and could only fit small functions, say up to 50- 60 sitting and 80-90 standing it was not suitable for most weddings but being adjacent to St. Mary's Church there were not many weeks, especially in the season when there wasn't at least one wedding service a week, sometimes up to three on Saturday. The bar trade and occasionally pre-food requirement were astounding although this could create a problem when it came to the car park. If there was a or more than one wedding or funeral at lunchtime, say 12noon and the guests all came in cars, which would usually be the case, the car park could soon fill up leaving no spaces for the pub customers which meant that during the church service no other customers could park and frequent the pub at the busiest part of lunchtime, no customers, no revenue. To prevent this I would patrol the car park, only allowing bona fide lunch customers to park which did cause me a few problems and I was called a few choice names, but you know me, broad shoulders and thick skin especially if it kept the tills ringing. Of course I got 'oh we'll be in for a drink later' or 'I'm a regular customer,' having no idea who I was I'd say 'when was the last time you were in' they'd reply 'I'm never coming in again'. With extra staff, if available or by utilizing existing team members, again if available we'd get through these stressful days and at the end count the takings. Not everything always went to plan as sometimes we'd be given the wrong information or no information. The funeral and wedding services were advertised in the monthly parish magazine but sometimes a funeral service was held at short notice so not advertised as on one occasion when we were asked by Finnerons funeral directors if we could accommodate a wake on the following Thursday, we said yes, but the funeral party arrived unannounced one day prior on the Wednesday at 3pm. The staff from lunch had departed; Grace and I were on our own, we hadn't got any food which would be suitable available and all the equipment was switched off. I contacted Alan Finnerons to be informed that the funeral had been previously arranged for the Thursday but had been brought forward, but they hadn't informed us. Ooops. Egg on whose face?
On another occasion another directors had enquired about a reception for 100 the following week which, yes, we could fit in, the booking was made. The day and time came and passed, so I rang the director to be told that the client had cancelled the booking. It turned out that the client had visited the Egerton Arms at Chelford to check on the venue, not liked it and told the barman that they wished to cancel their booking; the barman not knowing about the booking said he'd inform the manager on his return. They thought they had cancelled the arrangement, but at the wrong Egerton. As the booking had been made via the funeral director we insisted that they were responsible and in due course they paid the account, because the funeral was an early booking we were able to reset the restaurant and use it for luncheons and not all the reception food was wasted, I sent back half of the amount they had paid us. Everyone happy. Although this next story had nothing to do with us I must relate an incident that was shared with me by Martin Garside another funeral director who said that when a funeral party had arrived at the grave yard to bury their father the grave had not been dug which caused great distress to the family and friends and had to be rearranged, the other funeral directors responsible who's offices were in

Antrobus St. at the time were the ones previously mentioned and didn't survive much longer.

If we managed to get a day off, day off means, after serving breakfasts, getting the pub and cellar ready for the day and eventually about 11am getting out for the day, we could then go to one of our few favourite venues usually for lunch such as Bodysgallen Hall nr. Llandudno where Nicolette the restaurant manager took good care of us and always gave us the window table with a fabulous view of Snowdonia or the Arkle restaurant in the Grosvenor in Chester where we'd sit on table 10 and be well looked after by James the maitre de, they have the finest bread selection and cheese trolley ever, Rookery Hall nr. Nantwich, Est Est Est in Alderly or jump on the train at Congleton and go to Manchester where since the BBC had relocated their studios had become a Mecca for fine dining and novelty bars, it had rejuvenated the centre of the city. As we were travelling on the train we could enjoy ourselves and sometimes we would come home and think better of having another drink down in the pub. It was great when we could get the time to enjoy ourselves and we made the most of it when we did. One of our other favourite local eating places was and still is The Happy Garden Chinese restaurant at West Heath where from our first days at the Egerton have been well looked after by Candy, Nichol and their husbands who are the chefs.

Back to reality and work, more weddings and funerals which being next to the church are a regular source of business, as mentioned previously we have no control of their frequency but were notified in advance so we could staff accordingly but occasionally we could be surprised by the amount of guests attending the services, as when at one particular wedding the guests transport were several buses and in all 400 guests arrived. I thought we were appearing on 'Gypsy Wedding' as all the guests were very flamboyantly attired and they nearly drank the bar dry, both before and after the service, some never attended the service, just enjoyed the drinking bit before they moved on to their wedding breakfast venue. On one particular Saturday there were 3 wedding services and that was after a funeral at 9.30am. We unfortunately missed the trade from the funeral but guests for the first wedding arrived just after 10.30am for a quick one before the service at 11am as the guests from the second wedding arrived for the next service at 12.30pm. Oh some guests intended to make a day of it. The vicar Geoff usually stretched the service out for 45mins which meant that those guests came over from church whilst the 12.30 guests were still enjoying their pre-drinks and this was repeated for the 2pm wedding guests both prior and after. The pub was packed, the till was bursting and we were knackered. One of the major headaches we had was having a supply of clean glassware, there is never enough shelf space to store all the different array of glasses necessary on a very busy day so it's important to have a backup of boxed clean glassware close at hand, just in case, but on several occasions we had to inform customers to reuse their glasses. What do you do, wash glasses or serve beer? Serve beer means money in the till, wash up later. At this time, in one 10 day period we hosted 7 funerals, 2 on one day. We tried not to let these functions affect the normal business of the pub but of course hosting a funeral meant that the restaurant would be the venue for the wake, on some occasions because funerals were arranged at short notice and the restaurant had previously been booked for 1 or 2 small lunch parties I would ring up the parties concerned and explain that I had a funeral party wishing to book the restaurant and would they mind either dining in the pub or moving the date. I sometimes may have mentioned with a smile that it was my uncle's, fathers, brother or mother and would they mind? I always managed to accommodate everyone's needs. Well was I going to refuse a wake for 60 or 70 for 4 OAP lunches?

I always say a good funeral can be better than a good wedding.

During this year we managed to find, sorry make time to visit Bahrain which was hot but not much else and also Bangkok in Thailand staying at the Crowne Plaza. On our arrival at the airport we were approached by a lady from the Thai Tourist Board who requested that she would give us a free guided tour of the Golden Temple the following day, to which we agreed. Remember 'no free lunches'. The day dawned and as scheduled we were escorted around the spectacularly beautiful temples for all of 2hrs and then the real reason of the 'free' trip unfolded, a trip to the shirt maker, a trip to the jeweller, another to the jade shop and there would have been many more but I told the very nice lady that enough was enough and gave her a small fee to cover some of the commission she would have earned from any purchases we may have made. Bangkok was a fascinating city and gave us a great deal of pleasure exploring its many sites even if some like Pat Pong were a little lurid at night. We made a 3 day trip to Phuket on the coast, thankfully well before it was destroyed by the tsunami a year or two later.

That years trip to the Lakes staying as usual at Gilpin Lodge gave us the excuse to visit Sharrow Bay for lunch which was always the highlight of the trip, but in order to get there we had to embark on the road over Kirkstone Pass that Grace did not enjoy, sorry dreaded, and by the time we arrived at Pooley Bridge my arm was black and blue where she had squeezed it during the trip. On our arrival we always stood under the flag pole on the banks of Ullswater looking down the length of the lake towards the mountains and Angletarn Pike in the background, often covered in early winter snow. What a fantastic lunch, the service by the waiters, often helped out by either Mr. Slack or Mr. Coulson who by now were getting on a little which showed when Mr. Slack asked us six times if we required more bread, forgetting that he had only just asked us. Apart from the excellent food the atmosphere in the restaurant and bar was quiet elegance and the view from the windows was stunning, so much so that although on entering the dining room the waiters would insist on leading us to a window table with a fantastic view. I always requested that we be seated in the middle of the restaurant as we were there to enjoy the food, not to be distracted by the view. What made the dishes stand out at Sharrow Bay was the finest beurre blanc cooked by the head chef Colin Askrigg who had been at the hotel for many years. On one occasion I did have to mention that on the outside of the windows the spiders had been busy overnight which obscured the view this was unusual for their standards were always very high. I bet someone was dispatched to clean the windows tout suite.

At this visit we were asked to buy a cute little teddy bear wearing a red jumper on which was emblazoned the name of the hotel, along with a book of charity raffle tickets, the prize, a weekend at the hotel. We recently gave that teddy to Zoe in'21.

In '99 we acquired another teddy bear when we took a journey on the Northern Belle from Crewe to Bath with Haley and Michael her long term boyfriend. We knew that James from the Grosvenor and some of his colleagues had joined the staff on the train. When we arrived on the platform we were greeted like royalty and it wasn't long before we were seated with a glass of champagne in hand from the bottle that was included in the ticket price which I knew wouldn't last long, but I needn't have been concerned as the champagne just kept on flowing, quickly followed by breakfast consisting of crumpets topped with scrambled egg and smoked salmon, Danish pastries and hot drinks. The views from the windows were amazing and because the train was not travelling at high speed we had time to appreciate the beauty of the Welsh Marches, but this was interrupted with a caviar and Bellini sampling and more champagne. Bath is always stunning but this trip was glimpsed through a haze of champagne and there was more to follow with our dinner on the return journey which culminated with us all going home with a bottle of champagne each and another little charity teddy dressed in a blue jumper, thank you James and team. We gave this teddy to Joshua in '21. The two grandchildren mentioned are well in the future.

As previously mention the general public do not and why should they comprehend how much thought and organisation goes on in the background, our job is to make the running of the hotel appear seamless which in my opinion is nigh on impossible for a single person to achieve. Grace and I tried to keep our roles separate, she the catering operation and mine the bar and cellar and general dogs body, God help me if I tried to interfere in the kitchen, not only from Grace but Edi kept from interfering if he could unless they needed me when I went in to wash up on busy days, I was then called the Polish pot wash. We changed the menu once a year, a. so that the customers didn't get bored with it and b. because it kept the chef's from getting bored cooking the same dishes every day, however customers don't like change so amendments were made to the non essential dishes and we'd keep the classics perhaps with subtle changes to either improve the dish or for financial reasons. So instead of increasing prices we didn't serve bread with all starters as had been the case for many years but only with soup and pate was accompanied with toast and we took out bacon from the previous lambs liver dish and augmented it with onion which of course was a cheaper option. Grace put together all the main menus and discussed with Edi the OAP and Today's special menus so that we could move any ingredients we had too much of, which meant we diminished any food waste and the customers got a very good meal at reasonable prices.

Sometimes Grace and I disagreed on her choice of dishes on the main menu that she had devised, but I didn't / wasn't allowed to interfere and I was usually proved wrong.

2000 and the Millennium celebrations were fast approaching and I had had plans for years of a magnificent party on New Year's Eve night of 1999 going on into 2000 so as the year '99 came in I started to finalise the ideas I'd tentively enquired about over the last few years, but no one would put pen to paper because they wanted to see how much they could actually squeeze out of us, which left us in limbo. The prices for acts and DJ's rocketed, what had been £400 was now £1000, but what became the worst problem, was staff, none of our staff wanted to work over New year and even after an offer of 3x wages they were still not interested, so in the end all the well laid plans went out the window and we organised a private party in our apartment for a few friends, great do.

In '99 two sad events occurred, my mum Ada died and Auntie Marie also passed away. Mum had a cremation service at Longridge Crematorium as did Marie; Ada had her ashes interred at the crematorium but Marie joined Bernard, we scattered her ashes on the sand hills behind the hotel at Beeston where we'd previously scattered Bernard's ashes.

When we'd signed the contract for the Egerton in '95 I'd noticed in the contract that Robinsons were obligated to keep the external walls and paint work in good order and contracted to paint the outside every 7 years but all the other Robbies landlords said 'you'll be lucky' so when Tony started back to work around Easter I gave him the good news that I wanted him to paint the exterior of the building pink, yes pink. As we'd been touring Greene King country looking at their pubs I noticed that a lot of their properties had thatched roofs and pink pebble dashed walls which looked quite stunning, so I thought why not, it did give people something to talk about and our pub became known as 'The pink pub'.

Our holidays this year took us to Abu Dabi which although very hot was very commercial and the Crowne Plaza Hotel at which we stayed was in the city, full of business types. Also in May we visited Madeira with Brian and Pauline at their suggestion, well I should say Pauline's as she was always the driving force behind many of the holidays we took together, Brian was just happy to be where ever. The break was really a freebie which meant that the hotel we stayed at for 5 nights was complimentary but we had to fork out for the flights. Remember 'no free lunches'; well the catch was that we were all expected to go for a talk about time-share which we managed to wiggle out of and enjoyed the island holiday, which in May was still very damp, but of course that's why the Island is so

74

lush and green. Reeds Hotel, overlooking the Ocean was a trip back to an old fashioned era, men had to wear jacket and tie in the restaurant and ladies had to be suitably attired, not too much skin on show. I remember the meal was ecstatic, unlike the dinner we had in an Italian where Pauline and I contracted salmonella after eating a Chateau Briand together, I went back 2 days later and demanded our money back or I would have gone to the Health Authorities, well it worked. We managed to fit in a week at the Elysium Hotel in Kato Paphos were we met up with all our old friends including Lagis and Jesus. Our visits to Dubai averaging at least once a year were always the highlight of our holidays and by this time we had met and befriended quite a few people, both staff and ex-pats who frequented the numerous eating and drinking establishments in and around our hotel. We always stayed on a club floor in one of the Captains Suites which then entitled us to use the Club lounge and its myriad benefits such as free drinks, breakfast, light lunch, complimentary early evening hot and cold buffet which if you were only staying for a few days would suffice for dinner but we'd have a pick at some of the delicacies and then go out for dinner. The manager of the floor was Nihall who with his team of girls could not do enough for us and certainly made our holiday. We made sure we treated all the staff with dignity and one particular guy Dave, a big black man who guarded the entrance to Trader Vicks, a Polynesian cocktail bar and restaurant. He would always greet us with a huge smile, flashing his brilliant white teeth and saying 'welcome Miss Grace and Mr Norman', he'd then show us to a seat at the bar, moving someone if necessary and the boys behind the bar would serve us in no time with a chilled bottle of wine. What a welcome. Grace and I would always get to know the management by introducing ourselves, often asking questions of interest which in the end paid off as we'd get invited to managers cocktail parties and as the staff saw us talking to their managers they looked after us, just in case. On another floor was the piano Bar which was a wine bar looked after by Clifford the barman cum pimp. I say this because at any time of the night there were always one or two scantily clad young women drinking at the bar who Clifford controlled and he would tell them to get off a bar stool when we entered, so that we could sit at the bar. He was a very gigarios character, obviously a little Oscar Wildish with lots of interesting information. One of the male regulars was Binladens brother Mohammed who dressed differently every day, mushti one day, jeans and T shirt the next and a suit another, always with a different young lady on his arm with glasses filled to the brim with premier champagne.

Later that year we'd visit the Lakes staying at Gilpin Lodge, I'd try and get there by noon or 1pm so that we could enjoy a roast Sunday lunch for me and perhaps seabass for Grace at 2pm and after a little tiffin and about 7pm order a taxi to take us down into Bowness for a visit to 2 or 3 or 4 drinking establishments. On another day we'd go over Kirkstone and have lunch at Sharrow Bay, Still our No.1.

There are several reasons I like to visit the lakes at this time of year, the fantastic Autumnal colours of all the trees and mountains with perhaps a touch of snow on the peaks. The lakes and waters quietly flowing with the late autumn sun on them, the many high class hotels and restaurants, top class service but most of all the quiet roads, not clogged as in the height of the season with caravans, but most, most of all there are no kids because they are all in school, just grand.

Talking about school, well in Haley's final year at Heath field High she was involved in the senior prom to which she went all dressed up in not a lot and heels so high, us hoping she wouldn't fall off them, but then worse things could happen. Half way through the evening Grace got call from Haley's form teacher asking for one of us to pick Haley up from the prom. Of course we were concerned and Grace duly set off to collect her and on arrival was asked to take her home in disgrace as Haley had been distributing booze to her mates, which of course was not allowed, I say distributing, what I really mean is selling.

74

She had nicked the bottles from the cellar and proceeded to set up a business, making good profit 100%, I wonder where she got that idea from?

When the boys in the pub heard about Haley's escapade they all cracked up laughing much to Grace's disapproval, well you can't blame her for trying.

Some months earlier in the year Grace had lost, we thought stolen, her wedding ring and engagement rings and after claiming on the insurance we purchased replacements from Gordon Bank's, the jewellers shop in Preston that the originals had first been bought. Our rector Geoff Cuttel from St. Marys church in the village had agreed to bless the rings for us in a private service, so Grace, Haley, Michael, Haley's new boyfriend and I went to church and the rector duly blessed the ring but during this short service the kids couldn't stop giggling which mum and I were not happy about. Well Geoff's 3 legged dog had been sick in the corner which caused us all to smile a little and then Geoff instructed me not to step back, which I duly did and fell ar.. over tip, lying on the rectory floor, very distinguished in my best suit. Went back to the hotel and had a glass of champagne or two, one of the finest things I've ever done.

2000, the unfounded and unexplained catastrophic problems that were supposed to befall us all over the New Year didn't happen and we soon settled down to a new millennium and work carried on as usual, just as trying, just as tiring and stressful but often with a surprise around every corner, some pleasant and some not so. By now we'd acquired a professional team of competent staff who included Edi, Sara, in the kitchen with a group of young waitresses and behind the bar James, David, Lee, Dan and Pam, a team of 3 housemaids to keep the bedrooms and pub in tip top shape and also two Sunday cellar boys who cleaned the beer lines and maintained the car park and other odd jobs which at one time gave us a staff total of 26. Many of the younger staff were still at school and they would change on a 2 year basis as they went off to Uni at 18 and came back thankfully at busy times like Christmas and during the summer break. We paid all the staff well over the recommended rate which meant that after all the time we spent on training they stayed with us, that is unless they didn't make the grade, in which case they moved on. The major problem I had was with the 2 cellar boys who I eventually reduced to one boy because each week there would be something not done, each one blamed the other, so with only one I knew who to blame.

I was always being asked by varied charities if we'd put one of their boxes on the bar for customers to deposit their loose change, we allowed 3 only, usually for local charities as we had an old gallon whisky bottle on the bar which punters placed their loose change around and inside and when full we donated the monies to a local charity after we had a knocking down ceremony which was featured in the local press.

At this stage I should mention that Astbury village had a May Day every year which had been going on since the year dot. There was a May Queen Procession prior to a service at church and a garden party on the vicarage lawns where you could enjoy sandwiches and cakes supplied by the Women's Institute, all washed down with lashings of tea. It had been decided well before our time that the alcoholic drinks should be left in the hands of the professionals; i.e. the pub, which made for a very busy day, thankfully. From about 10am I would block off the side entrance gate so that all traffic had to come up the main driveway where I would park them in an orderly fashion with the help of 2 or 3 Rotary members, that is after the motorists had paid £1.00 to park which some argued about, but it was pay or go away, the money collected all went to church funds. Regardless of the weather, which often rained it was always well attended and we sold lots of beer and other drinks to the parents, grandparents and aunts and uncles who just had to come to see their little Sophie or Billy walking in the procession, thankful for an umbrella and then a visit to the Egerton.

2001 was a year that few will ever forget. Pauline rang us in July and informed us that she and Brian were planning a visit to New York and would we be interested, well of course we were but she didn't mean just New York she envisaged a tour of the East Coast of America, taking in New England. Our first stop was Manhattan staying just off Times Square in a huge hotel that Pauline had found on line. We stayed for three nights, did the sights, went up The Empire State and had lunch in The Twin Towers after taking in the astonishing views of Manhattan, found one deli and went to see Henry Winkler in The Dinner Party on Broadway after visiting Stratton Island on the free ferry. After picking up what should have been a rental car we actually ended up with a 4x4 Chevvie, the lady said 'just take it' and after taking Brian 30 mins to get out of single gear we travelled thru Falmouth, Hyanas, Buffalo and Rochester staying a few nights at each before going over into Canada visiting Niagara Falls which were stunning. Some of the places we ate or stayed were places that Brian had found as cheap offers advertised in local rags with a voucher redeemable at the outlet. Of all the restaurants we ate the worst was a Chinese in Falmouth where a prawn ball was the size of a golf ball and on biting it oozed nothing but grease, ugh! In another American bar we were not allowed to moved tables because 'You're sitting at my table' said the waitress anticipating her 10% tip, 10% , I ask you. That was our memories of New York in July and later in the year they would come flooding back to us. Our flight home was from Boston and on the last night our chosen hotel was in Salom not far from Boston Airport, we felt safe because they'd stopped burning witches in the 18c. Our rooms were tiny but functional and whilst sitting at the bar I noticed a big sign saying no smoking which I thought a bit excessive for behind a bar because surely that would have been obvious, I enquired and the barman said 'not just behind the bar but in every public place, footpath, park, anywhere other people might be. Wow that's some no smoking regulation, but what a good idea.

We visited Menorca with B & P in September of 2001 and on the 11th we had been out for lunch in Fernaise, on our return to our hotel we were greeted with the vision of an aeroplane smashing into the first of The Twin Towers. Our shock was indescribable and then for the same to happen to the second tower was beyond comprehension, everyone just stood around not believing what we had just witnessed, taking in the possible repercussions that this act of sheer terrorism would incur. Now with hindsight we can look back and see what this evil incident caused, so many deaths, for what?

In this year another Rotary club asked if they could hold their meetings with us on a Tuesday evening and so after some negotiations the Congleton Dane Rotary Club joined us for their weekly meetings. Having club nights on the two quietist nights of the week was certainly a bonus and encouraged other trade because we must be good to have two Rotaries. Congleton Dane was a mixed gender club which in time would present its own unique problems.

Peter and Lesley still had their villa in Caviero which we'd visit from time to time and they would come to stay with us, we'd usually go out for dinner and as both Peter and I were into port at the time we'd often enjoy a fine port later at home. I'll just set the picture of our bathroom which Tony had built, floor to ceiling blue and white tiles, corner bath, navy blue towels and a bright canary yellow carpet. Well one night after a dinner out and more port than was good for us Peter didn't feel well, he rushed to the bathroom nearly making the loo but not quite, the carpet was ruined, have you ever seen what port does to a bright yellow carpet? We changed the carpet colour to dark blue and we're still best of friends.

Later this year we took another trip on the Orient Express or Northern Belle as it is called when making tours in this country, this time to London. The route tended to steer clear of main lines and because of the slower speed we found the scenery quite fascinating, unlike the usual hi speed trains that everyone wants these days. The service was extraordinary and again we were treated like royalty with lashings of champagne and on our arrival we were escorted on a trip to Harvey Nicks to be lavished with free gifts and mementos of our visit, another fabulous day in the city.

It came to my attention that I had been wrongly accused by my sister when we were much younger that I had purposely allowed her big white pet bunny to escape, this I knew nothing about till this time. It was Rowland who now informed me that the bunny was actually served up as Christmas lunch when Sylvia was about 6 or 7 and I was blamed for its escape. Well things must have been tougher than we ever realised in the early sixties.

On a Friday in 2002 Pauline rang us and said that she had found a good deal for a trip to South Africa and would we be interested but there was a drawback, takeoff was on Monday, well what the hell. So in a mad, desperate panic to organise staff, supplies, wages and pack, off we went flying British Airways via Heathrow to Johannesburg where we were met by a combi and driven to Sun City a vast hotel and gambling complex based in the middle of the desert, just like Las Vegas. We were asked to deposit our guns in a locker before we entered the gambling hall, deposit our what?

After a few days we flew down to Cape Town and stayed for one night at the Intercontinental but because the hotel was fitted out in a businessmen's style we decided to move to the Lord Nelson Hotel on the sea front which was much more to Grace and I's taste but I'm not sure about Brian because he thought it a bit flash, Pauline liked it.

We later went on to stay at the Peninsular Hotel on Camps Bay which was quite outstanding with crashing waves onto white sandy beaches where stood the magnificent Camps Bay Hotel, all yellow, white and blue awnings fluttering in the sea breeze. One of the best trips we took was to Vakalaken in the wine area which of course we all enjoyed although the wine at the wine tasting was not memorable, or cheap. This area was built by the original Dutch settlers from the 1500's who built Dutch style houses above the bay amongst saplings of Sagole Baobab that they planted and now were huge trees some 80ft in circumference and 80ft high that can live to 1200 years. The first Governor built his house in such a position so that he and his men could see any ships about to come ashore and they were first there to victual the vessels. Grace and I took a walk around the capital during the day after being told not to venture near the bus station were we might find trouble, so we avoided this area until we rounded a corner to find ourselves bang in the middle of the bus station, well too late, so we walked quickly over and quickly back to our hotel. Phew. We had been informed that it was not advisable to venture out on the streets at night and always went everywhere in a combi. Nice holiday, lots of poverty adjacent to the expensive districts and always that sense of bubbling trouble, I'd recommend you go before you can't, it is a beautiful place but I wouldn't go again.

Willy Shaw and that gang were all part of a group called the Toss Pots who appeared on various local stages in clubs and school halls collecting money for charity, but this year they decided to take their show to Blackpool. The show consisted of the members singing and dancing, miming to old and modern music, generally acting the fool but very professionally, some were good singers. The Metropol Hotel was the chosen venue both for the show and our stay and although our room was a little dilapidated it didn't matter much as we weren't in it long because of the drinking. Many of the crowd had come well prepared as the drink prices at the hotel bar were exorbitant so they had bought bottles of spirits from the offi and just purchased coke from the bar to put in their Bacardi, some came with that as well. Great fun night which came with a sore head in the morning.

On one of our days off we visited Manchester in the spring and booked a table for lunch at the Portland Hotel overlooking Piccadilly Gardens where the cherry trees were in full bloom. We were seated in the window and had full view of the blossom being blown from the trees by a stiff breeze; it looked like a pink snowstorm, quite beautiful and enhanced our ecstatic lunch served by properly dressed white tie waiters on white crisp tablecloths as we sipped Montrachet served in handmade French crystal glassware.

Our little village just off the A34 about 1 mile south of Congleton was made up of a circle of large and small cottages around a village green which had a large oak tree at its centre. Over the years these cottages had served many purposes as for instance the first cottage name Royal Oak had up to 1881 been a pub as its name suggests, then a further 6 premises, all with small fronts and long buildings and gardens at the rear, then you come to the 16c Egerton which looks over to the huge mainly Norman church and grave yard. Now running down the other side of the village we start with Black and White cottages which had at one time been 3 farm workers hovels and had since been developed into one large timber beamed cottage owned by the Carter family. Next door to that is a Georgian house built in-between B&W cottages and the farm next door to that for the daughter of the farmer when she married, thereby filling in the gap, making the whole row a terrace. The old farm which had been converted into a large house was now owned by Audrey an older lady who ran it as a village shop and P.O. where most things were available but not always fresh or in date. On one occasion Grace bought a bottle of pop for Haley which, when back at home found that its best before date was the previous year and also a reduced price sticker from Tesco was still half attached, we didn't shop there again. Before our time there had been an old cottage next door which had been knocked down and a modern out of place and style detached house erected, it had been designed by Keith Carter a local architect and Parish Councillor, tongues still asked how and why? The bottom property was a large house facing the green and at one time had been the local police station, it still has the cells to the side next to the last building in the village, the garage where you could have your cars repaired or serviced or even buy a second hand vehicle, this property used to be the village smithy, how times have moved on.

What best to do about some financial security for Haley, Grace and I discussed the issue and decided to take out a life insurance policy for her? Well you'd think we wanted to murder her as the companies we approached gave us the impression that we wanted to take out a policy, knock her off and claim the money. After a lot of discussion we finally managed to convince them that we wanted to give the benefits to Haley on her 25th birthday, which we did, it came in very handy then and helped her and Tony purchase a house.

Just on the outskirts of the village were Glebe Farm which was to the side of the church and across the Rd. from the gigantic Rectory, it was owned by the Lomas family. Denis the father was big into Holstein Friesian and Charolais cattle breeding and had taken first prize at many of the local and national agricultural shows, he was well known around the area and when he passed away this year the wake was overwhelmed with mourners, not only friends and family but guests came from the many farm associations he had been involved in and the clubs such as Rotary that he had been a member of and every local farmer wished to show their respects to his family. The wake was held next door at The Village Hall where the mourners could pay their respects to the family and take a drink of tea and sandwiches. I've never known a farmer be happy with just tea and cake so of course as soon as the pleasantries were out of the way they exited and came to the pub for a proper drink and a chat with their farmer friends, that's the way to celebrate Denis's life. The bar was pulled out by 2pm and there was a fantastic sense of camaraderie amongst the assembled crowd, most of them farmers all talking about farming matters. I called Grace from the kitchen and said 'what can you see, and what can you smell', she looked and remarked 'cattle market'. All the farmers had come in their best Sunday best macs, white shirt, tie and clean shoes, but they couldn't get rid of that farm aroma.

How do you tell a farmer by looking at him? Well his ears stick out a little and he's going a little bald on the right hand side of his head. Why? Because during a deal when the price is mentioned he'll say 'how much?' whilst putting his hand behind his ear and then saying 'bloody hell' running his hand thru his thinning hair before enquiring about how much luck money was involved, deal done.

The Egerton came with about 1 acre of outside land, 1/3 car parking 1/3 paddock and the other laid out to pub garden and grassed areas, all of this grew at an astonishing rate and needed cutting every week from March to end of October. This operation took me approx. 4½ hours which I split into 3, fitting the job in whenever I could find the time. Many people asked me why I should cut the grass and not employ someone to do it, as they thought the task was beneath me. Well there are two reasons, 1. If I employed say Tony to do it, it would cost 8 months x 4 weeks x 4½ hours x £10 per hour = £1440 per yr, that's a lot of money to cut grass. 2. I've never been a keen gardener, never had the inclination, time or space to grow flowers and veg. But I bought myself a new mower and found time to think and get some fresh air which I didn't find in the pub. Any problems I thought we might have I could run round in my head with no interruptions from the telephone, customers or staff wanting answers there and then, peace, away from life's tribulations and the fresh air stimulated my inner being whilst I counted out the number of steps I'd done and the remaining I had to do, 2001- 2002, just one foot in front of another, dodging the daffodils in the spring making nice straight lines in the lush green grass. The daffodils were a sign of spring, warm weather and return of customers in the garden, just about doubling the seating area, yippee.

In the beginning Harold from Biddulph had supplied all our plants, both for our winter and summer shows which usually were adored by many punters but his selection was limited so I had recently been getting our plants from Congleton Garden Centre but this year most of the hanging basket plants had started to die within weeks. Charles, the boss replaced them immediately and on investigation found that whoever had made them up had left the baskets on the floor and slugs had got into the base water reservoir and eaten all the plants. A much better amateur gardener than I was Terry De Pledge who lived in the village; he'd been a long time local and had been there for many years. He owned a fishing tackle shop in town where he sold everything from maggots to air guns and catapults, well you needed them to put the bait into the middle of the water. Terry known as Fishing Terry was rather a large man and had come to rely on either walking sticks or a wheelchair to get around but that did not deter him from growing a myriad of garden vegetables and flowers. We didn't often run out of supplies but at weekends, after say a busy Saturday I would pay a visit to Terry to replenish any salad products we needed, always fresh at a reasonable price. It helped us and gave Terry remuneration for all his hard work. Terry was one of the old locals who remembered the Creswell family who had kept the pub for 40 years and were renowned for their pork pies which they made themselves from the pigs they reared in what was then a small holding and pub. Terry liked a drink and when closing time was nigh, then 10.30pm he would order 4 or 5 pints which he would consume before he went home at about 11pm, some drinker.

Est Est Est had now changed its name to Gusto and after many months of trying to get used to the change, not only in the menu but their operation we often used to visit the 'Nose' instead. A small eclectic restaurant in Wilmslow opposite the Police Station which had quite a comfortable feel about it. The menu encompassed Pan-Asian and Italian style dishes, the only problem was that the chef had a thing for chopped parsley which he would scatter on every meal including cheese and biscuits, this really did P... me off.

This obviously didn't seem to bother Posh and Becks as they were regular customers who sat in the window with baseball caps pulled down over their faces trying to be discreet, oh yes, then waving to all the remaining customers as they left.

Another holiday, suggested by Pauline was to Tenerife staying in Los Christianos after spending the first two nights on the island of La Gomera where the weather turned out to be challenging and the trip even worse because the sea was turbulent to say the least, we only just managed to get on the last return boat before the authorities closed the harbour because of the rough seas. I think La Gomera was a cheapo and would not be on my future wish list but the hotel on the main island was fabulous and the black sandy beaches were a novelty. Not far from our hotel was the small town of Los Gigantis and standing high above it was a large hotel named after the town. At the entrance to the hotel stood the famous T. J's cocktail and music bar which opened daily and held live music events every night. The proprietor and compare Miss Joanne Love was a tiny lady, probably a size 8, she kept the audience amused with her lady side kick who was just the opposite, size18. There were many very professional live acts that would entertain us throughout the night. Joanne would make comments thru the evening about her friend's size, saying that she wished she wouldn't keep borrowing her outfits, think about it, size8 and size 18 and there'd be a Destiny Child tribute group entertaining us singing 'you can make my hole again'. Went down a storm.

In June we were invited by Kevin and Edi to attend South West Australia Day in London at Australia House which is situated on the Corner of the Strand and Melbourne Place. The function started with a church service at The Savoy Chapel which is situated at the rear of The Savoy Hotel and is owned by the Queen. The chapel was built by Henry V11 in 1512 and although damaged in the war has now been restored to its former glory. Four male choristers sang like angels after a reading by the rector and prayers were said, these consisted of unusual requests, like praying for billabongs, lakes, islands, tempestuous seas as well as red sands of the earth. There then followed a buffet at Australia House to which we walked, but, the route there took us past the Savoy and who can pass there without visiting the American Bar? Certainly not us. Kevin being the Australian Agent General obviously knew a vast amount of influential people from industry and politics and they all gathered there to celebrate this special Australian day and we were introduced to many of them including Lord and Lady Digby Jones or Lord Digby and Lady Pat, who when we got home sent me a copy of his book and tapped me for a donation to his charity. A few hours later Grace and I made our excuses and retired to our hotel The Ritz before going out on the town. I'm not name dropping but we stayed at the Ritz because as we had an American Express card which gave us a favourable room rate with breakfast and £70 credit on our bar bill in the very grand Tivoli Bar. £70 meant 4 drinks. Over the next few years whilst Kevin and Edi were stationed in London we would be invited to many similar events and the doorman at the Ritz got to know us by name, 'welcome back to The Ritz Mr & Mrs Smith', now that is name dropping. During their time at the embassy Kevin was allocated a car with the number plate WA1, Western Australia 1 you might think but in effect it had once belonged to a famous piano player of the 50's. Can you guess? Yes, Winifred Atwell.

Unknowingly to us, this was to be the last time Mel Scholes was to bring his Sunday lunch Signal Radio show to the pub, because later this year he passed away. We had tried to keep in touch with him by visiting him at whichever digs he was staying at, usually some back room at a pub, he'd gradually slipped into ill health over a period of years since he and his lady had split up and the drink didn't help. This had started to affect his show on the radio, so much so that he was either pushed or he jumped and took some leave which then sent him into a downward spiral. The man was a genius at comedy and you could not stop the jokes just gushing out, so much so, that after only a short time your stomach muscles were aching. Within a few days of his death we received a phone call from Mel's P.A. requesting our presence at his memorial service to be held in two days time in Stoke. She said that although she had not met us Mel often talked about us and he had written about us in his diary, we were very honoured.

End of an era.

One of our favourite places for lunch was the Chester Grosvenor ever since our first encounter prior to us taking the Beeston. We would either drive there or be collected by Alison to enjoy a few hours shopping in Chester and then a fabulous lunch in the Arkle Restaurant always sitting on Table 10 which was our preferred table due to its location. We could see the whole room and were near to the kitchen doors thru which all the dishes emerged and they enabled us to see what other people had chosen for lunch, very interesting. Two of our favourite courses were the vast selection of breads which we later discovered were baked by Paul Hollywood. My favourites were soda bread and banana bread. The cheese board was delightful with more choices than in any other restaurant we ever visited especially the smelly/ripe French selection.

The leisure industry is full of pit falls to those that just treat it as a job, it is not a job it is a way of life and those that think you can just go to work, do the 8 or 9 hours, go home and switch off should find another vocation. One of the biggest problems in the industry is drink; well you might say that is what we sell, but to some in the trade it wreaks havoc. Many of us like a drink to relax after work or when we're out enjoying ourselves but when alcohol creeps, sometimes unaware into our everyday life, that's when it becomes a problem. Drink is all around us and so easy just to have just one and then another. During my time in the trade I've seen so many landlords and ladies who have found it so easy just to put glass to optic or just keep topping up a half pint glass as they work. In my opinion it's spirits that do the most damage. Of course staff are not immune from having the odd tipple and spirits are quick to pour and quick to knock back when your back is turned or if you are not around. When we first arrived at the Egerton a cleaner of many years was found to be helping herself to the whisky and so, had to go, she knew why but her son didn't and fell out with us big time not knowing the truth. A girl called D... worked in the kitchen at lunchtime as a waitress, all the customers loved her for her smile and friendly manner but what they didn't realise was that she was a registered alcoholic which didn't affect her work in any way, although I believe from gossip she was a very different person in her off time. One day she did not turn up for work, which had never happened before and it as with great sorrow when later that day we were informed that she had been discovered dead lying in some bushes in Antrobus car park from an overdose of alcohol. Grace sometimes had help from a cleaner in our apartment and one such lady named Idi who was the mother of two of our waitresses came in two days a week to clean what Grace had already cleaned up, which basically left the dusting and Hoovering. Tony the odd job man commented that she was a drinker and that she carried her handbag everywhere with her, as to each room she was cleaning. One day Grace went upstairs to discover that all the furniture in the lounge was in disarray, the Hoover in the middle of the room and Idi missing, we never saw her again, someone had seen a bottle of vod in her bag and perhaps that explained her close connection to the bag. We employed a middle aged respectable looking lady in the kitchen whose work seemed OK except she would keep excusing herself saying she needed to go to the loo. The Monday of the second week she came in early and once again disappeared to the loo in her own time, but 15mins after she should have started work we became concerned, so Ash went to find her. She was locked in the loo with no response, so he climbed in over the top to find her slumped drunk on the toilet and a half empty bottle of vod in her bag. He lifted her up and escorted her outside to sober up and wait for her friend to collect her, she remarked 'well that's another job I've f'd up'.

Please do not imagine that I don't drink or disapprove of it, let's face it I've been peddling it for years sometimes to customers who couldn't handle it and they let it take over their lives with dire consequences'. Certainly later in life I have tried not to drink in the day and kept my first tipple till 'cowboy time' or 10 to 10 pm. Ten 2 ten ten 2 ten. Got it? Except when on a day off (I've explained what a day off means) or on holiday. Cheers.

In previous years I had learnt to write with a white marker both straight and backwards on a shop window, this experience stood me in fine feckle for writing on Blackboards to advertise food specials, OAP lunches and general information about upcoming events like Mothers Day. Unfortunately this was the extent of our advertising at that moment for three reasons 1.I've never believed in advertising externally for many reasons, where do you place your ads, in which region, spread over how far and how do you know the results? 2. How much do you layout and what is the ratio money to return? Also once you advertise every advertising hack in the country is on the phone because they know you are interested in advertising, but if you don't advertise you can inform them so and eventually they'll get the message. 3. By now the internet was becoming big business but I didn't at this time realise how much influence it was to have in the future and I did to some extent stick my head in the sand. I've always thought that the best form of advertising is word of mouth that is if you're good; watch out if you fall foul of Jim's auntie or her sister because they'll tell the whole St. and everybody at work.

Going back to sign writing, at this time we had two big black boards and a smaller free standing board which was the OAP menu on which we had a choice of up to three courses at a very reasonable price, one of the other boards was used as a specials board and the other for information. Each day Grace and the chef would discuss what dishes were to go on the OAP menu, on Monday it could be whatever had been left from the weekend such as roasts or prawns for a prawn cocktail or chef would make old time favourites like stuffed hearts or liver 'n' onions. The pensioners enjoyed these old fashioned dishes which they wouldn't make at home but enjoyed at a very good price, by 12noon on most days the pub and restaurant was full.

As previously mentioned that is the trade that's out there at lunchtime, grab it.

The specials board was used as an alternative to the main menu where we introduced dishes which were in season and gave us the opportunity to buy meats etc at good prices as products could fluctuate dramatically when in season and this of course affected the profit margins. Empty boards are a missed opportunity to let the punters know what's on now and what's up and coming, always keep them informative, clear and up to date. Old, out of date information is history and the other waste of space is menus only printed on one side.

For many years I've thought that menu boards were a good way of informing customers of what we were about but there was one major problem with this idea. Mainly it was because of a few spelling mistakes that crept into my script. Well OK I did pass English Language but just occasionally I would make a faux pas, but at least it meant that the customer had read the information.

Tony was still our handy man who worked two days a week mending, fixing and painting but I still insisted on cutting the grass. I've never believe in saving grass cuttings so I never put the grass box on the mower which means that the mulched up grass returns as fertilizer to the lawn. In the autumn because we have many trees surrounding the site there is a problem caused by the fallen leaves. Some I swept them up and the others covering the lawns were mulched up when I cut the grass. The downside to this was that we had many molehills which I was informed by Jim the mole catcher was as a result of the soil being very rich and full of worms which encouraged the moles.

On my birthday in 2004 Grace arranged a surprise trip to Madrid at the end of January where snow lay on the pavements and boy was it cold but that didn't stop us enjoying the various tapas bars in the city. Tapas bars in Spain have no connection to the suedo tapas bars that operators attempt to put on in this country. In Spain a little tit bit is given from a glass fronted selection with even one drink, then the tit bit getting larger the more you drink, up to a small snack. The selection could vary from a few chips to fried meat balls, gambas, patatas bravas with aioli, mantaditos, pimientos de padron and chiporones, all free of charge, good business, the more you drink the more you get.

Later in the year we celebrated our 10th anniversary at the Egerton and to show our appreciation to all the customers we invited them to a garden party with a DJ and buffet which Edi had put together and laid out in the kitchen as this was the biggest table top space available for all the food he'd made to cater for 250 to 300 guests.

Over the previous months there had been lots of rumour and gossip in the village concerning the love tryst of Rob the farmer and his wife Jackie who had reputedly split up and each taken up with the others partner. So what, we liked Rob and after talking to his new partner Lesley invited them to the party, she was a little hesitant but with some encouragement they came, which helped put a stop to all the gossip and helped cement her position in the village as Rob the farmers partner, soon to become wife.

Within months David her 15yr old son came to work for us on a part time basis and continued till we retired, also his brother came for a short period and later their sister Lucy who also stayed with us for many years becoming a great friend.

Although the village was only a mile from town it was on the whole quite idyllic being surrounded with green fields, a small local school nearby, the church standing majestically in the centre of the village and of course the village pub. However we did get complaints from some residents, what you might call townies. These included the noise from the church bells too early in the morning and that the church clock chimed every hour, even thru the night and the noise of the farm animals, especially the cock crowing in the early hours. Some of the more southern townies especially those from the big city thought they could just walk outside and hail a black cab and didn't understand why they had to book and wait for a taxi.

On our trip to the Lakes in autumn, staying at Gilpin we encountered three traumatic experiences which didn't put the Gilpin in a good light and made us consider not staying again. On booking we always requested the Troutbeck suite which we preferred to some of the other suites, but on arrival we were escorted to one of the smaller rooms where on opening the cupboard drawers found ladies underwear in them. So down I went to reception mentioning the underwear and why had we been given a different room? When I mentioned the knickers they thought they were Graces but when the situation became clear to them I saw the lady receptionists face drain of colour and she immediately shot off to instruct a maid to clear the room; however the change of room had come about because the original booking had not had a little star put next to it instructing other receptionists not to let the room to any other guest which had happened, the mistake was rectified the following day. More was to follow as the following day when Grace was taking a leisurely hot bath she turned on the Jaquzzi to find masses of hair pumping from the jets filling the bath with a mass of hairy goo, not nice. I heard a scream and on entering the bathroom saw the situation and immediately got Grace to have a shower in the separate shower cubicle washing all the hairy slime from her body. Reception was contacted and within seconds a maintenance man arrived along with a member of the management who was very apologetic, saying that they would 'sort it out', which they did. I hadn't realised that Jaquzzi baths have a reservoir tank built into their system and it was this that had caused the problem. They need checking regularly which obviously had not happened. Without being prompted the hotel knocked off two nights stay and apologised unreservedly and the incident was forgotten about, till now. Question, what happens to the water in the tank when the bath is working normally and whose water is it really?

Christmas of 2004 as always was a hectic time of year giving us all lots of extra work both business and personnel to attend to. I would have already ordered 200 or so Christmas cards, written and signed them in ink well in advance ready to post on the 30th of November, ours were always the first cards to be delivered and first to be remembered, just a little PR trick. When at the Cattle Market Ken Iddon had introduced me to a saying by Anon which I thought was as poignant a message at Christmas and ever since we've had it printed on the fly sheet of our cards. Never a Christmas Morning, Never a New Year Ends, That Someone Thinks of Someone, Old Days Old Times, Old friends.

Decorations would go up in the last week of November with at least two trees making the whole pub like Santa's Grotto and our private lounge would be decorated in the second week of December with the tree shining brightly in the window overlooking the church and grave yard. Grace had control of the catering operation and had ordered all the stock needed for the festive period so that everything ran smoothly and all the many extra parties went off successfully. Over the years we had become popular with the older members of the community and attracted many Christmas outings from the local retirement homes, mostly at lunchtime, A. because we offered a reasonable price, B. the size of the meal was manageable, older people hate waste C. we talked to them with a smile and sometimes I'd tell them a joke. Over the years we'd got to know many of the residents and become pally with some, of course it's inevitable that on these trips I'd notice faces missing and on inquiring found that Hilda, Mavis or John had passed away, which was sad but we always made any newcomers feel welcome and all the staff waved them off as they departed.

Christmas menus were Graces dept. and she had them ready for the printers by early July. What caused the problem was trying to keep the price competitive as every other hotel and pub were trying to attract the same clientele. Of course there are horses for courses, just little local pubs, others with a small separate dining room and us a separate dining room which could cater for a private party and of course some are just decorated with that je ne sais quoi. Prices were dependant on which of these establishment styles you fell into. Out there are a myriad assortment of punters, some want to spend as little as possible, others are prepared to dig deep in order to achieve their ideal Christmas meal along with professional service, which doesn't come cheap, especially if you understand all the preparation necessary to achieve it. At this time prices for a three course meal ranged from £10.95 to £30, we being about £20, some included coffee which we had dropped many years previously 1. to keep costs down, 2. to stop the customers from dawdling over their coffee; therefore enabling a quicker turn round and reset.

By the time Christmas Eve arrived we'd cracked the festive season, but Boxing Day still had to be endured as this was the busiest day of the year although by now we didn't open at night as we'd found the evening a waste of time, if honest we'd got used to having the night off and we also closed on New Year's Eve night after 5pm. So Christmas Day, although we opened for two hrs at lunch, 11am to 1pm for drinks only, Boxing Day night and New Year's Eve night were the only times we closed and I cannot remember closing on any other days during the whole of our time at the Egerton. Ever.

Periodically we'd get visits from both the health inspector and the weights and measures dept. sent from our local council who would turn up unannounced at any time of the day, though always during office working hours, refer to Blackpool.

Health inspectors would turn up about once every two years unless they thought you had issues but we seemed to be in the good category so when they appeared Grace would suggest that they change into their white coat in the laundry which gave us time to check that everything was in its proper place as it usually was; i.e. rubbish bin lids on and all food covered. Hand sanitising was and always is an important part of kitchen hygiene so Grace would make sure that the inspector was asked to cleanse their hands before entering the kitchen sometimes to his or her surprise. We'd often get an Asian inspector who although very thorough was also fair and helpful with advice if necessary. Weights and measure inspectors who came very infrequently were totally straight down the line, assuming you were on the fiddle from the start, no smile and certainly no excuses. On one visit they found that a bottle of gin was not 100% pure Gordon's as Pam had poured ½ inch of Bombay into a nearly full bottle to top it up; therefore the bottle was not pure Gordon's, I thought they were going to hang, draw and quarter me as it was my responsibility, but in the end I got a warning. That was all they found but I suppose it justified all the paper work they filled in and after all there are some rogues in this trade. Out there prior to the 2003 Licensing Act we could be visited at any time by a Magistrate and a deputation from the Police to check on your premises about once a year but after the act it was up to the council to attend if they had received a complaint from the public, this never happened, so never a visit.

Over the many years as a licensee I have endeavoured to keep my pubs clear of trouble from drunks or addicts which at times has been a hard task because let's face it alcohol and sense are not good bed mates. Regular punters get to know how far they can push you but 'only there for the day customers' think what the hell I'm not going to be here tomorrow, these are the ones that need careful attention. As I've mention before you are the guiding light of your business and must firmly and politely show that no nonsense will be tolerated, your only other option is to involve the police which should only be used as a last resort otherwise you become known as a house of trouble, not only by the police but by the whole town who then don't feel safe coming for a visit. I only drink in pubs where I don't have to keep looking over my shoulder.

Grace often remarks that as her birthday always falls on a bank holiday she has to work where as my birthday is at the end of January I never have to work and we are often on holiday as was the case in 2005 when she organised a surprise short trip to Cairo, this being our second visit to Egypt. I knew nothing about the trip till we arrived at the airport, although if I'd opened the card from Brian and Pauline it might have given the game away as it had a scene of pyramids on the cover. The hotel was in the city centre on the banks of the Nile, I like cities and we made the most of some other quality hotels and of course a visit to the pyramids via a taxi supplied by the hotel which picked us up at 7am to avoid the crowds. Well that was a waste of time as it took only minutes to travel the short distance to the edge of the city and we found that the site did not open till 8am. On the short trip on tarmaced roads, both sides of which being built up with 2 to 3 story apartments and houses I looked to the right and suddenly the pyramids appeared, Grace was looking to the left and did not see them until I remarked that she should look to the right, 'Oh wow'she remarked, there they were just behind the houses. On we went through some old rickety gates onto a rutted sandy road where we alighted the taxi, paid our fee into the site to an Arab in a ram-shackled hut and made our way with no instructions to view two of the wonders of the world. What a letdown the Sphinx was, so small compared to the picture I had in my mind's eye from the pictures I had previously seen in print and on tele, the pyramids were bare and small. However the trip was not to be boring as we picked up a scruffy man who latched on to us trying to give us a free gift and even when I had said no thank you several times he carried on saying he didn't want anything for his free gift. He was a pure nuisance but his patience paid off for in the end I gave him a few Egyptian Pounds for a tiny scarab beetle and a Nefertiti on a chain, what a mug, some free gift.

On reflection the Egyptian authorities don't seem to have any idea of what a gold mine they are sitting on and with more subtle development of this site I'm sure it could be appreciated by visitors with easier access and a lot less hassle, perhaps the local Mafiosi don't want change as they already have great control over its finances.

To support a charity auction at the George and Dragon pub in Holmes Chapel we made a bid on a weekend at a hotel in Bedgellart, North Wales, surprisingly our bid was accepted and in due course we set off on a trip to Wales for the weekend. Grace was not looking forward to the trip as she thought it would be leek soup and lamb which she cannot stand, but although it rained all of the time we had an enjoyable time. Dinner at the Castilian Hotel, with no leeks or lamb in sight and lunch at Port Merion Hotel was excellent. This hotel stands on the banks of the river Afon Dwyrd in the midst of Port Merion Village where the t.v. programme the Prisoner starring Patrick Mc Goohan was filmed in 1967-68. Also in this year we visited the island of Palma staying at the Hotel Melia Victoria adjacent to Titos night club and opposite the marina in which were moored many very expensive yachts including the King of Spain's boat. We would often walk into the city which was a 15min stroll, along tree lined Ave's and there enjoy a cerveza and a wine at a road side bar or in a small tapas bar amongst casually smartly dressed customers. The atmosphere was eclectic with an overriding aroma of garlic and sometimes seafood which was always fresh from the Mediterranean Sea. Walking round the old town was a revelation especially when you compared the prices of drinks and food to our hotel and venues along the sea front. A glass of wine 1 euro with a little tapas included against the hotel at 10 euro. All luxury hotels worldwide charge exorbitant prices a. because of their location, b. the staff required to maintain a high level of service which is demanded c. their expected superior furnishings and c. they can, as once you've crossed the threshold most customers stay within the confines of their hotel, why wander out when everything is provided for you, at a price. We like to wander out and discover the locals and all that is on offer whilst still enjoying the first class service provided by the hotel, if you don't want to pay the price, don't go there.

Later that year we visited Muscat staying at the Crowne Plaza overlooking the Qurum beach, the hotel was constructed to look like a cruise liner, so I suppose that that is the nearest I ever got to taking a cruise which I've never fancied. It was a good job we were not wishing for lie ins as early each morning the hotel swimming pool which was situated beneath our bedroom window was utilised by local schools for swimming practice and later in the day the pool became a playground for a platoon of young airmen much to Grace's delight. One morning around 6.30am I heard this strange noise from outside in the grounds and on peering through the window saw a groundsman spraying smoke from a very noisy blower into all the bushes and trees, presumably to eliminate any bugs and flies, who thought that would go down well with the residents at that time of the morning. The finest hotel in the area was the Chedi Hotel where we sat at the bar overlooking an infinity pool with views to the sunset, gorgeous. Like all hotels there was a small but well stocked shop with a plethora of luxury items from headscarves to beachwear and handbags, no women can ignore shoes or handbags, well of course there was this divine little wicker bag which couldn't be ignored and oh there's another one that Haley would love, well and truly stuffed. Later we went on to Bali and then Singapore. In Bali our hotel of choice was a Hilton hotel which had a grand colonial feel to it with afternoon teas under canopies in the gardens and waiters in long flowing robes. However it did have its mishaps, the first for Grace when she slipped on a set of steps and badly grazed her leg which necessitated medical treatment by a doctor who swabbed the affected area with lashings of iodine which stung like hell. I should have known better than bite on local delicacies which were rock hard which of course broke my false teeth. They needed repairing by a dentist in Dempster the capital about 5 miles away, the cost of both these treatments was neglishable but necessary. As was normal we'd have a bottle of wine with our dinner, the cost about £20 but I was not impressed when the waitress commented that the cost of the wine equalled her monthly salary. On to Singapore staying at the Grand Hyatt Hotel on Paterson Rd. just off Orchard Rd. in the centre of the very clean and tidy city. A must visit of course is Raffles a hotel dating back to 1887, built at the height of Empire and today boasts many iconic bars, restaurant, cafes and delis including the Tiffin brassiere and Long bar which is renowned for peanut shells covering the floor and the Singapore Sling which disappointedly is today served from a soda style gun, not shaken before your very eyes. The hotel was used by the Japanese in the war as a concentration camp for prisoners, a long way from the luxury of the 19c and of the present day.

2006 was a very eventful year as we were to discover when half the village were up in arms about changes that Rob the farmer had become involved with a haulage company based at his farm. Farming in general was going thru a rough time and farmers nationwide had to diversify. Large wagons were thundering thru the village at all times of the day and night and this had caused uproar amongst some of the villagers especially the Carters and Gresty's who sent letters of complaint to all and sundry including the council. There were three men involved in the haulage business Rob and the other three we'll call John, Paul and George, all of whom being blamed for the debacle with no thought for the environment and disruption to the village which was and always had been a rat run or short cut for the local car users and now these huge wagons trying to get through our tiny village Rd.s. From our point of view there were extra drivers with money to spend in the village and this new found business brought extra cash into the area and into our till, we didn't get involved in the argument. When it came time for John to renew his car insurance the insurance co. asked him to name which drivers he allowed to drive his top of the range car. He said Dave T who at the time was just 18, the insurance co. said definatly no because of his age, this was a major drawback for David as he lost his chauffeurs job which he really enjoyed but he was still working for us.

With Brian and Pauline we visited further afield for lunches out, places we'd never thought of like Albrighton Hall and Albrighton Hussey on the outskirts of Shrewsbury, we'd also visit our old favourites such as The Grosvenor where if given enough notice Jonathan Slater would send Alison to pick us up in the hotel car. Another firm favourite was Rookery Hall near Nantwich were we would often see the Beckhams and whilst in Nantwich I must mention Church's Mansions in the centre of the town where extremely good food was to be found. Rookery Hall was owned by the Kings who always recommended champagne cocktails on arrival at about £10 a pop, they later went on to run Lower Slaughter Manor in the Cotswolds which we visited once, it again was very grand but without the champagne cocktails.

One of our holidays this year was to Bahrain an island in the Persian Gulf lying just north of the Tropic of Cancer and north of Quatar in the United Emirates, an area we like to visit because of the sun and great service, however this did not prove to be a favourite as we found it as yet an under developed holiday destination. We later visited our favoured Emirates holiday to Dubai where we are always spoilt by the Crowne Plaza team. If there's a fault it lies at breakfast which because of the local religion pork is not allowed and can only be prepared in a separate kitchen with separate utensils but bacon can be acquired if required. One morning I asked for boiled eggs which I required to be boiled for 3mins, sure enough I was presented with two eggs and soldiers, on cracking the shell out poured the uncooked contents. I called over the waitress who went to see the chef; he told her he had cooked the eggs as requested, putting the eggs in cold water and cooking them for 3mins. Some chef!

Later in the year we returned to Kato Paphos in Cyprus staying at the Elysium Hotel. We set out to find our old friend Lagis at his village in the mountains, I had lost his address but remembered the area, after making enquiries from the locals who were very wary about us, Lagis eventually appeared and invited us to his house which was literally just around the corner. We had previously met his wife who insisted on us sharing dishes of Greek fare, hard cheese, olives, bread, salted fish and cold chips straight from the fridge with a glass of local wine, thank god it wasn't retsina. We really do enjoy Cyprus but the food is so repetitive.

Over the years we have always collected money for charities, always local and for children, never for overseas as I think it a pure waste of time and resources, how much actually ends up at the intended destination because of official overheads and corruption. What happened to all the money raised by Geldoff and other such charities, those countries are still in the same mess as they were or even worse.

On the bar we placed an empty gallon Bells bottle on a board around which we encouraged (you don't want that spare change do you?) customers to put any spare change either around the bottle or in it and when it was full we'd knock it over, count up the change and donate it to a designated charity, the amount was usually in access of £1000 over a period of about 18 months.

The beer garden was a great asset to the business as was the patio which was always well used on warm sunny days, there were in the region of 25 garden tables dotted around these areas each seating 4-6 people, you do the maths. The waitresses sometimes used to complain about carrying heavy trays of food and drinks out into the garden, but it paid their wages. At some pubs the garden furniture is neglected to the extent that the tables should not have food served to them, you wouldn't serve food to a dirty table in a restaurant and therefore Tony always kept our furniture well painted. Some were the original tables we'd bought from Denis Leah at Beeston, perhaps with new extended legs because the original legs had rotted away with being stood in the damp turf. Some years prior Tony had constructed a brick built BBQ on the patio which was used by the Rotary clubs for their annual BBQ's but unfortunately not as often as I would have liked because of the vagaries of the British weather. An idea I introduced was covered ashtrays which consisted of a 3inch plant pot unturned on a saucer, this kept the astray dry and the fag ends out of site. Nowadays I see these ashtrays on many pub patios.

Two stories come to mind about the garden, I kept the grass cut but Tony had the job of keeping the hedges trimmed which he did twice a year, a job I did not do. One fine lunchtime with the garden filled to capacity a grandma came into the pub ranting that her grandson had cut his finger and that it was entirely my fault, of course I enquired as to what had happened and could I be of assistance. 'He's cut his hand badly and needs medical assistance, your holly is too prickly'. A plaster was applied and grandma was consoled. A similar accident happened with a child who had grasped a nettle, our fault again not the parent who was supposed to be looking after the child. On those hot sunny days the garden was a god send, customers would come from far and wide because we had this outside space for them to enjoy our food and drinks and the kids could play safely. Of course this sometimes meant that the pub could be empty inside and one such day some punters entering thru the front door remarked how quiet we were for such a nice day, they were served with their drinks and went out onto the patio and garden area, returning a little while later to order food, they said' bloody hell it's like Blackpool out there', we smiled.

2007 dawned and in my opinion the legislation that had been passed by government had one of the greatest effects over the whole country and its people, especially the licensed trade and many of the punters were up in arms about it; smoking in enclosed spaces was banned, which in my opinion was well overdue. Grace and I had smoked in our youth; I went on longer than her with the occasional sniff of snuff and then went on to cigars but I saw the light of day when we visited Barbados in '98. Instead of bringing back some of the finest cigars I just stopped, not really saying anything to anybody, I just stopped and believe me there is nothing like an ex smoker. I now loath the smell of smoke and feel pity for those that practice the habit and wonder why they can't see the error of their ways, especially now with all the irrefutable proof that has been laid out for all to see. To placate the customers who could no longer smoke in the pub, hooray, I erected a smoking shelter on the back patio with electric lights. This was done by connecting two garden gazebos together and facing them with plastic sheeting to keep out the rain but not the cold. They wanted us to install gas heaters, no way, if you want to smoke, that's your problem.

In January for my birthday we went to Abu Dhabi, the financial centre of the Emirates staying at the Crowne Plaza Hotel, our preferred hotel group, a. because of the excellent service and b. because we acquired IHG points which we could redeem on future visits. The hotel was in the business district and the clientele were either business men or workers out there to fill a contract, some for many months or years, not a destination we'd revisit. In May we rectified that mistake by once again visiting Dubai. As it was Grace's 50th Birthday whilst we were there the hotel pulled out all the stops and lavished her and I with champagne, birthday cake and other surprises throughout our visit. People ask us why we go to Dubai so frequently, that's the reason, the service and the sun.

In the summer the haulage business at Glebe farm came crashing down around all the partners' ears and was the talk of the village. As much as we had tried to sit on the fence we were drawn into the fiasco that followed when we had a visit from the police asking if we had recently been in touch with John, as we had not they then asked whether we thought that he could do himself any harm, to which we replied 'definatly not'. It transpired that the haulage co. owed money to a lot of people for services rendered and to some friends who had invested in the co. some of those had previously been enjoying the party. What they didn't realise was that it was their own money they had been partying with which should really have been in the bank, not in John's glove compartment. Just to show what a kind person John was was illustrated when he provided a holiday for a lady and her family whose husband had terminal cancer. This came about at one of the gatherings at Glebe Farm where this lady was a waitress, she looking glum, John asked her what her problems were, she told him her story and he asked what would help, she replied 'just one last holiday for all her family', he said 'book a holiday and I'll pay for it', he did.

Over the next few days there was much excitement and speculation as the police helicopter flew overhead searching for John partly because he had reputedly once belonged to the SAS and there was still no sighting of him. It was said that he owed a great deal of money to the wrong people, after a while this was all forgotten about and the haulage co. was no more. It would be some years later when John reared his head again, as a town councillor?

Later that year we visited Peter and Leslie in Feragudo which lies on the banks of the river Arade opposite Praia de Rocha in Portugal where their walled villa is situated. It was to be a great few days celebrating their anniversary in the garden with a luxurious swimming pool where most of the guests ended up in at some stage of the party, due to the vast amounts of Casal Mendes rosé that was consumed.

Instead of a lavish birthday party for Grace's 50th we decided to take a trip to the Maldives flying with our favourite airline Emirates staying on the island of Bandos which lies in the beautiful Indian Ocean surrounded by rings of azure and pink coloured waters. The facilities were fantastic but I did not like all the sand, it was everywhere, in the bar, the restaurant, in the chalet and even on the beach. You know what they say about sand, 'it gets everywhere', not for me. We were there for a week, a week too long and then went on to Dubai and as it was Grace's birthday whilst we were there the hotel pulled out all the stops and lavished her and I with champagne, birthday cake and other surprises throughout our visit. The bars wouldn't allow us to pay for drinks or gave us 50% discount. We are known in the hotel as Miss Grace and Mr. Norman because of the first names on our passports and they don't half look after us. On one occasion Grace wanted to make a reservation for dinner in the Polynesian restaurant, she gave a time and was about to give the waiter our room No. to secure the booking when he remarked 'Miss Grace everyone in the hotel knows your room No'.

People ask us why we go to Dubai so frequently, that's the reason, the service and the sun.

2008 was to be a very eventful year, some good and some not so. There was a big hoo-ha about a housing development around the mere that Gladman construction were trying to get passed by the council, which all the towns people were up in arms about as it would spoil the aesthetics and beauty of the area. After much heated discussion in chamber, many planning applications for the development being put forward it was eventually thrown out much to the relief of all concerned, not Gladmans. The land and water was bought by Crewe Angling Society who did cordon off much of the Mere but the grassed areas were still available for the 1000's of dog walkers and locals who used the space on a regular basis for recreation. This was the year that Haley and Tony had decided to tie the knot at Astbury Church on the 4th July which was to be a grand affair, but before that I suggested to Grace that she and Haley should take a mum and daughter trip to Palma staying at the Hotel Vittoria where Grace and I had been before and I knew they'd enjoy. I believe they had a great time, especially enjoying the jugs of sangria, after which memory of the trip went out of the window or what went on in Palma stayed in Palma. The wedding day was getting closer, Haley and mum had all the arrangements in order and paid for, coming in dead on Haley's budget at about £18.000 but Grace and I had added on a few little extras which brought the total up to £20.000 which at that time was well worth it.

Two weeks prior to the wedding however our world was turned upside down when at about 4.30am we were awoken by the security alarm going off alerting us of a potential break in. I jumped out of bed in my shreddies and ran down stairs to find our upstairs kitchen in disarray, the till draw gone and also my bunch of keys which I kept on the kitchen table, out of the way and where no one could see them. Looking out of the window, as by now it was light I could see 3 or 4 balaclavad men in the car park struggling with the downstairs safe. By now the whole house was awake, tony in Haley's pink dressing gown, me in my shreddies. Haley was on the phone ringing the police explaining in no uncertain terms exactly what was accuring and Grace saying not to get involved and wait for the police, thinking of our safety. No way, that's not me, so running down stairs with Tony following we tackled the balaclavad burglars who were blocking the side fire escape door whilst attempting to get the safe into a car. I picked up a fire extinguisher and threw it at them, Tony poked them with a brush stale and then they broke off and jumped into their moving escape car disappearing down the drive way onto the main Rd. After catching our breath and taking stock of what had just happened we realised that things could have been worse. Missing were the takings in the till from the previous day, money I had saved in a savings box in the kitchen, my bunch of keys and most importantly the main safe which they'd pushed across the downstairs tiled kitchen floor, out onto the patio and into the boot of their car. They had managed to open my car and boot but it was parked further down the car park, that's why they'd used their car which they had backed up to the back door, having to knock over and destroy several of my planters. Most upsetting. About 20mins after the 999 call two traffic cops arrived to take a statement, traffic you may ask, they were the nearest.

Some months prior I had heard that the Rising Sun, Tarporley had been broken into, the thieves gaining access via a skylight on the roof. We had a similar window in the loft so I asked a friend Alan to install bars, which he did saying in his gruff voice 'nobody ull get through that' as he screwed in the last 6 inch screw. Guess which way the burglars came in? Yes you're right, smashed their way in thru the skylight which gave them access to the kitchen, the money and the keys. This then enabled them to gain entry to the pub, only setting off the security alarm when they were 10ft from the safe in the catering kitchen. I've never been one to broadcast our problems to all and sundry so after we'd cleared up, put the flowers back in the planters, patio tables straight and generally tided up no one would be any the wiser. The last thing I wanted was for the press to get hold of the story as it would have been The Great Congleton Pub Robbery and every Tom, Dick and Harry would want to know all the grimy details. Eventually that day two police detectives turned up to take further statements, which we did as privately as we could, away from prying eyes and speculative customers. The usual questions, what time, how many men, what was taken, what we did and finally would you recognise these balaclavad men again? Oh yes! One of the detectives found a torch which had been left by the robbers; he commented that as they had been wearing gloves (true pros) there would be no finger prints, but had they worn gloves when changing the batteries? Two days later the empty opened safe was found dumped in Frodsham; boys on their way back home to the big city on the Mersey. Sure enough some week's later the detectives visited again informing us that they had identified culprits from finger prints on the batteries and would we attend an identity parade and if necessary go to court. Did they not understand that the robbers were balaclavad and no, we could not identify them? Just to make matters worse the junior policeman told us in great detail what hardened criminals they were. This was in front of both my girls, which I knew had unsettled them. I took the senior detective to one side and told him to control his junior and never upset my girls again. They asked us if we'd been traumatised and if we wished to claim compo, we said no, they said they'd keep us up to date, we never heard from them again. I was convinced that the robbers had inside info about our upstairs kitchen, where I left my keys and the site of the downstairs safe. A few weeks prior we had employed an upstairs cleaner/housemaid for a short time and she would have had that knowledge but she had left after a few weeks. No one followed that up.

I'd had dealings with insurance Co's a few years previously when one of the hot water tanks in the loft had over heated causing damage in that area, so having that experience I was prepared for their questions and meanness when it came to parting with compensation. Always make sure you itemise every single item that is either damaged or stolen, don't miss the smallest thing, even if you think it is not worth bothering about because the loss adjuster will screw you down to the ground for a penny. It's their job. I'm not suggesting that you lie or exaggerate your claim, but don't give an inch unless it suits your cause. For instance we went out after the robbery and bought a new safe for £450 which they said was too big and too much so they adjusted the amount down to £300, and yes I could have bought a smaller one. Neither was I recompensed for the cash taken from my savings pot.

After the break in of 2008 we had increased our security and purchased a Chubb safe which we placed upstairs for our private heirlooms and as extra security for cash if we'd had a very successful day's take as the insurance Co. limited us as to how much we held in one safe. Every day I'd count the cash and go to the bank every other day but just occasionally the amounts didn't add up which I couldn't understand. There were only one set of keys to the safe and the till count every morning were within reasonable limits. I decided to ask Clive a R/T friend to secretly set up a small ct scanner above the downstairs safe where the cash was kept. The scanner was hidden in a fire alarm casing for secrecy but he let some of the staff discover what I was doing and on the first trial day Pam Evans the barmaid didn't turn in for work. Her husband Dave rang to say she was ill and several days later that she would not be returning. It dawned on me that when we went out she had access to the safe keys in case she needed change and it later came out that she had been giving free drinks to her friends in the afternoon when I was not there, some of whom certainly did not need free drinks. The money situation returned to normal.

In 2008 one of the bar girls that worked for us was enticed by extra money to work for a bar cum night club up town, well, she had been trained by us. She told us about a white van that turned up late at night with large plastic containers full of some white clear spirits that were decanted into well known branded bottles which then went into the cocktails late into the night, by then who'd know? That same operator is still in business today and after rumours and reports in local and national news papers of many dodgy deals he must have nine lives, but they seem to be diminishing at a great rate after leaving many conned business's laying in ruins.

Prior to the wedding Edi had asked Haley who was giving her away on the big day, of course Haley quick as a flash said 'my dad of course' he replied 'that ull be unusual, he doesn't give anything away'.

4th July dawned bright with the threat of rain later, which we hoped would wait till after Haley and Tony's drinks reception at home (the pub), wedding at St. Marys next door and reception at Alderly Edge Hotel. All the guests looked in good form, smart and colourful with the wedding party in top hat. Dear John Seddon in morning suit gave a reading and Rector Geoff Cuttel took the service, all went well and thankfully the rain had passed over during the service. The wedding car awaited and the bride, groom, Grace and I started our journey to the reception at the hotel but just as Grace and I had done on our wedding day we decided to stop for a quick one in Alderly at Gustos where we had arranged for a chilled bottle of champagne to be awaiting us. We arrived at the reception shortly after, to be greeted by the guests and the flashing lights of the photographers who had come over from Italy, how much you might ask? Don't. Photographers are the bain of all caterers as they have no concept of time and take hours getting all their photographs just so, with no thought to the food being overcooked. The reception went well and the speeches didn't disappoint. Horace, Tony's best man recalling his first meeting with the groom, not at Portofino's Spanish restaurant as most people thought but from the back of a lorry, joke. My few words featured on a paper that extended to many feet when I let it drop down much to the consternation of the guests but I kept my speech short extolling how proud Grace and I were of Haley's achievements to date and wished it to continue with Tony's loving assistance. The night went as expected, drinks, dancing and more drinking, in the morning many guests needed Alka-Seltzer not breakfast but some did attempt both.

Haley and Tony continued to live with us until they had saved up enough for a deposit and with a sizeable donation from the bank of mummy and daddy they moved into a four bed roomed detached house in Kenilworth Dr. just off Park Lne.

Some years prior to Haley and Tony's wedding a young lady called Amy called on us at the pub representing Diageo as she was their Pimm's lady and had been given the task of promoting Pimm's on a national advertising scale. Her responsibility was for all of the North West and Cheshire and she had a £1 million budget. Little did we realise at that first meeting how much of that budget would land on our pub. After a long discussion with her we planned a major Pimm's extravaganza for the summer of '06 and boy did she come forward with the promo materials. In the end we ended up with 25 red Pimm's umbrella's for the garden and patio which really did stand out, two large double deckchairs, boxes and boxes of jugs, stirrers, glasses and swizzle sticks by the thousand. On the end of the building we draped a huge Pimm's promo banner and one lady asked if the pub was called the Pimm's pub. Every time Amy visited us there would be more promo material and as that summer came to a close we were asked to promote winter Pimm's which we mixed with hot fruit cider or hot ginger beer which went down well on a cold winter's day. This creation went so well that Pimm's actually sent another representative to suss out exactly what we were doing differently to be selling so much hot Pimm's. I didn't tell them but I can tell you that the secret lay in the whole cinnamon sticks that we put in the finished drink along with sliced lemon and cloves which gave the drink a warming glow. I had managed to lay my hands on a generous supply of bundles of cinnamon sticks for next to nothing which would have cost a fortune in the shops and would have made it impossible to create our unique winter Pimm's concoction. Just before the wedding Amy turned up with more goodies, a pop up gazebo, out of which we constructed an outside Pimm's bar and some white picket fencing with a roll of artificial grass which was rolled out on the patio. Last but not least she also supplied us with two urns to heat up the red aromatic liquid to make the cocktails. I told Amy and many of my friends that she was the girl who gave me everything except s-x.

Another co. representative that I had built up a friendly rapport over many years was Mike Smith who represented Famous grouse and whenever he called which was about every 2 months I would always order a selection of whisky/malts from him as after all that was his job, to sell. He introduced me to a vast selection of the finest Scottish malts, in the first place by presenting us with a malt bar stand which held six bottles. Lagavulin, Talisker, Oban, Dalwinnie, Craggamore and Glenkinchie which encompassed Scotland's finest. Gone had the days of huge whisky sales that we'd had at the Cattle Market in Preston and Mike would give me odd bottles to try to resurrect whisky sales by way of special offers like 2 for 1 but gin sales were rocketing, taking over the spirit market. Perhaps whisky sales will make a resurgence in the future but I wouldn't put my hat on it.

After all the excitement of the wedding Grace and I decided to revisit Palma later in the year, for three reasons; 1. because Grace had enjoyed it so much earlier with Haley 2. to apologise to the hotel for their antics on that holiday 3. I wanted to go as I'd enjoyed it so much on our previous holiday there.

This year a new bar came to Congleton, DV8, opened by Chris Carson and his friend James who Haley had gone to school with and James's father an accountant was the money man. They had previously run the Bubble Bar in Alderley a very busy establishment popular with the gay community; I don't know how Congleton would have got on with that, at that time. DV8 was novel, different food ideas and expensive with strict rules to keep out the riff raff and it became the place to be. Chris had great ideas and lots of ambition for himself, not necessarily for his partner who disappeared after a short while but the money man stayed as he could see Chris going far with other people's money and ideas.

Ever since I had acquired the Billsborrow Hall lithograph and had it framed I'd had several people interested in purchasing it, it was now in pride of place hung on the wall in the front lounge of the pub and it had many admirers and still offers came but I liked the picture and at that time had no interest in letting it go. I may change my mind but not yet.

We had a loyal staff, still some of the originals like Edi, Sara and Tony the gardener cum handyman and others who had joined along the way, James and Becki, Dave T. Lucy T. Ash, Alan Coppock, several Hayley's, Rachael's and Emma's. The older ones tended to stay as we paid them over rate and looked after them. The younger ones tended to be students when they started at16, worked two years and went off to Uni, then returning during the holidays, some even came back after Uni.

At one stage we had 26 staff on the books, only 1 or 2 full timers, the rest part timers; we tried to keep them below the National Insurance level which saved them and us paying N.I.

I remember this figure because over the Christmas period trade was spectacular and we tended to limit the menu choices to the main menu and the festive menu whilst still offering the OAP's selection Monday to Friday. So that left one of the two big blackboards empty and as you know I don't like wasted advertising or information space. To this end I would write all the staffs' names in chalk on the board wishing Merry Christmas to all the customers with Grace and my non-de- plume in lower small case at the bottom, with a very sincere Thank You. This always went down well.

In September Grace and I went to Sorrento once again using the same chauffeur service and stayed at the same hotel renamed the Sorrento Hilton which had recently had a major refurbishment, new suites and club floor with a private pool for club residents only.

We enjoyed the Italian sunshine and la cordialita which shone thru when talking to the locals be it in a bar, restaurant or just on the street especially with the hand and arm gesturing. From Tasso Sq. you can take a tour of the city in an open topped horse drawn buggy, one of the horses, a palomino took Grace's eye, she wanted to take him home, she called him Harry but I talked her out of taking him home whilst sitting at a bar in the middle of the square, bellissimo. On all our holidays we like to visit other local bars and restaurants or in this case trattoria such as Lanterna where the waiter gave my girls freshly picked flowers. Oparrucciano off the main St. where they made the most fabulous panzenella which we devoured under a canopy of vines. Ilbuco a truly magnificent Italian restaurant and Caruso trading on the great singers name but not fulfilling its countries cuisine although the Italian singer did manage to rip me off, 10 euro for a tape of his music. Sounded good in the atmospheric restaurant but not so when played at home.

Each November we'd put on a bonfire night, I'd build a huge bonfire in the paddock and display fireworks for all who wished to attend. I got great pleasure constructing the tower of branches, pallets, old household rubbish that people were glad to find a place to dump and the carpet boys were happy to get rid of their old carpet tubes which gave great shape and height to the towering heap. I think I must have had pyrotechnic tendencies especially when it came to letting of the fireworks; some were supplied by the families attending. Our hotel insurance came due on the first of November and I set about getting quotes as you do and was concerned when asked by one Co. if we had a beer garden and did we put on any outside events i.e. music, carnivals, markets or firework and bonfire events, to which I answered yes. OK no problem, could you give us the no. of your firework and bonfire certificate so that they could validate that we had had training. Well of course we'd never been asked for this information before and had no such documents. I was then informed that if I were to go ahead with bonfire night as planned our insurance would be null and void. Oops what to do now? Several solutions and more problems presented themselves.

1. Take down the pile and then have to dispose of it, probably at the expense of 1 or 2 skips and after that trying to explain to hundreds of excited kids and parents, why, making me the man that destroyed their bonfire, not a good scenario.

2. Go ahead and ignore the possible consequences, let's face it we'd been doing it for years with no thought to what might happen if a child was injured by a wayward rocket or firework, but times have changed and where there's blame there's a claim so perhaps not such a good idea.

3. What would happen if the bonfire was mysteryaly set on fire by kids two days prior to the event? Problem solved, no bonfire, no firework night and someone else gets the blame. Just remember if ever you have to tell a little white lie, never tell anyone, even your best mate because somehow the truth will leak out. Always keep a poker face.

At the beginning of December we boarded the train to Manchester in order to visit the Christmas market which extends from the Town Hall throughout every St. and alley in the city centre. We have been here many times and the market as always based on a German theme of frankfurters and Bavarian beer served in steins by ladies in Tyrolean dress with Umpa music blaring from loud speakers. The funny thing is we never actually buy anything because most of it is Christmas tat and as we are going on to enjoy a lunch and a glass/s of wine either in an Italian or Chinese in China Town. The ambience and atmosphere of the market sets us up for the day ahead but I don't like carrying shopping bags around when I'm out on the town, but if I have to I always make sure that any cheap bags are inserted into a bag with a premier name; say Primarni in a Selfridge's bag, especially Primarni as it is made from paper and could fall to pieces in the rain. It rains a lot in Manchester. On this trip we stayed two nights at the Radisson Hotel on Peter St. whilst we enjoyed the delights of Manchester including the newly opened Albert

Scholsses Bar, very unique and packed to the rafters. Back to the hotel cocktail bar where a party of hotel guests were enjoying a variety of expertly mixed cocktails made by a professional cocktologist, god help them in the morning. Grace and I stayed on the wine. As always plans for December had been executed well in advance, the cellars were bursting at the seams with alcohol and beer and Grace had confirmed her provision orders from our suppliers which would be delivered throughout the month with the possibility of changes if necessary. In order to encourage us to place our orders well in advance the suppliers often offered us either discounts or extra stock such as, order 10 doz mince pies for the price of 8 or 10 cases of tonic and receive a bottle of spirit free if you ordered by 15th November, this of course gave them time to make up their requirements and finalize delivery logistics. I always ordered Bacardi if it was one of the spirits offered free because it sold for a premium price to say vod and sometimes I would end up with 2 to 3 doz bottles of it by the end of the November. All extra free stock.

We catered for a wide variety of parties over the period, from OAP's, Rotary, sometimes more than just our own, works do's, family get togethers and just couples trying to find a table on a quiet night if they could. This is not forgetting the residents, some attending the parties and staying over or the business guests who endeavoured to tie up their business well before Christmas and this trade would dry up after the second week in December. We had great fun with the OAP's

During this period we must not forget that people still passed away and their families tried desperately to arrange funerals for their loved ones with little notice and couples still got married with their receptions having been arranged well in advance at their final destinations, we still coped with the pre-wedding and after drinkers. It was all good for trade and the takings but wow, we all worked hard and were beat by nightime. As always on Christmas Eve we'd go to Midnight Mass, afterwards put out Santa's port, Rudolph's carrot and mince pie before having a quick one before bed.

Up at 6am. tidy the pub, open presents then burn the wrapping paper, ring distant friends and family, then get ready to open at 11am, that is if we hadn't had a few regulars like Chris Naden in at 10.30am which we usually did. Grace, I and Haley didn't stop till 1pm when I would ring the pub ships bells like hell and after shouting Merry Christmas in some foreign language I would tell them to GO HOME in a jovial but not very polite way and by 1.30pm the pub was cleared and we'd go out for lunch, more often than not to the Yellow Broome at Twemlow. After lunch a taxi would take us home at about 5pm and we'd watch tele and perhaps take a little nap before venturing down to the bar reminiscing about lunch, good or bad and perhaps take a little tincture before I made bacon and egg butties for all on thick white bread with Lurpak butter at about 10pm. Yummy. Things don't change much.

All the provisions we'd pre-ordered were by now well depleted and you may think that Christmas was over but believe me it wasn't over yet, Boxing Day as expected was to prove one of the busiest days of the year, the other being Mothers Day. Every table in the restaurant and bar booked on a staggered basis from 12noon to1pm and at 2 hourly slots thereafter with work-ins if they were lucky. Some years prior I had found that after we'd fed the crowds during the day they'd disappear off and we'd be left with a few locals who on one year Lee Mc. the barman had taken £40 from 6pm to 10.30pm, what's the point. So I decided not to open and Grace and I would venture out searching for some other foolish restauranteur who thought it good to open. One such was at the Holly Bush Inn in Wheelock which we found open after a trawl round several closed premises. It's a pub with separate dining room where there were a few other desperate diners. It has now been demolished and replaced with a few houses. Grace ordered grilled fish, I a Sirloin, mine was fine but Grace's fish smelt of bleach which off fish does in time. Called over the waitress who took the dish to show the chef who said there was nothing wrong with it and the girl said that all their fish was delivered fresh every day. Are you there yet? It was Tuesday, the last catch would have been no later than the previous Friday and there had been no deliveries since Saturday, fish mongers don't deliver on Sunday or Christmas day and certainly not on Boxing Day.

I asked them to show me a delivery note for that day, they didn't, and we left.

When Christmas and New Year's celebrations fell in the week it's like having 5 weekends in two weeks so you must make the most of the opportunities. I know that people budget how much money they have to spend over the Christmas period, but that's what c/c's are for.

If you can capture advance bookings early by being prepared say from July you will be the venue that is busy and you get the footfall that may have gone elsewhere. If Jack usually goes out with his mates on a Friday for a drink but his wife has booked a Christmas party with you on a Saturday he will probably be talked into not going out on a Friday, their loss, your gain.

Karen, one of our waitresses who had worked for us for sometime had left us to take on a pub/restaurant near Stoke with her partner who was a chef. The premises were a group of joined up quaint cottages situated in a small village with a large play area outside, bar and separate restaurant with low ceilings and a rural atmosphere. We were partnered by Brian and Pauline on one of our regular trips out and we were pleasantly surprised when we arrived for late lunch at The Village Pub in Endon half way between Leek and Stoke which turned out to be OK but not quite what we'd expected after all the bull s...t and build up that Karen had given us about her partners supposedly fantastic catering abilities. We commented how nice the place looked and how quickly they'd managed to get the pub up and running, Karen commented that she'd been at it all day and had taken particular attention that all the light bulbs were in working order as I'd once told her that if light bulbs were out it meant that the establishment was not being cared for properly, some people do listen. I shouldn't call light bulbs bulbs because on numerous occasions I'd been told by electricians that they are lamps not bulbs.

Why do people really go to the pub? That is a very complex question and may take some time to explore as I know why I became a landlord, if I hadn't I'd have probably been found propping up a bar somewhere, anywhere as I enjoyed the atmosphere of pubs, so I decided that I could make a living whilst enjoying that atmosphere and hoped that I could encourage customers to enjoy it with me. I accomplished that ambition with Grace by my side. Now customers visit pubs for many reasons, some just to drink because they enjoy the taste of hops and barley, others the alcohol and its effect which can get out of hand if not kept under control which sometimes means that the landlord has to step in and assert his authority. In our case this was a very infrequent necessity as our regulars knew how far to go. Putting drink to one side punters came to socialise with their friends to discuss local gossip, sport, national and international affairs, last night's TV and the weather. Of course the pub was a central point where they could congregate to celebrate their good fortunes, birthdays, anniversaries and sadly a place to commemorate a person's life after their death and commiserate with the family. Some customers came to the pub to escape from their home life or perhaps they are on their own at home and come to seek just a friendly smile or kind word to escape their loneliness. One such older unkempt gentleman was Cyril who came in about lunchtime, had a pint then took his leave saying he was driving home to have a sleep. He regaled us of when he was a joiner working for Seddons builders and what a good Co. they were, but then he cottoned on to the fact that John S....n was a customer and wouldn't leave him alone which I know John didn't like. The next day Cyril's in again, same stories, again, leaves and returns 1hr later telling us about his sleep, but another customer remarks that Cyril has only just left the Blue Bell where he'd had two pints. This went on for several weeks with Cyril sometimes visiting three times a day to us, so how many other places was he going to and how many pints was he consuming? The situation came to a head when late one afternoon another customer came in and said he'd nearly hit Cyril's car when turning into our driveway. At his best Cyril's vision was not A1 and with a few pints I couldn't imagine what he could see. I don't usually get involved in customers private lives but on reflection I could imagine the trouble Cyril would be in if stopped by the Bill and in time when would he knock someone over, so I had a quiet word with a Gerry a retired PO who had a word with a serving PO who went round to Cyril's address and warned him that he shouldn't drive and perhaps it was time he surrendered his driving licence. Job done quietly and no one got hurt, good conclusion. Our job is to be there for everyone, to listen, to give guidance and if necessary a shoulder to cry on but not there to lend money, as this is the quickest way to lose your money and the customer when the loan is not repaid. After a hard day at the office or on the building site some like to relax with a pint or glass of wine before heading off home, some think that their partner at home wouldn't like this so they'd say 'if anyone asks I've not been in' and some didn't care and would stay far too long, so that on more than one occasion wives have brought the guilty parties evening meal into the pub and thrown it on the bar saying 'if you want to live here you might as well have your meals here'. Oops!

Several times I've been accused of encouraging their partners to stay drinking too long to which I would remark 'that I hadn't chained them to the bar'. I've never been very sporty so football and other games have never been highlights of my life as they are for many of the punters who often encouraged me to get a bigger TV, get Sky for the all the sport but I didn't want the Edge to be a sports pub, it is a rural country Inn and the loud raucous sporting events would not have gone down well with all our diners who were our bread and butter (sic). Grace and I had agreed at the outset that there would be no darts, dominoes or pool as at the Beeston, I wanted our pub to be a home from home, perhaps slightly exaggerated with warm open fires, bigger pictures on the walls, a little library with your favourite authors and a friendly welcome with home cooked meals, a place you felt safe.

In summer months the outside areas create a great place for families and friends to meet up and kids to play and enjoy the outdoors within a controlled space. Unfortunately at times parents forgot that they have to look after their kids and at times I had to step in and suggest that there could be a problem if their young child fell from the top of the 30ft trees in the garden that they had not noticed, perhaps after a few beers. Oh don't worry kids will be kids they said.

I got great pleasure seeing all the plants in full bloom during these months; this was achieved by my strict watering and feeding regime.

Paintings are the heart of a good home but in pubs they never get changed so they are the same on every visit and become invisible so I hit on the idea of asking local artists to exhibit their works of art in the hope that they would sell thereby getting them an income and the pub a variety of pictures. I say works of art, some I was very dubious about, perhaps not my scene, but in general many did sell, those that didn't were replaced on a regular basis at no cost to us. The artists were happy and so was I.

At the end of March '09 I heard that an Interim Planning Application had been put before Congleton Council regarding the ring Rd. or By-Pass as it was now being referred to and from what I understood it was to have a major impact on our surrounding area. On the second blackboard in the pub I sketched a detailed map of the consequences that the development would have on our village which would join up the A34, A54, A534 and back onto the A34 which travelled thru Congleton town centre and then onto Leek Rd. which would take you to the vastly expanding town of Biddulph. The route shown would double the width of Bent Lne. come directly over the village green, taking out the 100 yr. old oak tree with several cottages being demolished and the church grave yard wall being taken back 10mtrs. to alleviate the pinch point in the centre of the village. All these changes to the original plan may come as a great shock to many of you, so if you have any concerns please contact Mr. Roadrunner or Mrs. Streetwise at Congleton Highways and By-ways dept. to discuss this issue. It was only at this point did most of the very concerned readers realise that they had fallen for an April fool's joke, those that didn't were assured on the 1st April that the planning application had been scrapped.

Grace and I love going abroad for the sun but we do enjoy visiting this country especially the Cotswolds so a few days away were planned for Grace's birthday in May staying at the Swan Hotel at Bibury, half way between Burford and Cirencester on the A4425. Thru this beautiful Cotswold village flows the river Colne and on higher ground above the water meadows sit Arlington Cottages which are built of quintessential Cotswold stone. There is a bridge crossing the small river and if you lean over ever so carefully 100's of trout can be seen in the crystal clear water. These trout may have escaped from the fish farm that has developed from the old pools belonging in years gone by to the water mill which used to be powered by the river. From this was devised a thriving trout farm, the mill being turned into a very busy novelty shopping experience and alongside it a flourishing cafe for the 100's and 1000's of visitors who descend on the village as it is on the 'must see sights of Britain' and was described by William Morris as the most beautiful village in England. The trout farm sells fish food to give you the pleasure of feeding their fish. Unbelievable. The Swan Inn sits on the banks of the river and was originally a coaching Inn but is now a very popular wedding venue and popular with Americans. On our visit a wedding was in full swing so Grace and I found a quiet corner at the end of the bar where, when he had time we chatted to the head barman who showed us his fine array of very expensive brandies, sorry should say cognacs. Just then three guys, the groom and his two best men came to the bar and asked for three of the best brandies he could offer; I thought this could get messy. The barman showed them a bottle of fine brandy and asked large sir? So as not to be thought mean the groom said 'sure' and the barman poured as requested. The boys sipped the golden liquor with reverence and at this point the barman asked if the drinks were to be added to the wedding a/c the groom said yes but then enquired as to the amount of the three drinks, to which the barman replied £150. The groom and his friends were shell shocked and the groom said that he would pay because he didn't think his new father-in-law would be too happy if he put it on the wedding a/c. The barman said no more and as we left he smiled and winked. Isn't it fun people watching?

50% of our trade was food oriented and the restaurant was in need of a little TLC and reconfiguring so after discussions with Robinsons who agreed to finance the building work on condition that we pay for the refurbishment which would cost us in the region of £15.000. Of course the restaurant had to close during the works and remembering the last time building work had been carried out I insisted on a completion date which I'm glad I did as they tried to move the date back, but I said no as we had taken a funeral booking a day later, good job we got a booking nearer the date. On completion we were overjoyed at the outcome although our costs had ni' on doubled as the designer Neil Stanier Robinson just seemed to pay the prices that the suppliers asked for without thinking of putting them out to tender. Was it jobs for mates? I hadn't asked enough questions.

About this time the AA decided to recategorise their hotel star rating system. I understood why this was done as you couldn't really grade us in the same band as the Savoy Hotel in London, so we became an Inn and during this transition period I decided to rename us as The Egerton Country Inn which I thought painted a picture in people's minds when they came to looking for somewhere to stay. We had been an AA client since '95 and had found the inspectors suggestions and advice very helpful at times but all these changes made me look at the cost of having an AA sign outside and being on their internet booking site. Booking sites were 10 a penny now and after checking the proportion of bookings coming via the AA their £450 yearly cost seemed to be extravagant, when we'd joined in '95 it had cost £75 per annum. When I say 10 a penny, internet booking sites took in the region of 25% of the booking price dependant on which booking platform you decided to use, so although it was a cost we could have done without this was the modern way of booking rooms for many people and all hotels were forced, to some extent to use this system or miss out. Also by now Trip Advisor was being looked at by most travellers before they made their reservation and I've always thought that this business, their opinions and recommendations were open to abuse by the corrupt and sometimes manipulated feedback represented in the information given in their star ratings and I can say that Grace and I have never taken any notice of it. Possibly because I think we are savvy travellers, if we find something we don't like, complain and move on. It's all part of life's great experiences. After saying all that, our trip advisor star rating was 4.8 / 5 and we worked hard to maintain that high ranking which took a lot of smiling, hand shaking and just being helpful. Customers have a hard time complaining whilst you are smiling at them and in all honesty I can't remember there being many of those, if any I did my best to resolve them.

I remember on one occasion a Rotary member came to me and asked if we could make slight alterations to the usual way that their club nights had operated in the past, I assured him that what he was suggesting would be no problem for us to arrange in the future. He remarked that we always seemed to make problems disappear and nothing was too much trouble. I thought that that had been one of the nicest comments anyone had ever made to me. I've said many times 'it isn't important that people know what I'm doing , it's important that I know I know what I'm doing'. Also at this time Congleton Rotary club asked if they could perhaps host their club meetings at the Edge on a Wednesday instead of the Bulls Head in town as it had changed hands and they were dissatisfied with the new landlords. Of course we would have been happy to comply with their request but their headquarters said that they didn't want too many clubs to be based at one location, so that idea went out of the window, shame.

I had been a customer of National Westminster Bank since the year dot and had since the early days with Bob the BM at Penwortham always had a good relationship with whichever bank manager was in charge at the time. They did seem to get younger (or was it me getting older) and no sooner had I got to know them and build up a repartee than they'd be on the move, working their way up the ladder, I think it's called fast tracking. All of my business life I had an overdraft facility to be able to dip in and out of whenever funds were needed to either purchase some necessary equipment or stock or pay for tax and VAT bills when due in January and July. Always expedient to have a back up.

The BM at the time sometimes wanted to visit the pub to check we were still viable or we'd go to head office in Preston to discuss the following year's plans and needs, as in financial needs and often we would be treated to lunch somewhere in town. However I realised that there must have been some belt tightening in the banking industry when on the visit in '09 the BM suggested we go for lunch at a little Italian restaurant in Guildhall St. where they were doing a budget lunch; we declined, making an excuse that we had to get home.

In June of '09 we visited Palma, our room at the Victoria overlooking the Marina filled with the most amazing boats or is it yachts' and as always we enjoyed the 4 day break sampling the delights of the tapas bars and small cafes. At breakfast in the hotel which was a buffet affair with a lady chef cooking any style of eggs on a hot plate there was also a choice of wines and champagne for us to help ourselves which most mornings I did, usually champagne. However I said to Grace 'who's going to drink red wine at breakfast time' but no sooner had I said it than a client came and poured themselves a glass of red wine. There's no accounting for taste.

I always think that the local men and women dress so casually smart when walking around town, is it the sun or just the Mediterranean influence?

August took us to Barcelona, another last minute Brian and Pauline cheap short break which had us staying on the Ram Blas right in the centre of the city in a pension hotel which was a 4 storey building with small rooms kitted out with large plastic storage boxes, like Tupper ware as storage units and a horizontal pole on which to hang your clothes, very minimalistic, but as Brian said 'it's cheap'. The city with all its Gaudi architecture was fantastic and worth a visit but most of all I loved the Tapas bars especially the Mitre bar situated in the corner of the square opposite Gaudi's cathedral. I'd never experienced a tapas bar where you just helped yourself to any delicacy you took a fancy to from a grand selection of cold plates, order cerveza from the bar and hot dishes from a man behind a counter with no idea of how we paid. Each cold dish had a cocktail stick skewered in them and when I'd eaten that particular morsel I threw the stick on the floor with the many other sticks, it only became obvious when we came to pay what the sticks were for. Each stick had a coloured tip which indicated to the cashier the price of the individual dish we had consumed, some more expensive than others, the barman remembered what drinks we'd consumed and the hot service man also had perfect recollection of the hot dishes, but they didn't know how many sticks I'd thrown on the floor, very strange. At the hotel on the following 2 mornings breakfast was a help yourself to a very frugal Continental affair, fruit, cereal, ham, bread and make your own coffee, well it was a cheapo.

After we'd developed rooms 1-3 with ensuite it became evident that we needed to crack on with rooms 4-6 because by now everyone was expecting their own facilities. Bedrooms were a major contribution towards the business, not just because of the profit from the rooms but they also enhanced the need from other events that we could cater for like restaurant functions, christenings, weddings, funerals, music events at Glebe Farm like Astonbury and Capesthorn Hall where a Rewind music event was held each September. Walkers and sightseerers came calling, some visiting St Marys church and not forgetting the many business men and general workers looking for short and long stays. This type of trade could sometimes be very trying as their bosses often got their booking dept. to cancel at last minute as they'd got a better deal somewhere else or the goods to do the job hadn't arrived and they expected you not to charge, even though you were left with empty room/s. One guy actually left us and went to the Plough as I told him that we required at least 24hrs notice or we'd have to charge. As we only had six bedrooms it wasn't worth while getting in a chef to do the breakfasts so if the beds were full Grace and I would do them together or if quiet I could manage them on my own.

One night guests tended to have full English but long term guests soon decided to have a simpler affair like scrambled eggs on toast or just bacon, we did whatever they wanted. After Haley and Tony's wedding the previous year Geoff the Rector had left to look after naughty boys in prison and was sadly missed by all. In 2009 he was replaced by Jonathan and Ellie who were to bring about great changes, both to the village and the church.

At the end of August, straight after the Bank Holiday Grace and I went off to Santorini staying firstly at Akritiri then moving to the capitol Fira which is the picture that represents the island in all its worldwide advertising with white and blue painted houses high on the mountains above the beautiful blue sea inside the old volcano, this is called a caldera. The journey there was by a Greek Airlines plane to Athens and then a 10 people mono plane to the island which sounded like the propeller was being driven by an elastic band. There was one pilot and one stewardess who gave us a bottle of water and a bag of peanuts, great in-house refreshments and then we were down in bright Mediterranean sunshine. Our hotel, in the centre of Akritiri village was deserted and we had the run of the pool most days, visiting the beautiful sandy beaches which lay just a short walk away where we found several rush strewn tavernas at lunchtime and at night there was Harry's' bar in the village for drinks and snacks. If we asked for a drink he didn't have, say Baileys he'd looked along the Rd. to the corner store 50mtrs. away and if it was still open he'd say 'yes we got Baileys' and someone would be dispatched to get a bottle. Fabulous lazy few days.

Then off to Fira staying at a marble clad hotel overlooking the centre of the water filled volcano with as many as 4/5 gigantic cruise ships at anchor every day. Imagine all those passengers, most of them Yanks, disembarking every day and engulfing the local shops and bars, the small alleys are packed and prices are sky high all day but then by 6pm the day tourists leave, return to their ships for dinner and life returns back to normal for us holidayers. Peace and quiet. We'd commented about the vines which grow low across the barren parched landscape and we were informed it was because of the high winds in the winter, the grapes produce a sweet wine called Vin Santo. It became obvious to us that winter starts early because by the first week in September the wind was howling and the rain was sideways on, we sat on the balcony with our coats on, time to leave. Back on the elastic band driven plane and an 8hr stopover in Athens which I don't recommend.

We were asked to get involved with the government work experience for kids which seemed an ideal opportunity for us to give local school children a taste of the realities of the leisure industry. The scheme was spread over a two week period giving them an introduction of what would be in store for them if they decided to join the industry when they left school which we hoped they would do. They were placed under the care of one of the more experienced member of staff and shown every aspect of the trade, at the end of the fortnight I would give a report of their time with us. This carried on for 2 or three years quite successfully, one or two of the students being taken on to work part time but then we were informed that the scheme was to be shortened to just one week. One week would not give us enough time to give the students a comprehensive taste of the job so I ended the association with the scheme which I thought was a great shame.

Christmas was just around the corner and as always we managed to visit Santa's Christmas grotto in Huddersfield to stock up on larger than life decorations to fill the pub with festive cheer, giving the customers a Christmas home from home in front of a log fire, which by now was fuelled by natural gas. The cards, all 250 of them were addressed and most importantly signed in ink, I always dispatched our cards by the 30th November so that they would be the first card that anyone received, everyone remembers their first card, good advertising. On the 1st of December I'd put up the trees, one in the pub, one in the restaurant and one in the window in our private lounge upstairs. Because some of the decs were quite big I'd found that using a stapler was easier than pushing drawing pins into the walls which left me with very sore thumbs. Tony the handy man played hell with me for leaving holes everywhere when I took the decs down in January. I have to say I made a good job of the decs and it looked very festive both downstairs and in our private quarters.

Over the years we'd made several changes to Christmas, the major one was that we no longer celebrated it in July as we had done at Beeston and other changes had been made to save money especially when it came to the festive menu. Each year we agonised over the price we needed to charge and still make a decent profit, so instead of increasing costs too much over the last few years we had not included coffee as part of the meal and we found that most people didn't notice and also it meant that they didn't linger which in turn gave us a quicker table turnover. We also had found that the mince pies we provided were often wrapped up and taken home because the diners were already full and the novelty cardboard party hats and poppers were taken home for the kids, so what was the point? We made sure that the upgraded cracker provided contained a hat, novelty and joke which seemed to satisfy the diners and enabled us to keep our costs down.

We attracted a wide selection of guests over this period and each group had different demands which we hopefully managed to satisfy. There were the shooters who wanted a big meal and seconds, and they often came with more than their allocated numbers even though we had told them we could not fit any more in but always did, their bar bill was enormous and they never wanted to go home. The OAP's were happy with a smaller meal, at a reduced priced and the veg needed to be well cooked, not al dente. Clubs always had someone in charge of proceedings who knew how to cook and organise better than us, we just said yes to everything they asked and still did it our way. Edi chef didn't like being messed about or words to that affect.

Couples and small parties were easy and we bent over backwards to make sure their experience went well. With parties the one thing I hated was when 30 of them wanted to pay separately and even though it was printed on the menus that the account should be settled by the organiser the so called organiser still insisted they pay separately, I insisted more. Each week in December was different and as most parties liked to dine in the 2nd and early 3rd week we'd encourage the OAP's to dine in the 1st week by offering a discount for a smaller meal, which from experience is what they wanted. We always made a fuss of these groups, greeting them with a big smile and at the end off their trip always waved them off. Might be me one day.

At the end of all this on Christmas Eve we'd attend Midnight Mass at church just over the Rd. finished off with a quick drink and then after Christmas days usual routine, Boxing Day had to be tackled and put to bed before we could really say that the season was completed. All the tables had been booked for months, some from the previous year, the bar tables were all booked at 12noon and walkins thereafter, the restaurant bookings were staggered from noon till 1pm with reservations later in the day till 4pm. It was the busiest day of the year and when the day came to a finale we were all absolutely shattered but satisfied as too how many customers we'd helped to enjoy their Christmas celebrations.

Bedrooms were often booked at weekends by wedding guests which was good for business but sometimes brought us problems as on the occasion of one couple, the groom an army captain had had their reception next door at the village hall. They'd made it clear to them that the bar closed at 11.30pm. So the Groom, now husband decided that he'd bring some of his wedding party over to the pub for a few drinks, well he was a resident. Being a resident did give him the right to have a drink after time, him and his wife, certainly not a wedding party. He didn't see it that way so he argued the t..s with me and at one stage I thought he was going to get violent. Let's face it, he was losing a lot of face with his guests to whom he'd probably said 'oh come on we'll get a drink back at my place, don't worry it'll be OK'. They'd all had a fair share of drinks and common sense was thrown out of the bath with the water. He got more vociferous and it was only when I threatened to inform his senior officer of his conduct did he suddenly calm down and his party disappeared into the night. Grace who'd been present at this debacle said she was surprised that I still had my head on my shoulders as she thought I was going to be hit, hard. Sometimes you have to stand your ground. In the morning the wedding guests who'd stayed the night came down for breakfast and nothing was said.

On a slightly more comical note was the occasion when a couple stayed, she being a rather large lady and he of very slender build. You could have said 'little and large'. Nothing out of the ordinary happened and after breakfast they departed and the chambermaid Pam went to strip the bed and clean the room. Later that morning Pam came and informed me that she had found an item under the pillow, what I enquired, a piece of ladies apparatus which needs batteries. She was embarrassed and asked me what she should do with it as at present she'd put it in a carrier bag and it was in the laundry room? I commented that when they'd finished their shift that she should put it in the dustbin outside as surely no one will come back to claim the item. I was wrong, within the hour the man came and asked me very sheepishly if we'd found anything in their bedroom as his girlfriend had misplaced 'something'. I replied I was unaware of anything being found but I would go and see. By now all the staff were aware of the situation and they all came to see this very brave man who'd probably been coerced by his lady to come and get her item. You could just imagine the conversation that must have taken place. Well after a while I picked up the heavy carrier bag and returned it to him, he was out of the door in a shot. We always referred to this story as 'batteries not included'.

One other situation that arose was one night in the early hours the pub alarm went off and I duly jumped out of bed, down the stairs and after turning on the lights went into the bedroom corridor were I found socks on the carpet, then pyjama top and bottoms followed by a pair or men's undies, down stairs to the pub area where I was confronted with a near naked male, yes definatly male. In a drunken stupor he had been seeking the toilet and had ignored his en-suite facility and remembering there was a public toilet downstairs he had gone to find it. Grace had been concerned about the alarm and had followed me; she looked quite bemused at the sight.The man was returned to his bedroom after he'd picked up his clothes on the way. You may ask why? At breakfast he was oblivious to the charade.

2010 heralded in a year when many changes came about. It's important to gain new customers and to look after your existing clientele who are the backbone of any business, no more so than in the leisure industry. Many of the groups of regulars had changed in size and moved to different areas in the pub and new groups had taken those places, such as the builder boys who had taken over the spot nearest the back door, this group circulated around Mick the boss of Meadowside builders, a busy general building company and it was Mick who did the hiring and firing, so an important man in their eyes. If the weather was inclement or too hot it would be an excuse to down tools early and a perfect excuse for a drink before going home, where better than the pub that appreciated you and occasionally gave out a few tit-bits, a bit like tapas. Well after most of the wakes there were usually sandwiches etc. left over and rather than throw them away Grace would put them on the bar for the boys to eat, good business.

Many of the old regulars had been coming to the pub since the year dot and some did keep reminding us of this fact, telling us that it was their pub and they were letting us look after it for them for a while. One of these was Chris Naden who'd actually worked there well before our time and didn't let us forget it and he'd recently been joined by Mark Forester who later became known as 'p..s head Mark' for obvious reasons. His wife and sister-in-law actually asked me to stop serving him. If I did he'd only go somewhere else.

There were many foodie regulars, some dining 2/3 times a week, and when they had celebrations like anniversaries or birthdays they'd bring their families to join in the fun. Some that spring to mind are Dave and Kath who at lunchtime always sat on table 9 and Roy and Carol T7. Clients are creatures of habit and have their favourite tables, so why not try and oblige them. Alan and Sylvia Hulme were great supporters of ours and over the years came to dine regularly on T15 and had many family parties usually with them paying for the event; they have since become great friends. The Jacks came every Sunday night regardless, Mrs. Jacks always an omelette. This is what I mean when I say look after your bread and butter because these customers are the backbone of your business and they will repay you in spades as long as you are there for them, whatever.

Some people move to an area because there is a pub nearby but what they should consider is that pub landlords regularly change, say every 3 to 5 years. Some can't hack it and go out of business, some move to improve their prospects and this means you may end up with a landlord/lady that you don't get on with and at the end of the day they are the heart of your local.

After Christmas and New Year I would take the dec's down and carefully pack them away as I remembered how much they had cost in the first place and I would need to know where they were for next Christmas. One year I had made the mistake of letting one of the young staff pack the dec's away, I should say they were thrown into boxes without a care, young un's that have never had to buy commodities have no respect for their worth.

For many years Grace and I would take time every year to conduct an AGM sometime in January to thrash out what we intended to either change, mend, construct or purchase that year. Ideas were put down on paper and ticked off as each task was accomplished during the year; it saved discussing ideas each week. The major plan for that year was the refurbishment of the restaurant which was well overdue and would need some building work, the cost of which would be met by Robinsons but only any actual construction work, not the carpets, curtains or furniture that cost was paid for out of our bank a/c. In order to make sure the work was completed on time I told a little white lie by informing the builders that we had a funeral booking the day after the completion date they had given me. The work was completed on time, just, and the wake went ahead as planned. A lot of customers assumed that the brewery had paid for the alterations but I soon put them in the picture. In fact it was our cash along with a helping hand from the brewery that kept their premises in good nick which did need to be done to keep ahead of customer's expectations and therefore our scores on the doors and Trip Advisor comments.

Every four years our tenancy contract became negotiable, when I say negotiable I mean due for an increase. I would get a phone call from Mr. Peter's secretary requesting a meet, he was chairman of the Robinson family brewery and he had the final say on all rent issues. Unlike all the other younger family members he was a very down to earth guy and at the said meeting would ask several relevant questions, scribble on a scrap of paper his findings and within a few days a letter would arrive with his suggested rent increase. Over the years I always found his decision to be fair and reasonable which would alter when the sons took over his role in the Co. because they had been accountancy trained and had an eye to the bottom line which isn't what pubs should be about.

Briton the frozen food and dry goods suppliers that we'd used since 1995 had to be contacted because a customer had found pieces of shredded plastic in a bread roll that they had supplied to us, made but not baked. There first response was 'oh sorry about that , please send us the item and we'll look into it', I remember the Holland's pork pie from way back in the chip shop days, so we sent them half of the roll and kept the rest as evidence. We were well recompensed by the bakers as it was a fault in the manufacture of the bread and a lesson had been remembered from years ago.

Staff wages as always was a major expenditure and I tried to limit the no. of staff to a minimum but we could get caught out if we didn't have enough bodies and on really busy days, which were often, it left Grace and I to work even longer hours than our average 90 to 94 hours a week. We paid all the staff above minimum pay, some like Edi, Sara and Ash who had joined as a chef in '04 were remunerated well over the odds in order to keep them and because they were good at their jobs. Finding and keeping professional staff is never easy as other unscrupulous business's let you train members of your team then steal them away which saves them the expense of training them so they can at that stage pay them more. Naughty.

Sometimes if we needed to recruit we may try the local Labour Exchange to see if they had anyone suitable on their books. This was usually a waste of time as they would send any Tom, Dick or Harry for an interview just to get them off their books and the applicant would often not turn up at the allotted time, in one instance a guy turned up for the post of barman looking like he'd just been working under a car bonnet, I told him I was not prepared to consider his application. He'd only come to show willing so he could claim his job seekers allowance. I did ring the Labour office to put them in the picture as I always did if one of their applicants didn't turn up

In April of '10 we again visited Dubai as always staying at the Crowne Plaza on Sheik Zaied Rd. on the club floor being looked after by Mr. Nihall the manager. All the years we had frequented the hotel he had been referred to as Nihall but now it was Mr. after a promotion. One of our favourite hotels to visit was The One and Only Hotel on the Palm where we always dined in their seafood restaurant overlooking the beach on the Persian Gulf with the huge Hotel Atlantis Complex in the background. Grace always goes for the seafood platter which consists of a vast array of shell and fresh fish but on this occasion the waiter came to our table to apologise because they had run out of oysters and could they replace it with some other shellfish, say another half of lobster, Grace, quick as a flash said that would be fine, so Grace got a full lobster not half, thank you. We have never stayed at this hotel but it is certainly a must place to visit but only stay if your girl has got a very small, very expensive bikini and you an Adonis's body.

As was our want, on most days whilst staying at the Crowne Plaza Grace and I would venture down to breakfast at about 9.30am and have a little breakfast from the buffet selection, a hot drink and toast. This morning I asked for a boiled egg which the chef was to prepare, I asked for two 4min eggs to come with toast. Sure enough the eggs and toast appeared and I cracked the tops of the eggs to spoon out the centres. The egg white was clear and uncooked, so I called the waitress over and showed her, she was unsure why this had occurred but went to enquire. On her return she assured me that the chef had cooked the eggs for exactly 4mins as requested which puzzled me. After further enquiries we found that yes the chef had boiled the eggs for 4mins after first putting them in cold water and heating for 4mins. Some chef. After this debacle we retired to the swimming pool where our sun beds were reserved with towels already laid out by the attendant.

This day the 16th April 2010 was a day that would be remembered by us and many for the rest of our lives. We'd settled ourselves on the reserved sun beds to soak up the sun when a quiet murmur could be heard passing amongst the other sun seekers scattered around the pool, which grew louder and louder till the news reached us that a volcano in Iceland had erupted and that the ash spewing from it was jeopardising air flights around western Europe, little did we know how devastating this news was to be for millions of worldwide travellers as all flights were eventually grounded in Europe and North America thereby affecting worldwide travel. Sure enough our flights were cancelled from Dubai to Manchester so we decided to sit it out for a few days until the emergency was over in a few days, but by Sunday the situation had worsened, the hotel was jam packed with cruise passengers who could not board their flights home, so we decided to make our way home as best we could on the Monday. It was very pleasant having an extended holiday but the business needed us and VAT had to be paid by the end of the month so after many phone calls to travel Co's Grace managed to get us two seats on a flight to Barcelona via Moscow, yes that's right Moscow on an Aeroflot flight. When we told the hotel staff we were leaving and flying with Aeroflot they burst into hysterical laughter which surprised us as the first class one-way tickets cost around £3000. The cabin crew consisted of one elderly bespeckled gentleman who regularly insisted that we eat and tried to flush us out with vodka. Moscow airport was under major refurbishment and the 1st class lounge was still under construction so instead we were given a roubles voucher each worth about £5 which would buy us a small burger but definatly could not be spent on alcohol. Why? After a short stop over we continued on to Barcelona with the same air steward who continued to insist we eat something and drink vodka. After arriving in Spain and discovering that one of our suitcases, the large one was still in Moscow and with no real plan of action we decided to travel up the east coast by train with many other displaced travellers all trying to get home. This local train was taking us to France where we hoped to board an express to Paris but as we crossed the French border the train came to a holt and the conductor pulled a few switches turning the lights off and informed us that all the French rail workers were out on strike. Typical of the French to go on strike when there was a major worldwide air disaster. We trekked like refugees to the nearest village Portbou which was on the Spanish/French border to find lodgings for the night as there would be no trains till the morrow. We managed to get the last bed in a pension which looked fairly rough but we had no other options open in this small village in the middle of nowhere. We slept all night with the light on to discourage any creepy crawlies. After a very simple continental breakfast we boarded a bus to Perpignan were we caught the high speed TGV train direct to Paris which travelled so fast the view of the country side had passed by before you could see it. On these travels we kept bumping into a variety of travellers we had come across prior and we all wished each other good luck and safe journeys. When we arrived in Paris we had no idea where we should go but fortunately for us we met a guy who seemed to know his way around the Paris Metro so we followed him which took us to Amiens by 11pm but by then there were no more trains so we decided to split a taxi fare by 3 to take us to Calais were we could hopefully board the Thursday night ferry to Dover, which we did. If it hadn't been for John our guardian angel we'd have still been wandering round the Paris Metro.

On arrival at Dover there were long queues waiting for transport to London and some bright entrepreneur had laid on London red double decker buses at £50 a go as transport to the capitol, we were the last two to jump on the last bus. There were no doors on the bus and the only space for us to sit was on the stairs which was like a wind tunnel from the cold night air so I gave Grace my jacket to keep her warm. Travelling at 50miles an hour on a London bus was not the best journey I've ever taken and going round corners or bends was scary as I don't think these buses were designed to go this fast. We arrived at Victoria bus station at 4 in the morning and then trudged our way to Euston train station and after finding the booking office were informed that the first train was at 6.30am at a cost of £450 one-way, but if we waited till 9am it would be half that amount. Grace and I were exhausted and all we wanted to do was get home so we opted for the 6.30 train and paid the money. Thank goodness for credit cards. We both fell asleep on the journey home and on arriving at Stoke boarded the Manchester Piccadilly train which stopped at Congleton where Haley was waiting for us. If I could have got down on my knees I would have kissed the ground as I was so relieved that our adventure was at an end. At the time both Grace and I were absolutely knackered but once home realised what an epic adventure we had accomplished and now I smile at our experiences and have many happy memories of the people we met especially our friend John who vanished into thin air, perhaps he was our will of the wisp guide sent to keep us safe. Thank you whoever you were.

The adventure cost us £4345 some of which we claimed on insurance but we found to our cost that I had not read the small print and although Am Ex Insurance were very good to us the maximum we could claim on their insurance policy was only £2000. Lesson learned.

Early in the year I had read an article in the Caterer that the government were to introduce a plan to regulate how allergen information was given to the public, so I looked into this huge minefield of misinformation and little known about subject. To be ahead of the game I devised my own easy to understand grid using the first letters of the 14 allergens which most people had never heard of, which could have major detrimental effects on people's daily lives. The responsibility for getting this information to the public was going to be left to the provider i.e. the landlord and there were to be heavy fines for those that didn't comply. The people who have suffered for years with these allergen effects should take some responsibility for informing the provider who intern bears the responsibility of having up to date knowledge of the ingredients in the dishes and drinks they provide.

Of course you have the customer whose allergen list does not appear on any official paper but in their head, as was the situation with one lady who was allergic to lemon and broccoli and would inform of this whenever she placed her food order which was often fish on the OAP's menu. Another older lady was adamant that she was affected by 'thrice cooked chips', so we assured her that ours were blanched and then finished off in hot fat, she was happy.

The new Rector and his wife had made some changes to the Sunday services, introducing a more family friendly morning event, what I'd probably call happy clappy, with the congregation joining in, this did not go down well with some of the older church goers. It became apparent that Jonathan had been an amateur thespian in his former life and he intended to introduce an adult nativity play next Christmas which would involve locals participating in the story whilst visiting various locations in the village, one of them being at the pub where I would take on the part of the grumpy Inn keeper saying 'no room at the Inn'. Would you believe it, me a grumpy old Inn keeper?

Grace and I always enjoy Palma so once again we visited in June, after that families from the Spanish mainland fill the hotel all thru the summer which forces the hotel prices up and it becomes uncomfortably busy which neither of us enjoy.

Over the years I've often been asked what it's like to run hotels and if would I recommend it to other people, well the answer to that is, all I can say is, I have enjoyed fulfilling my life's ambition which I've had since being a teenager. Grace has supported me all thru our married life and I know that I have had the easy part of it. Edi once asked Grace why we married, to which she replied 'because Allen loves me', Edi's reply was 'na it's because he couldn't afford to pay anyone else for the amount of work youse do'. As much as that may be true, I love and have always loved Grace with all my heart and cannot thank her enough for supporting me and helping me fulfil my dream.

There have been rough patches, arguments and we've seen hard times when money has been short but we have battled thru putting in long hours, help from friends and with determination we have won thru, it isn't easy, you've just got to make it look easy and don't burden customers with your woe's, it's your job to listen to theirs. Everyone has their idea of their perfect pub and there are always 'horses for courses' but my ideal hotel is in a village, with bedrooms and a restaurant, not forgetting some land and a large car park for the cars attending the events at the adjacent church. I suppose you could say that describes the Egerton. Lucky me.

There are two/three other bits of advice I always give to any prospective publicans, if either you or your partner have a jealous nature then this is not the path you should tread and if you have even the slightest drink problem then don't even go there, it will only get worse and lastly I could not have managed the job on my own, you need a committed partner to be there for you at the end of the day.

By the time Christmas had come round once again the new Rector Jonathan had rehearsed us in the Nativity production we'd all or as many as he'd managed to coerce to join in. I was as mentioned before to play the part of the grumpy Inn keeper who tells Mary and Joseph that there is no room at the Inn. I had improvised a short sketch following roughly the biblical story whilst wearing typical landlord's garb of the time, a tea towel on my head wrapped round with string and long flowing robes made from an old sheet. This was definatly low key Am/Dram and I was surprised when about 200 people turned up on the first of two nights. They had assembled at the church for a short service and then on crossing the Rd. to the pub had espied an Angel at the top of the church tower. No one had realised how strong the wind was and the Angel was nearly been blown off, with his wings acting as sails, he was pulled back by a junior Angel. The crowd then congregated on the patio at the rear of the pub and I did my bit telling them all to clear off as 'there was no room at the Inn'. After this they next went to the village hall where shepherds 'washed their socks by night' and then over the Rd. to Glebe Farm where baby Jesus lay in His manger surrounded by Three Wise Men and they all sang carols after having a hot toddy for the adults and a soft drink for the kids. The production was a great success and in later years I wrote a different script for myself, obviously sticking to the general Christmas story and my dress became more true to life with me eventually having full dish dash as a Jewish landlord would have which I'd purchased whilst visiting Dubai.

In the years to come there were more and more clients buying tickets till in the end it became a sell out with a maximum of 400 tickets available. Some changes were made as I think at some time a risk assessment was carried out and the angel in the tower was strapped down and a spotlight shone on him to highlight his presence. Of all the situations at the pub this was one of my most enjoyable even when the young kids booed and hissed at me for telling them nicely to 'clear off'.

In 2011 we lost two dear friends, Brian Lang our great friend from the beginning of our association with the Egerton who along with his wife Pauline we had had many memorable holidays. I was asked to do a eulogy at his funeral which was well attended and afterwards we celebrated his long life with a few drinks and buffet back at the hotel. Brian for many years had been a bridge husband as Pauline was absent from home playing and teaching bridge which took up much of her time, this suited Brian as he could venture down the pub whenever. This was another nail in the coffin for his group of pals who met together in the snug, one or two of his friends had already passed away and two of them had moved out of the area. Others were waiting to move into that space.

The other sad loss was Steve Mercer our accountant who along with his wife Sue lived in Houghton Nr. Tarporley and he had been our money man since our first days at Beeston. He had never been a best mate but we bumped into Steve and Sue in and around the local pubs inTarporley and Bunbury, especially the Nags Head which I think was their favourite drinking hole. He had been an invaluable asset to the business and had dug us out of a few run-ins with the HMRC. Thank you Steve. His funeral was a testament to his popularity. The crematorium was chocked full and some mourners had to stand outside the building. Steve must have known in advance of his early demise and had sold off his flourishing business, Mercer & Co to Barrington's of S.O.T to safe guard Sue's future, Barrington's took over looking after our a/c's. By now our bookkeeper had ceased doing our wages and bookkeeping as she had become unreliable, often turning up hours late with the wages and also she lagged behind in the internet world which the HMRC were encouraging us to use so Grace and I had taken on an on-line bookkeeping service which worked out our wages and day to day a/c's. On Thursday mornings we set to and after making many mistakes eventually came to grips with the system and within a short period became proficient bookkeepers.

The government had brought in several new legislations at this time apart from the allergen bill; they had tightened up on fire regulations, MGD or machine games duty, employee pensions and online payments. A new signage system using a running man was introduced to inform guests of the safest and quickest way to evacuate a building and other new regulations brought in, which had to be checked every day, like does every door close properly, of course all these rules were adhered to? MGD was just a nightmare and employee pensions just another drain on our profits, little as they were. Sound like a farmer, don't I?

By now we had introduced allergen information for all our menus of which there were quite a few, main menu, OAP's, breakfast, buffet, Christmas, specials board and Sunday luncheon. When the Health and Hygiene inspector came to do the annual check he was most impressed and commented that he had not seen a more comprehensive allergen display. He asked if he could take a copy to show his colleagues, I told him to take a running jump after all the effort I had put in to discover the necessary information. He took it in good part and gave us a top mark of five hygiene certificate which we displayed proudly in the window for all to see.

One of the pieces of equipment that he checked was the ice machine as if not cleaned regularly could get a build up of mould caused by moisture, warmth and dust dragged in by the air cooler which then goes on to become pink bacterial slime. This can also happen in dish and glass washers which also have the added pollutant of scraps of food which can go on to cause salmonella. No one ever thinks about ice buckets and water from the mains made into ice, when left can go on to leave black or pink slime, wash out ice buckets and scrub tap spouts regularly.

In April of 2011 we took a trip to the Lakes for a few days and whilst there drove over Kirkstone Pass for lunch at Sharrow Bay at the top end of Ullswater. The boys had by now passed away and they had left the hotel to their Head waiter who immediately put it up for sale, I thought, he's not daft. Sadly it had been bought by an investment Co. and had deteriated to a pitiful state with all the antiques, pictures and antique furniture being sold off or left to go to rack and ruin. Obviously the head chef Colin Askrigg had left and the food was not to the standard it used to be. We were disappointed and very sad. Things change and unfortunately not always for the better but we have many happy memories of times past.

On our return home we had a couple of nights at the Radisson Hotel in Manchester where one night we dined at San Carlo a fantastic Italian restaurant behind Kendal's on Deansgate and the next night at the New Emperor in China Town as are usual Chinese restaurant Wong Chu was no longer. Manchester over the past few years has developed into a thriving metropolis caused I believe in part because of the BBC moving their HQ from London. New restaurants and leisure venues have sprung up all over the city, never more so than in Spinney fields and the Northern Quarter, this area catering more for the younger clientele, but in and around the Crown Court a myriad of eating and drinking establishments have sprung up of which our favourites were Manchester House, Alchemist, Australasia which was concealed below ground under a glass pyramid next to John Ryland's Library, Carluccio, Oust house, Neighbourhood, and Harvey Nic's, all good with varied exciting and innovative menus. We started visiting Manchester many years ago from Beeston where at that time we'd pick up catering supplies from a Chinese cash-n-carry on Oldham Rd. which was called Wing Yip. Although we'd visit local c-n-c's the Chinese c-n-c's offered products in larger sizes at much cheaper prices and a more varied oriental selection. For these trips we needed a car with large boot space and this had always meant that when we changed vehicles this was always critical; that was until in 2011 when a new car was decided upon. We went to visit our friend John Coppock who was the manager of a group of Volvo garages in Stoke. We viewed and decided to purchase a Volvo saloon which suited our needs, so whilst John filled out the paperwork Grace and I had a walk round the garage and espied a Volvo coupe which we both immediately fell in love with. John on seeing our reaction to this car just ripped up the paperwork he was filling out and said 'that's the car for you'. I said 'I can't afford or want to pay that much' (£40.000) he replied 'you are friends or family and get 25% off' we bought it. This was to be the start of a new era for us and changed completely the way we purchased our supplies because the boot in this new car was none existent so we now changed to having our supplies delivered which sometimes cost us a little for transport but when the cost of petrol and our time was taken into account it worked out cheaper, especially when you take into the evaluation that when we shopped at the Chinese c-n-c we'd often also have an authentic Chinese meal at the Tai Pan restaurant above Lungs c-n-c on Lower Brook St. just off Oxford Rd. Saved all round.

With these exciting Asian ingredients Grace and the chefs were able to augment our menu's with oriental flavours which gave us an edge that some of our competitors hadn't thought about but soon began to copy. Some of our dishes were copied by other pubs and hotels as was pointed out to us by some of our regular customers who did dine at other establishments. From our holidays in Cyprus we had over the years become competent in cooking Greek style food such as Beef Stifado, Arni Ttavas, Pork Aphelia and Lamb Kleftiko, at one time building an authentic Kleftiko oven in the garden. These dishes would appear in many other local pubs, I wonder where they got the idea from. Imitation is the greatest form of praise.

One of my favourite, no my favourite TV show was All Creatures Great and Small which I enjoyed because of its gritty story line showing the realities of farming with a heart rending touch and Siegfried had the same impression of farmers as I especially when it came to 'owt for nowt', they wouldn't come to pay their accounts but would show up in droves for a party and a free pint. I don't know if I should not have been a farmer because my other favourite programme is on Radio 4, the Archers which I listen to avidly on Sunday morning at 10am. This is the longest running daily series on any programme; it was first broadcast in 1950 as a light hearted way on getting progressive farming and agricultural information to the farming community after the war.

After cooking and serving breakfast I'd get all the jobs done that needed doing and by 10am be ready for my daily bath where I would settle in the warm water and listen to the Archers omnibus where the life of this mythical country village came to life, sometimes very close to the happenings in our village and surrounding area. I often used to comment that I could write the script for the programme.

One fine morning just before we were to open, a big tall man appeared asking to see Grace and I, it was Mark a lad we had employed at Beeston all those years ago, at the time he lived with his mum and dad in Tiverton and had worked p/t for us as a barman. We were surprised to see him and after the niceties had been exchanged we asked to the reason for his visit. He said he'd gone to Uni and progressed thru his chosen career and was now head of the children's care service in Leeds and that as a lad he'd been shy and undetermined and it was because of our encouragement when he was younger that he had managed to progress to these busy heights for which he was most grateful.

Grace and I were close to tears when we parted.

On 29th April Prince William married Kate and Haley organised a village fun day to celebrate the occasion, there was supposed to be a village committee but no one stepped forward to do the organising so Haley stepped up to the plate and within days she'd got a plan in place and encouraged people to join in with her plans which included a fancy dress parade, stalls and tea tent at Glebe farm where she was working at the time as farm shop manageress, then followed by a music festival later in the day. It was a gorgeous day and all went well for the event with us providing car parking facilities on the paddock, we had some spin off trade as no alcohol was sold at the fete and people parking their cars had to pass us on their way home, some people would call that passing trade, I call it stopping trade.

In May of 2011 we drove down to Oxford staying at the Randolph Hotel in the centre of the city which is synymous with Inspector Morse. A very grand hotel, as it should be for the price. I had booked a junior suite for two nights and as we arrived early I didn't expect the room to be available as was confirmed by the concierge who informed us that Miss Harry had not vacated her room, so we dropped off our bags and toured the city stopping off for a drink or two. On arrival back at the hotel we were escorted to our room on the 1st floor were we discovered what Miss Harry did all night in her bedroom, smoked. The room stunk of cigarettes, so down to reception to explain that we required a non smoking room which they soon obliged us with. So you see, I never slept in Debbie Harry's bed.

Later in the year we visited Palma, flying with Monarch Airlines which was shortly before they went bust due to many worldwide factors which also affected other airlines, but as always the short holiday was much appreciated and at the time unknowingly our last flight away for some time as Dereck our Dalmatian became ill and we did not leave him for more than a few days until he passed away in 2013 aged nearly fifteen which was a great wrench to both Grace and my heart strings. We did manage to sneak away for one day on the Northern Belle to Bath were we had a great day being pampered by James the train manager and his staff, arriving back home slightly squiffy from all the Champagne they'd poured down our necks. Fabulous day out.

By now other new regulars had joined the different groups around the pub, Nigel who drank copious amounts of cider had joined in with Mark, Ian Tate,(Tattie) Chris Naden and the builder boys in late afternoon, Dick and Val, Keith and Jane became friends with the group on table 4. As much as I tried not to get involved in customer's private lives, just occasionally they step over the line and I got drawn in as was the case with Mark because one day a restaurant customer saw him fall out of his car when he was attempting to get in it to drive home. I assured her I would deal with the situation, as the last thing I wanted was for her to ring the Police. I took Mark to one side, took his keys off him, sent him home in a taxi and on his return the next day told him in no uncertain words that if he did that again I would bar him as I was not having him put my licence in jeopardy. Yes your right, he did, so I barred him and it was only after many weeks Andy Mount begged me to reconsider, I let him back with certain conditions, one being that if he came in his car he left the keys behind the bar. Mark drank like a fish, but had worked out that over several hours he lost so much alcohol from his blood stream naturally that after say six hours drinking he would be sober. Codswallop. How his wife put up with him I'll never know and in the end she didn't. Over the years I'd known Mark he'd had numerous jobs selling commodities from kitchens to carpets(his nick name was now 'carpet Mark') he always seemed to leave jobs owing money, on one occasion he put £10.000 on a friend's c/card,(silly friend) he eventually ended up sleeping on a friend's sofa. The other long standing local was Noggin who gambled to the extent that he'd put all his wages in the one arm bandit and although I kept telling him there were only two winners, the Landlord and the Brewery he continued, sometimes borrowing money from his friends and sometimes the girls he used to bring into the pub only to leave them chatting to the other locals whilst he carried on filling up the bandit, he knew better than to tap me up. With gambling on-line now becoming big business I wondered how much he owed them. When we first arrived at Astbury Noggin had a good job working for an estate management Co. and over the years he worked down the ladder, ending up as an odd job man living with his mum. Gambling and drink has a lot to answer for, could I have done more to help save them both? If I'd barred them they'd only have gone somewhere else.

2012 our customer base had, as always, evolved for many reasons, after we arrived at the Egerton some of the older regulars departed to a higher place; the couples with young children who had now grown up became customers in their own right and of course new customers arrived with the advent of all the new housing estates being built around Congleton, new housing but no infrastructure. One such proposed estate was planned to be constructed on land just down the A49 ½ mile north towards Congleton on marsh land where Pedleys farm was situated. The developers held an open day at the pub where their plans were on show for people to see exactly what they were proposing and also as a PR exercise for future house sales. Many people were against the proposals and a committee was set up to object to the development and within weeks someone came to ask me to sign a form objecting to this development joining many other objectors. In my view new houses mean new customers and I was certainly not going to object to them.

An older lady, Audrey and her husband John used us to have lunch or just pop in for a drink and a natter, she was never short of an opinion or two, well she had been born in one of the upstairs rooms many years previously as her family at that time ran the pub when it was part/farm and part/beer house which many such premises used to be. She related many stories of how things used to be in the olden days especially why the hotel had a ghost which I never believed was true but some of the staff had supposedly seen, one being Tony the handyman who had seen a lady walk thru a closed door and Angie who had seen a lady in white upstairs whilst she was cleaning and Angie then ran tout suite downstairs looking as pale as a ghost (sic). This story originated from 1922 when a man murdered a lady in what is now room1, it used to be part of the cottage next door; he was later hanged in Broadmoor Prison in 1928 for her murder. I don't believe in ghosts but I've seen strange things which I cannot explain, perhaps a trick of the light.

Some years prior I had become acquainted with a guy called Lyndon Murgatroyd who had written a book called A Pub Crawl Around Congleton which was the history of every pub in Congleton and its environs since Methuselah which was a must have book for all people interested in pubs, many of which have now disappeared, the pubs not the people. As we were to be featured in his book he asked if we would sponsor his work, which we did and I received a signed copy and he went on to write another four books about Congleton of which I have signed by Lyndon.

Audrey who as I mentioned had her opinions, informed Lyndon that some of the facts stated in his first book were incorrect and that he had missed out some important information. He duly had the book reprinted in A4 size which was a sell out, giving all his readers a very interesting and informative read.

Haley had left Tony in '10 and had lived with us for a while then, rented a town/cott in Congleton for a while and then suddenly, out of the blue informed us that she was moving to Basingstoke to join up with a guy she'd met on line who I'd nearly bumped into on their first date on Boxing Day night '11 in DV8, I was told that in no uncertain circumstances was I to butt in. So within a space of a few weeks she was off in her little Ka car with her two dogs and loads of luggage, off down our driveway to pastures new with Grace and I waving, mum in floods of tears. Pom de Pom Pom - Pom Pom on her car horn.

In 2012 another Preston Guild was celebrated, but without us which I felt sorry about but I'm sure we were not missed. With the demise of the Trade Unions, the Town Guilds and the loss of the old manufacturing industries, especially the cotton mills there was not the interest or manpower to build the floats of previous years and of course Preston Council hadn't the funds due to the economic climate to decorate the streets as I remember in my youth. Let's hope that in 2032, the next Preston Guild will have a reversal of fortunes and the guild can make Prestonians proud once more.

During the summer rumours ran riot in the village about the sale of the vicarage which had stood empty since Jonathan and Ellie had vacated it when he had stood down from his post as Rector due to ill health. The new reinstated rector Geoff did not wish to live in the dilapidated old building and it would cost far too much for the diocese to repair and bring back to a habitable state so, we soon saw a for sale sign appear on the property, it would take some time before a brave purchaser was found.

Dereck our doggie was still not well and needed lots of TLC so we didn't venture very far and the vet Steve from Charter veterinary services came on several occasions to treat him. On one occasion he arrived at 9pm to give Dereck some medication which he insisted he required immediately after the blood test results that he'd taken that morning. His nick name was God because he'd saved Derek's life more than once. One day his wife came for lunch and I addressed her as Mrs God.

However later in the year I had to call Steve 'aka' God to examine Dereck because his condition had deteriated and we wished for his opinion. Vets don't make the decisions but they do give you the options and after his examination of Dereck he told us that yes Dereck could be helped to live a little longer but not with any quality of life so I was left with an unenviable decision to make as I didn't want Grace to be left in that position. Steve assured us that Dereck would feel no more pain and after I'd given him the go ahead I held Dereck in my arms as he put him to sleep. We were all devastated at his passing and although within the next few days we were offered 3 replacement dogs Grace and I decided that we never wanted to go thru that experience again. It was like losing your little boy. Within a few days Derecks ashes were returned to in an urn and I dug a deep grave in the garden along by the hedge where I didn't think anyone would disturb him if in future if the garden was redeveloped. I dug the hole with tears in my eyes and I knew this is where he would wish to be as he loved playing in the beer garden especially if any of the customers had any food and he would look at them as if he'd never been fed.

Every January Grace and I sat down with a piece of A4 and had a discussion as to our plans for the year; we called it our annual AGM. After setting down our ideas to do for 2013 Grace asked me what plans I had for my future, regarding my retirement. When this question had arisen before I usually shrugged it off by saying 'I'd go out in a box and Martin Garside the funeral director and friend had my measurements' but Grace was serious so I asked her if she would give me five more years when I would be 70 in 2018. We told no one but Haley and Edi of our decision and swore them to secrecy. Edi said that the news suited him as by 2018 he would be 65 and due to retire, which fitted in well with his plans. After that we carried on as normal deciding to be careful not to spend unnecessarily as we'd never recover the cost of any major investment so close to retirement.

Tim Brown from Browns Est. Agents came to see us early in the year and enquired if we'd be interested in holding a Jowett vintage car show in September as their present site had let them down. The decision to say yes proved very beneficial to us as several of the exhibitors booked rooms for the weekend, people viewing the cars visited the pub, perhaps for the first time and a dinner was held on the Saturday evening, all bringing in extra revenue. Each night of the event one of the organisers slept in a caravan to safe guard the exhibits which had been arranged on the bottom field next to the wood which was an excellent area to show off the polished vintage cars. The weekend went well and continued for many years.

In May of '13 we again visited Palma Majorca enjoying the early warm sunshine before the hotel became too busy with the invasion of mainland Spanish tourists who filled this popular hotel for the summer season.

After Dereck had gone to doggie heaven we made up for our lack of away days by visiting Dubai in June when the temperature was starting to rise to about 40 degrees which was just perfect. In all the years we'd been visiting Dubai we'd always thought that all bars were only situated on the first floor or higher because of alcohol laws that existed in UAE so it came as a great surprise to find that only 3 blocks from our hotel there was a bar at street level called Fibber Magee's which by its very name was an Irish bar frequented by many ex-pats. Drinks prices in Dubai, especially in hotels are expensive but this bar was slightly cheaper with different daily offers and regular music so it was always packed.

The beer garden at the pub was always popular with families when the weather was warm and sunny and often all the tables would be filled with punters drinking and eating. The only way to get more tables into this area was to turf the garden part of it which was planted out with roses and shrubs, so Tony and I dug up the plants and I collected many of the bulbs which I planted out in the grassed areas along the driveway. The fence was moved to keep the play area safe for the kids to play and this new patch was seeded to make a bigger beer garden. I hadn't been able to collect all the bulbs so the following spring there was a beautiful show of spring flowers shooting thru the grass.

I was asked by Biddulph Rotary if I would be a Judge at their annual school cooking competition for young chef's to be held at Congleton High School. Basically it meant that I and another chef would taste the dishes which the school kids prepared and mark them on preparation, appearance and taste. The other chef should have been Dave Cropper, ex licensee of the Bulls Head but his son had to stand in because David had had a fall so both of us were new to the task but after much deliberation we gave our considered opinions and the winner went on to quarter finals. I carried on in this role for many years with whomever or whichever guest chef they could talk into carrying out the task. I was proud to be asked each year to judge the young hopefuls and over the years tried to instil into the teachers and contestants the need to use local or at least British ingredients. One young girl who turned out to be a farmer's daughter told me that all her ingredients had come from their farm, chicken, vegetables, potatoes, milk and the eggs collected that morning. Another young person told me that all her products including lemons and sun dried tomatoes were all local as her mother had bought them from Tesco on Barn Rd. the day before. Cute.

Over the years I had never taken a 'sickie', let's face it when you're self employed you can't just take a day off, for a start it costs, 2nd you are letting the side down and it's not setting a good example to the rest of the team. There have been days when I've felt like death, perhaps after a few too many the night before or when a few years earlier the skin on the bottom of my feet just cracked open and made it difficult to walk but breakfasts wouldn't cook themselves, so I went and did them, then crawled back upstairs and put my feet up for an hour or so until opening time. It was when I was younger that most of any medical procedures were performed like visits to the dentists every week, listening to the belt of the dentist's drill and that smell that always pervades a dentist's surgery. Then later the operation on my foot at Wrightington Hospital and later contacting Typhoid in my teens which put me out of action for a week or two and taught me a lesson about girlfriends, look at their mother before getting too keen. The last medical problem I had which was caused originally by my road accident when I was 12 having my 2 front teeth knocked out was alleviated when I was 20 when I decided to have the remaining teeth removed and inserting a full set of false teeth which also alleviated the need for dentist's. In years to come I also got rid of the need for dentist's to repair or renew the false teeth by going to source and thereby missing out the middle man. So all in all my life from then on has been illness free and in later life that has been the case thanks to Grace looking after me and the odd tipple or two, but definatly not spirits.

In or around '86 whilst at Beeston Bass gave us the opportunity to get BUPA benefits for the whole family at a reduced company rate of £70 per month which seemed a good deal, but after being in the scheme for several years, about 12 I noticed that the monthly payment had increased to £168.80p so I suggested to Grace that we scrap the scheme and save the money in our own bank a/c, it took some time to convince her but eventually that's what we did and we never needed to use the money we saved as we remained in good health. Thank God. We also used this idea when it came to dog health plans, so instead of paying Pet Plan £40 per month I opened a Dereck bank a/c and when he passed in '13 he was worth £8.000 as he'd never needed any very expensive veterinary treatment. These were just two of the private bank a/c's that I used so that there were no bank charges and it was a way of saving.

Lyn and John had moved from Bunbury and gone to live in North Wales so we decided to have a lunch at Bodysgallen Hall near Llandudno which we have visited several times over many years but never stayed. Since 2008 this 17c hotel has been owned by the National Trust and is still being operated as a hotel but I've noticed that they have increased the room and food prices quite dramatically which are soon forgotten when sitting in the panoramic restaurant window seat viewing the Welsh vista with Snowdonia in the background eating a delicious innovative luncheon before retiring to the plush bedrooms to have a nap and tiffin before dinner. Heaven.

Willy Shaw had been diagnosed with lung cancer earlier in the year which really came as no surprise. All his life he'd been a heavy smoker and living on his own for much of it had taken its toll. He was the life and soul of any gathering, be it just the boys in the pub or a party and was a founder member of the Toss Pots, a large group who played music with lots of fun and hilarity to raise funds for charities. His deep gravelly voice and Rod Stewart persona was renowned in and around Congleton. He could be very mischievous especially with the girls, I mean grown up girls who all took his fun as fun and no one took offence. You always knew when he was around, especially when he greeted you with either 'eh up duck' or 'what you doing mucka'? After a short illness and a couple of weeks in hospital he passed away at Leyton Hospital in Crewe. At the time we had gone to visit Haley and Ben for a few days and whilst we were having a beer in Laarsens Bar in the centre of Basingstoke Grace received the news of Willy's death from Ian Tate a long time friend of Willy's, we were all absolutely devastated and the barman couldn't understand why one minute we were laughing and the next crying into our beer. Very, very sad. On our return home the wake was held at the pub and 2 weeks later we held a Willy memorial day to which all his friends came to talk about and commemorate the life of Willy Shaw.

What a man!

Ian Tate had supported Willy all thru his 3 year illness and to some extent had neglected himself so that he could concentrate on getting Willy better, which was never going to happen, but Ian never gave up. On Willy's death Ian was a broken man with no partner to support him so I encouraged him to get out and about, which is what Willy would have encouraged him to do. I admired Ian for his exemplary support he'd shown to Willy but it was high time he now regained his own life. Well within a few weeks sure enough he introduced us to several young ladies he was trying out, but none of them fitted the bill until one day he got to know a lady who popped in every now and then on her own and who drank pints of Stella, many pints of Stella. This lady was not the type I thought Ian would be interested in, some of his previous ladies were stunning and didn't drink like fish. She would end up biting us all on the bum in the future.

'13 turned into '14 and as usual Grace arranged a fly away for my birthday at the end of January which was to take us to Hong Kong and the New Territories, staying at the Crowne Plaza. I say Hong Kong but we didn't stay on the island as our hotel was a couple of miles inland which I'd reserved as I wished to stay in a Crowne Plaza hotel for two reasons, one being the level of service we'd become accustomed to and secondly we collected IHG points whenever we stayed in the group. Before we departed I had rung our friend Mr. Nihall in Dubai and asked him if he had any connections in Hong Kong, he said he'd see if he could get us upgraded and I never heard anymore, that is until we arrived at the hotel where we were greeted by a deputation from the hotel at the hotel entrance and then escorted to a suite on the top floor. The rooms were fabulous with views for miles over the New Territories where several complete high rise cities had been developed in which hospitals, schools, sports areas and residents were all encompassed in one high rise development. For the first time in all the flights we had taken around the world this was the first time Grace and I suffered with jet lag, presumably because on previous flights we had laid round the pool to sleep but in this case the pool was out of action, being cleaned because the weather was cool and the hotel management probably thought would not be used. Over the next few days it became apparent that Mr. Nihall had mentioned that we were higher management officials from Crowne Plaza head office and we were treated with great respect which is the way with the Chinese. One day a waitress asked us why we had chosen to come to Hong Kong and as a joke I said 'we've come for a Chinese take-away' she looked at me as if I was stupid. She had no idea what was I was talking about as they either eat food at home or go to a restaurant, no Chinese take-away. Later we boarded the Star ferry over to the island which was so busy, all the streets bustling and restaurants packed with local Chinese diners eating some most unusual dishes only seen where the Chinese live. We chose to dine at Jumb Island Restaurant, a 4 storey building packed with lunchtime diners on all 4 floors. The menu was very Chinese and I don't think we really knew what some of the dishes were, but it was delicious and for the first time we were introduced into the idea of eating with two different chopsticks, one set to pick up food from the serving dish and the second from that plate or bowl to your mouth. Very hygienic. When at home you will only get authentic Chinese dishes where the Chinese eat. This area is renowned for expensive hotels such as the Sheraton where we dined in the evening on a huge variety of oysters from around the world in the Oyster Bar and Restaurant. The view from the restaurant was to Hong Kong Island where at night all the high rise buildings along the coastline were lit up in a myriad of coloured lights, being reflected on the water with a specula reflection. Quite spectacular. Also we visited the Peninsular Hotel where outside stood 6 khaki green Rolls Royce's awaiting the hotel clients. Inside a vast palatial hall with huge white Corinthian pillars and a grandiose marble stairway swept you to the upper floors and bedrooms. We stayed there just for a drink and later visited the Intercontinental Hotel on the waterside in Kowloon where I could only afford to stay for a drink as the prices were exorbitantly eye watering. The following day another trip on the Star ferry found us once again on the Island which with hindsight is where I wished we had stayed especially after our visit to the Mandarin Oriental Hotel situated in beautiful tropical gardens. We tried to arrange for us to have lunch at about 2pm but were informed that all 3 restaurants were fully booked till 6pm so we had a drink at the highly polished oak bar served by smartly dressed waiters which reminded me what it would have been like in the old colonial days. If only?

That March just before Easter I'd asked David our new handy man to get the outside tables painted for the summer season, he told me that some of the table legs needed repairs due to the legs rotting after being stood in the wet grass. He did the repairs and painting just in time for the weather to turn unseasonably warm at the end of the month so that the customers could sit outside in the garden shaking off the winter blues. Good for trade. Grace called me out one day when the garden was packed with lunchtime revellers and said how unusual it was for on such a sunny warm day in March there were no leaves on the trees. Just goes to show, always be ready.

In May 2014 we were once again invited by Kevin and Edie to attend the South Western Australia Day celebrations at Australia House in London which as usual was a glamorous event with Grace and me paying our annual visit to the American Bar at the Savoy and later the reception at Australia House. Kevin introduced us to Lord Digby Jones and his wife Lady Pat who talked to us in depth about our job and they seemed interested in our thoughts on the licensed trade, he also gave us insight into his overseas charity work and Lady Pat kept telling Lord Digby not to drink too much, and not to spill red wine on his tie. Lady Pat asked us where we were dining that night, to which I remarked that no plans had been made, she told LD who recommended Bentleys Oyster Bar on Swallow St. opposite Fortnum and Masons. He then rang the Maitre de and made a reservation for us, needless to say we were treated like royalty and for dinner Grace had crab with morels on toast with samphire and salt and pepper squid for her main. I had two different styles of oysters and for main I had scallops with pancetta, apple and mozzarella on seaweed all washed down with an Italian Chardonnay, all was excellent and pricey. Later we finished our night in the Tivoli Bar at our hotel spending the £75 drinks allowance that was thrown in by Am Ex because we paid for the accommodation with an Am Ex card. That amount covered four drinks which were served in fine crystal amongst the grandeur of the Ritz Hotel. On our arrival home I received in the post a copy of Digby's book and a short note touching us for a donation to his charity, I duly sent a small sum and thanked him for his book with his views on the world of business.

People were getting behind the campaign for clearer information as to food sources ever since the Horsegate scandal of '13 when Irish horsemeat was found in Tesco burgers. I contacted Carl our butcher at Glebe Farm so that he could assure us as to the source of all our meats, which he did. I decided to take this a step further to assure our customers that the food and drink they were consuming were safe to do so and with that in mind I filled one of the big blackboards with the names of all our suppliers and what they actually supplied to us which had a good response from the reassured punters.

About this time Robinsons asked/informed us that they wished to introduce 3 new measures 1. Beer line flow testing which informed them exactly how much and what beer was being dispensed thru their lines 2. Bar codes on all alcohol, spirits and minerals they supplied to us 3. Mystery shoppers to see if our pubs were being run efficiently and effectively. We didn't have any option and as I didn't really have any fears about these new measures I agreed but I do know that some landlords would not be happy as for years they'd 'bought out'. If caught they were liable to losing their pub and livelihood which had happened to some landlords who'd been buying soft drinks on the QT when I worked for Bass in Blackpool.

Scores on the doors had been implemented by the council some years previously and now with Mystery shoppers it encouraged us all to up our game as the last thing any of us wanted was for the score on the door to be less than a 5 and as Mystery shoppers delved into every aspect of your business that they could see or taste what you had on offer these are the two most important aspects of their visit to your establishment. There are lots of other things going on behind the scenes that they don't see which if running smoothly help to make their experience a positive 100% visit. We did not experience 100% visits every time but were always in the high 90's and always managed to maintain 5 on the door which is no easy feat. We showed the reports to all the staff which helped them realise where, if any problems existed, it encouraged them to maintain better customer relations which as I pointed out to them led to greater customer appreciation and hopefully more tips.

On one of our trips to Manchester for lunch at San Carlo which is just off Deansgate I left Grace shopping whilst I ventured into Kendal's department store which was on Deansgate. My 2 favourite departments are the perfume counters and the lingerie dept where I liked to purchase little surprises for Grace, in the perfume dept the larger the bottle the more expensive it got, in the ladies dept. the smaller the item the more expensive it got but whatever I gave her it always produced a smile. Before going for lunch we'd usually stop off and have a pre-lunch drink at Mulligan's Irish bar just around the corner from San Carlo whose Italian food was absolutely delicious and expensive. It was a good job that after many years of driving into and parking in the centre of Manchester I'd discovered that the train was easier, cheaper and allowed me to have a drink or two with my meal and then not have to drive home which I had done on too many occasions in times of old. I remember the time we'd gone on the Orient Express to London for the day which as I've mentioned before we were always well looked after by James and his staff. On our return to Manchester Victoria railway station that evening about 9pm I didn't realise how much champagne had been forced down my neck during the trip and I really should not have driven home, but I did. The day after I swore that I would never put myself or Grace for that matter in that position again. Lesson learnt.

When we first took over the Egerton in'95 we had no previous hotel bedroom experience so initially we relied on the existing staff to show us the ropes but it soon became apparent that some of their actions and practices did not meet with our or hygiene regulation requirements; such as washing ashtrays in the glass washer at the end of the evening. The previous landlady used to wash her dog in the catering kitchen sink.

When it came to changing bed linen the chambermaids had been told to, presumably to save money and time to wash the bottom bed sheet and drop the top sheet to bottom thereby only changing one sheet. If the duvet cover looked clean it would be left on and only washed when necessary. What has always concerned me are pillows. OK so the pillow cases are washed every time that a guest departs but their bodily fluids, coughs and sweat must soak through and linger in the body of the pillow. As time has progressed there are now chemical sprays that are supposed to kill all germs but just the thought of all that gunk from hundreds of previous clients makes me think. Some customers even bring their own pillows.

In September it was time to change our car, I say ours because for years when purchasing a new car on a 2 or 2 ½ year lease it was easier to put it in Grace's name as she was 10yrs younger than me.

In all my business life I've never taken on any H.P.(apart from the tills at Beeston when I was conned by Malcolm) but Steve the accountant had said it was more tax beneficial to put a car on a short lease deal. In July realising that the existing car agreement would come to fruition in September we decided to look for another Volvo cabriole but were told by the Volvo dealer that they had discontinued that model so we visited the BMW garage in Wilmslow to see if they had a similar model which they did or could have because of the extras we required the car would have to be ordered from the factory and would take about 3 months. This was one of those occasions were the salesman was the man's friend and totally ignored Grace, it was only when I informed him that it was she who was buying the car that he changed his attitude and brought her into the conversation and listened to her requirements. He must never have been informed that it's the woman who makes the final decision when it comes to the crunch. Eventually the deal was done and to our surprise the salesman said that as we'd come in July there was an extra £1000 off, an even better deal. I've never been one to show off a new car so when the car was delivered at the end of September I just left it on the car park and within minutes Mick the builder came in and asked if that was our new car, I asked how he knew that and he remarked that I was the only person he knew that could afford a car like that. Not long after P... Head came in and said it was the nicest car he'd ever seen; yes it did look smart, the champagne colour shining in the late afternoon sunshine.

Later that month we took ourselves of to Dubai leaving Edi in charge, the weather in Dubai was just starting to cool to a barmy 35° which was very pleasant.

Grace and I enjoy each other's company and since Brian's death we never went on holidays with anyone else but now that we'd been at the Edge for 20years we'd become friends with many people but never too pally pally as we liked to go where and when we wanted, gone had the days when we were organised by Pauline. Of these friends I suppose we were closest to John and Claire, Cindy and Dave, Andy and Sara, John and Julie, Keith and Jane, John and Lyn and of course Sara, Dave T. and Edi not forgetting our dear friends in Portugal Peter and Leslie and from Australia Kevin and Edie. Of course we mustn't forget our families who by now had diminished to just a few members on Grace's side and now that brother David had passed away in a nursing home I was left with son Barry who had reconciled himself with me in '13 and brother Rowli and his wife Lyn who we only saw every blue moon. Haley was with Ben in Basingstoke, he was still engaged in the Air Force, often on overseas duties but later this year he came out of this job and signed up to work for the government in a civilian capacity. Sister Sylvia had not been

heard of for years and my last known address was in 'Lanzagrotte', none of the family had
forgiven her for not attending Ada's funeral who had brought her up after Harry's death
and also babysat her son Graeme whilst she went out on the town. In this year I was
contacted out of the blue by Cousin Dorothy and her husband Phil, she being the daughter
of Auntie Jessie and Uncle Jim who used to live in Leyland, I remember the smell to this
day.

Grace's family consisted of Brother Bill and wife Pat who lived on Blackpool Rd. Their
son Billy lived in Penwortham along with wife Judith who had married in '94. The last
time we actually saw one another face to face was at Auntie Graces' funeral in '12 which
was held in Preston, her horse drawn coffin held up all the traffic on Blackpool Rd.
Auntie Graces' daughter Sylvia along with her long lost half caste grandson Keira was at
the wake along with other hopefuls as is usual at these events. Grace's sister Linda did not
attend because she lived in Narberth with husband Peter, this village lies in deepest
darkest South Wales and as of yet the two sisters had not made up after their contatante of
'92 but was to have a happy ending in'15 when their disagreement was patched up and
they became luvie dovie sisters once again. After the funeral Sylvia went back to living in
her mother's house in Ashton-on-Ribble, we never saw her again and in the years to
follow at her death she bequeathed any monies left after the sale of the house to a donkey
sanctuary. Cousin Bill was pig sick; he was upset because many family pictures and
memorabilia were destroyed.

Over our lives just think how many friends and acquaintances we've had the pleasure to
have come into contact with and now how few are we still in touch with which is a great
shame. Many of these friends have been lost because they have passed over, some we've
just lost contact with for whatever reason, lack of interest, moved apart, busy lives, broken
marriages where the new partner doesn't want to know anyone from their old past as has
happened in one of our oldest members of staff and her new partner's case. When I look
back at our old Christmas card list of about 200 in '12 I remember so many names that we
are now not in touch with, but I can still visualize all of them and hope they still remember
us.

In our local area the pub scene was or had changed dramatically over the past few years
with several public houses closing down due in some instances because of the ban on
smoking. Some pubs were just smoking/drinking bars and had been badly affected, others
closed because let's face it, they were inefficiently operated and others couldn't stand the
competition from operators like Wetherspoons who sold nearly out of date beer (sorry, late
dated) for next to nothing which left the breweries with no beer to destroy. The houses that
survived had been forced to up their game because of the scores on the doors, mystery
shoppers and Trip Advisor which was good for the punter but not necessarily for the
landlords profits and although the customer deserved better conditions they did not want
to pay higher prices to enable wages of the employees to go up as the Labour Government
was demanding in a White Paper.

Advertising has never been the top of my agenda as I've always believed in word of
mouth, this being the Be All and End All to any business. Customers are the best
barometer of any business's success, if you look after and nurture them they will follow
you but let them down they'll be off down the Rd. like a flash however much money you
spend on advertising. Ever since I started in the trade there were always the advertising
agents trying to get you to place an ad in this feature or that but after many years of
rejection from me they finally came to the realisation that I didn't advertise, that is until
the agency took on a newbie who thought he or she should try their luck, but always got
the same response 'We don't advertise'. Eventually even they gave up.

Over the years vegetarianism has had its moments, in the 60's it was a Hippie idol, in the
'80's most people would roll their eyes at the mere prospect of someone saying they were

a veggie but now it's the 'in' thing to be described as an 'arian' or 'an' at the end of their name as in vegetarian or vegan. Are these people doing it for health, religious, taste or sympathy reasons is for them to decide, but I consider that many of them have jumped on the band wagon because it's a fad thing to do. How many consider when dining out how the food they are eating has been cooked, it may say produced from plants on the packet but how many non plant food ingredients or surfaces does it come into contact with during the cooking process and do most chefs/cooks take the regime seriously? The supermarkets do seem to be making a big play for the veggie market, is it out of a sense of national health or climate change benefits or is it because plant based food is cheaper to produce? Time was ticking on and as we rolled into '15, no one apart from immediate family and Edi knew of our retirement plans. Only essential repairs were carried out but David kept up the general painting and minor repair regime to keep the premises in tip top condition and allay any gossip which would surely result if we allowed the rooms to look shabby and equipment was only replaced if it could not be repaired.

On a regular basis we would carry about £20.000 worth of stock split between wet and dry, wet being in the region of £17.000 so I decided that we should reduce this amount over the next 3 years to less than £10.000 so that when we left the new tenants would not have to find such a large sum on changeover day. To accomplish this it was decided to sell off much of the large stock of champagne which was a slow selling commodity as customers had turned over to Prosecco probably because of cost and whisky sales had plummeted so the large selection of malts had to go. To accomplish this I sold bottles of champagne at cut down rates and malts at 2/4/1 which went down well with the punters. For many years we had had an extensive wine list with some quite expensive wines but in general our customers' expectation was for a fine wine at £11 to £20 not £30 to £40 so as the expensive wines sold out I reduced the wine list to give the punter what they wanted to pay. The country at this time was going thru a lean time and the populous were pulling in their belts which showed in the dwindling economy with still more pubs and other business's going to the wall. We'd noticed that for some year's night time trade had diminished with customers going home earlier than say 10 years since when although I never actually rang a closing time bell there were now no customers wanting a drink much after 10.30 and therefore we'd be closing by 11pm. I thought it was just us but after talking to other licensee's they said they'd had the same experience, that is apart from the weekend late night bars in the town centre and of course the Horse Shoe in the countryside where Charles and Mary catered to the farming community who relied on the pub being open late into the night after they'd finished working in the fields.

In this year I upset a customer over a trivial matter which would normally have been forgotten but she did not want to forget and placed the matter on Congleton Chat. The complaint went viral and the fire was stoked by the Stella drinking lady that I had barred in '17. Anyone that had a gripe joined in, even some I had never heard of.

I.T. has a lot to answer for. In the end we got it taken down by complaining to the Chat hosts.

For my 67 birthday Grace treated us to a visit to Gilpin Lodge in the Lakes where the weather was unusually wet with floods over the whole area. As one taxi driver commented 'Don't worry we've got plenty of big holes to put the water in'. On this visit we did find a problem with all the foreign staff that hoteliers were being forced to employ because of the lack of British staff who had decided that they didn't want to do the subservient tasks of waiters and maids. This caused a language problem as many of these staff had very limited English comprehension, which in turn caused confusion when it came to ordering food or drink. I understand why this situation had arisen but at times I did think we were in a Eastern European country and at times our requests were delivered wrong. Also I think that in general they have a sad demeanour, perhaps because of their hard lives but however much you smiled at them there was never a friendly response which does not make for a happy holiday. At the end of our short stay both Grace and I commented with sad hearts that perhaps we had outgrown the Lakes and that it would be some time before we returned. Little did we know that it would be August '20 before we did?

I've always believed that the way I treat people is the way I'd want to be treated myself whether the person I'm conversing with is a pauper or a king. Over the years this has paid off as we've been treated in so many unexpected ways, free drinks, upgrades at hotels, little tit bits that came out of the blue and people just going out of their way to be nice. Sometimes customers asked us to omit or change an ingredient in a dish which in most cases was possible but sometimes they requested us to change the whole menu as was the case when 3 family members came to see us about a wake for their deceased mother. After they'd perused our funeral buffet menu they decided that their mother would not have liked about ¾ of the menu and therefore could we substitute those items with choices of theirs. As much as I didn't want to upset these ladies at this delicate time I had to inform them that what they were requesting was just too much and as such as we didn't mind altering 2-3 items, what they had been offered was our menu. I think in the end they went elsewhere as I didn't hear from them again. Let's face it; whatever we'd have done it would not have satisfied their deceased mother. God rest her soul. One lady wanted us to do afternoon tea for a funeral reception which we were not set up to do and another lady insisted that her guests to another wake be given a 3 course sit down meal which although I tried to talk her out of she insisted and out of the 30 she booked for only 12 stayed and actually had the full meal which we'd prepared for. Because of our proximity to the church next door we received many enquiries about funeral receptions from funeral directors and often directly from the deceased family members. I always made a point of talking to them myself assuring them of our undivided attention during their sad time. I often find that the family don't know what they really want or what to expect as perhaps it's the first time they have been left to deal with the passing of a loved one. From the very beginning of this distressing time their first contact may be the funeral director who will be able to give the family the information they need to proceed and it is often the F.D. who passes the family on to us. In the case of Garside's F.D. they would contact us and between us we would arrange the funeral details thereby relieving the family of all the tedious red tape and worry at this sad time. As I often say 'leave it to the professionals' which was certainly the case when it came to Martin Garside funeral directors.

I had come to understand when talking to strangers why Dr.s, dentists and other professionals don't say what they do for a job as in my case when I gave people this information all they wanted to talk about was their pub, my pub, price of beer etc. When away from work I tried to stay clear of discussing it but the one bad habit I had picked up over the years was saying hello and goodbye to punters in other pubs, must stop that. Also I've developed a roving eye, no not looking at girls but being aware of who's coming and going and what's going on around me so that I am on top of the game. I've noticed this with other landlords and sometimes they don't seem to be listening to your conversation, perhaps it's an affliction that affects us all.

From the word go mobile phones have been an athama to me and I have not allowed them to interfere with the day to day smooth running of the pub which I see in so many business establishments all around. Staff oblivious to the needs of customers whilst they finish off a conversation with a friend or loved one. All our staff were asked/informed that they should leave there mobiles in their coat or jacket pocket in the cloakroom during their working hours and if a family member had an urgent message for them they could use our landline.

Haley had by '15 settled in Basingstoke with Ben, they seemed very happy, her working at Slater's Outfitters and Ben working for the government. Barry married to Rachel was now back in touch after he'd one day walked into the pub, out of the blue which must have taken some courage as we hadn't been in contact for many years and I don't suppose he knew what sort of reception he'd get, but everything went well and sad times were soon forgotten.

Later this year we had a couple of other short breaks to make up for our disappointing trip to the Lakes in January. London for 2 nights and York for 3 nights using some of our IHG hotel points giving us free accommodation. However visiting Sorrento and Dubai later in the year didn't come as cheap but fortunately the business was doing well and who knows what lies around the corner?

In the olden days Grace and I would often have difficulty in deciding which restaurant to go to or when it came to changing the car which model to choose or which holiday destination we should decide upon. You know, I'd say let's go to so and so and Grace would say oh no I didn't like that last time, so I'd say well where do you want to go and Grace would say oh I don't know so we'd spend ages before we came to a decision, by which time we'd probably had an argument. So we decided that when a decision needed to be made it fell to Grace this week and I next week with no dissent from the other. We did this with holidays, cars, restaurants, days out and just about anything that needed a decision. Ok sometimes one of us made a mistake but we put that down to experience and it did lead to a smoother life. I'm sure all husbands can relate to this scenario.

In January of '16 Grace arranged a surprise holiday for me to visit Vienna for my birthday, see what I mean about me always getting away for my birthday at the end of January and us not being able to get away for Grace's birthday because it always fell on a BH at the end of May. Well the weather was freezing and when we got there the city was under a blanket of snow about a foot thick which we're not used to. Getting around was a nightmare and the food was typical eastern European with goulash, boiled beef and bony fish like perch. They do seem to like coffee and sweet cakes and pastries, on every street corner there was a coffee shop. A taxi dropped us off in the city and we trudged thru the snow looking for a cafe or restaurant when down a side street I espied an illuminated red sign, reminiscent of a Chinese sign so we struggled thru the snow towards it, when we arrived we discovered it was an Italian restaurant which looked like it had been there for years. The boss was called Giovanni and he greeted us like long lost friends to his busy, steamy authentic Italian trattoria. What a lucky find.

On our homeward journey the flight was delayed because the plane had to be de-iced for it to be able to take off and the snow on the runway was cleared by 6 tractors with huge scrapers attached to their fronts.

What a lot of restaurant owners and maitre de's don't understand is that they could increase their profit margins if they only allowed or encouraged diners to have a pre-meal drink before sitting at their table ('would you like to have a drink at the bar sir or miss?) and perhaps even order their meal whilst doing so, then sitting down and ordering wine or drinks for the table, it makes for a far more relaxed experience for the customer. I suppose this would not be the ideal scenario in a fast food outlet as all they want is quick in and out, but then that's not where you're going to spend a whole night or luncheon dining experience. I personally like to stand to drink and sit to eat.

In May our itchy feet took us on a short trip to Monaco and Monte Carlo where we visited the famous casino, we placed bets up to £10 and beat the bank, we won £50, wow!

Of all the times that we've been to Dubai I've never had sunburn but one afternoon in the Mediterranean sun and I turned bright pink, so off to the hotel bar for happy hour. Our hotel the Meridian was situated on Princess Grace Ave. on the shore of the Mediterranean Sea about 20mins walk from Monte Carlo. After exploring the town we decided to take a different route back to our hotel in the afternoon sunshine. The road we took kept rising up and up with the sea always on our right which I knew was taking us in the right direction but not realising that it was taking us well past our hotel. We trudged on and on until we came to a little linear village called Roquebrune Cap Martin where we found a little cafe called Bacchus which tended to our needs, a drink. When we told the customers how we had arrived at their village they were astounded how far we had walked that afternoon and after a light refreshment we were given guidance to our hotel about 3 miles away which didn't take that long as it was all downhill, much of it along the coast where several luxury hotels were situated into which we paid a short nosey visit to see how the other half lived. That night we paid a return visit to the cafe Bacchus for dinner but went in a taxi.

Over the years we've employed many staff, some long term and young ones who disappear off to uni. when their time comes, often returning in the holidays which fitted in well with our busy periods, like summer and Christmas. Older staff tended to do the work as a top up to their full time jobs just for a bit of beer money or holiday fund as in James and Becky's case who worked for us for many years. Ever since Pam had left I'd tended to do the bar on my own at lunchtime and staff came in at night time, except if we knew that there was to be a wedding or funeral when I'd try and opt in some staff. One of the kitchen staff who'd worked for us for some time was Tom Jackson who on finishing uni had gone travelling around the world for the summer. In early August it was reported on the t.v. that a young British man had been injured in Australia whilst trying to stop a girl being attacked. The young man was Tom and unfortunately the girl had died from her injuries and Tom was severely injured and on life support. It was a very brave act for Tom to take and with no thought for his own safety he had waded in, which is just what we would have expected of him. His parents flew out to be by his bedside and we all hoped for his speedy recovery. Grace and I were flying to Dubai at the end of August after BH and we had just sat on the plane with the t.v. on when on the news we were informed that Tom had passed away in Australia. The stewardess's couldn't understand why we were crying but were very understanding when we told them the reason. It was big news all around the world and Tom was later awarded an Australian medal of courage for trying to rescue the girl. The funeral was held at St. Mary's and we hosted Toms wake where 400 family, friends and school mates attended to show Toms family in how much esteem he was held. What a brave man. Grace and I were proud to have known Tom and been part of his life.

As time went from '16 to '17 I realised that our time at the Edge was coming to a conclusion which I was not looking forward to but there was so much to organise before our move to wherever? It was a little like leaving Beeston, no one had any knowledge of our plans, we had nowhere to go and we had so much to do. After much deliberation between Grace and I we decided it would be wiser to go and live in our house at Westholme Cl. which at present was rented out and it was only fair that we should give the tenants plenty of notice to quit, which we intended to do in March '17 giving them 12 months to find somewhere else to live. We were trying to keep our plans private and we recognised that the tenants who were heavily involved in St. Mary's church could let the cat out of the bag, which in time they did. All this was done legally thru our solicitor RT Tony Birchall who had advised us on several other legal matters including our wills.

Prior to this in January we took a train journey to Edinburgh staying at the Crowne Plaza on Royal Terrace for a few days, the weather was bright and cold which gave us the opportunity to explore this magnificent historic city with the majestic sombre castle always standing to attention in the back ground. Princess St. is a Mecca for shopaholics along with the parallel St.'s of Princes St. Rose St. George St. and Queen St. There are also many bars where the Scottish au de vie or scotch is found in all its forms, no more so than the Whisky Club situated in the Balmoral Hotel where we had a delicious dinner in the Palm Court restaurant. The Whiskey Club bar room is surrounded with glass cases, floor to ceiling containing 1000's of bottles of the finest rare malts some costing a fortune, but I think the Scottish barman thought I was an uncultured Sasanack as I informed him that I had no desire to taste the array of malts as I didn't like it. Aye the nue.

I remember someone asking me when was the best time of the day to imbibe a fine malt whisky; I remarked that it went well with porridge. I remember in days long ago the west coast train line had been a pleasure to travel but both journeys to and from Edinburgh were a great disappointment, the carriages were unkempt and what service there was very sparse and unfriendly with a lack of snacks on the trolley, when or if it appeared at all on the long journey. Not to be repeated again for some time.

Our intention was to leave the pub at the end of our 4 year contract in June '18 but in April '17 Haley and Ben informed us that they intended to marry at Easter of '18 making it nigh on impossible for us to attend as a. it was Easter and b. she intended to invite several of the staff like Edi, Sara and others making the pub inoperable. Grace and I sat and discussed the situation we had been dealt and decided to go earlier than June, say March, but having traded thru this post Christmas period for 23 years I knew that we actually make a slight loss during Jan, Feb and March so why not go a little earlier, say November'17 just prior to Christmas, so the die was cast and now we really did have to get moving.

Although we had no H.P. or long term leases hanging around our necks, we had signed contracts so that we could get favourable prices by promising to stay loyal to certain suppliers like utilities and other services, amongst these were; B.T. Streamline the c/c Co. Sky, Spotify, Scottish Power, British Gas, Money Soft, United Utilities and Biffa Waste. Most accepted our notice of intention to retire from the trade but B.T. held us to our 3 year business contract even after we left, Biffa made us buy out of our 2 year agreement and Streamline sent a demand letter saying that we had not returned their equipment on our retirement and demanded we give hundreds of £'s in compensation to which I replied, telling them to get their act together as I had proof of return by Royal mail. Never heard any more.

I've never been a believer of taking out equipment or services on long term hire purchase or lease as say bathroom/toilet soap dispensers and air fresheners offered by Co.'s like P.H.S. who fit all the essential equipment at a lowish cost for each item but over a year that cost can amount to 100's of £'s and you could go and buy similar equipment for very little and over two years you'd have paid off the original amount, but the Co. will be charging you for that equipment for many years to come and if you hit lean times you still have to pay and you'll find you're tied into a very long contract. Well they have to make a return on their investment, that's business. Doesn't Public Health Services sound like a necessary government health authority, which I think is a bit of a con?

Just think how easy it is to set up a business by hiring, leasing or putting all the equipment on hock, but one day it's all got to be paid for.

In April we had a day out in Chester with Grace going shopping, me taking only a little time shopping and then visiting a couple of city boozers before meeting Grace at the Grosvenor Hotel for lunch in the Brassiere as the Arkle restaurant did not open weekday luncheons. However we did meet for an aperitif (glass of wine and bottle of some unknown foreign lager) in the Arkle bar prior to lunch. We settled in a booth in the brassiere, chose the food and asked to see the sommelier to give us some advice about our choices of wine. At 1.30pm, lunchtime we were informed that the sommelier was not available as he was on his lunch. On his lunch? I looked at Grace; she looked at me, each giving each other that look, we stood up and left leaving enough money to cover the cost of the bar bill.

Of all the restaurants around the world the Arkle has been one of the finest ever since

Simon Radley became head chef in '98. His finest dishes included foi gras and boned quail, the cheese board was to die for and the bread selection baked by Paul Hollywood was sublime as were the floating islands.

Over the years we have had the privilege to visit some of the greatest restaurants in the world, one being at the Sharrow Bay Hotel where Colin Askriggs beurre blanc and Sticky Toffee Pudding put them in a class above all others. On our visit to Barbados the Sandy Lane Hotel produced the finest, lightest tempura vegetables and in Sorrento we had panzenella at Oparruchiano, so simple and tasty. In Dubai our favourite restaurant the seafood bar and grill situated in the One and Only Royal Mirage Hotel on the banks of the Gulf serves up a sensational seafood platter and octopus tentacle simply grilled. Last but not least is Maxims where the Grand Marnier soufflé was as light as the clouds even if the pheasant was slightly over shot. With hindsight I wish I'd claimed for these meals as business work development outings on our tax returns, but perhaps the HMRC would not have been too happy. Who knows?

The date we had settled on to leave was the 30th November so at the end of May'17 I sent a letter to Mr Peter Robinson giving him 6 months notice of my intention to retire from the Egerton. The cat was by now well and truly out of the bag, we did inform one or two senior staff of our intentions asking them to keep it quiet for the time being, but of course the news slowly crept out and soon became common knowledge. Remember never tell a secret to anyone and not expect it to not become common Knowledge very quickly.

To get away from all the gossip, rumours and concerned questions we took off to Dubai to enjoy a last holidays before returning to concentrate on our leaving plans which were by now well underway.

During our period at the Egerton I had been approached to join by all the three local Rotary clubs, Biddulph, Congleton and Congleton Dane, also Congleton Masonic Lodge but I had always politely refused because if I had a decision to make about a plan to do this or that I would make the decision myself, after of course consulting Grace. I could not wait for a committee to decide whether I should proceed with the said plan. That just isn't me.

Over the years we had collected so many items, like pictures, books, ornaments and general bric-a-brac and I knew we had to unload it somehow.

We had made a decision that we were not taking the pub to the house, so many of the pub ornaments and pictures would stay with the pub, for which we would be recompensed as F&F. Little did we realise how little recompense that was to be as the value for these bits and bobs would be what they would fetch at auction. I had once been involved in a book club and over the years had amassed a great collection of books, the sets and private ones I kept but sold over 400 to customers @ £2 each. With hindsight I wish I'd kept some more books and other items which I left. Ash and Lesanne threw out much of what we left when they took over, but more of that later.

Later in the year we organised a car boot sale to be held in the pub car park where I managed to off load a stack of goods for 5 bob here and 10 bob there, with some pieces going for good money but some seasoned car booters tried to knock down items for silly money but in the end I achieved good money and was happy with the outcome but sad to see some of the pieces I'd collected over the years go, such as a set of Babycham bambis and old style Babycham glasses which would hopefully go to other happy homes, but probably to other car boot sales. Life and bric-a-brac go round and round.

I advertised an old roll top cabinet which I'd picked up at Beeston Auction that wouldn't fit in the new house and a bent wood coat stand that had spent the last few years stored away under the eaves at the pub. The huge array of Christmas decorations stored away since last Christmas had to be left because they suited big rooms and our new abode was tiny in comparison to the hotel but we did take one small tree and all our private dec's and fairy lights including the old fairy that had adorned the top of the tree since the year dot. Sara had a root thru the dec's and took some items to decorate Sandbach Cricket Clubs pavilion where she had the rights to do the catering on club days and other club events. She was to retire when we left but Edi had decided to stay on with most of the staff. Robinsons had advertised for a new licensee to take on the Hotel or as by now called Inn and after several interested parties had been escorted around the property the list was whittled down to Ash and Lesanne. Ash had worked for us for 14 yrs. and in Robinson's eyes probably appeared to be their best bet, but we were just keen for them to find a suitable candidate to take the pub on so we could vacate before Christmas. Many of the other interested parties had dropped out because they could see that there was a vast amount of hard work involved and they would either have to pay staff to do the tasks or do it themselves, which Grace and I did. Ash however did not appreciate all the work involved because he only worked 4½ days a week, never on a Christmas Day, New Years Day or a B.H. and never started before 10.00am when much of the work and prep had been done, including the breakfasts. This was to prove his and Lesanne's nemesis.

Many people underestimate how much work goes on behind the scenes, not just in the leisure industry but in the running of any successful business, they only see how smooth everything appears but in the background, staff and management are beavering away in order to make the operation appear flawless, but you've got to put the work in to reap the benefits, or work hard to play hard as Grace and I did.

In the summer of '17 the owner of one of the properties of the Billsborrow Hall picture I'd had since Preston Cattle Market days came back to ask if I was ready to sell the lithograph print of the hall and estate properties. Well what an opportune moment as on our retirement the picture would have had no interest to anyone else and would probably have been worth very little, but he didn't know that. After a long discussion and lots of head shaking and hand wringing we agreed on a price of just short of £1000 with £30 luck money. That really wasn't a bad investment, 2 pints of Toby Light to just short of a grand. Another picture I sold for £250 was a rather raunchy skiing picture we'd been given by Art and Maggie after their trip to Brackenridge skiing resort in America. The drawing showed nude skiers in comical poses with artistically placed skis and other equipment saving their embarrassment but leaving the viewers to their imagination. Although the picture was placed in the entrance to the gents' loo, away from easily offended view it attracted a lot of attention from young boys and some ladies. Bit of harmless fun.

By now Robinson's had appointed Ash as the new licensee to take over the hotel, now classified as an Inn by the AA so as not to confuse say the Ritz Hotel with the Egerton Country Inn which I thought sounded quite nice and summed up what we were.

In September '17 the brewery sent a valuer to value our fixtures and fittings which Ash was to pay us on the removal day or so we assumed as that had invariably occurred in the past. The few items we wished to take with us were put to one side and the valuer went from room to room assessing the value of everything from curtains, carpets, chairs, tables pictures, ornaments, anything that wasn't nailed down that belonged to us. In the 23 years we'd been at the Edge we had collected and paid for many items including kitchen, restaurant and bedroom fittings, some getting on a bit but still essential to the running of the business and to us worth their weight in perhaps not gold, but certainly silver,

However the valuer did not have quite the same idea and some items he was disparaging about, valuing them at little more than fire sticks which was depressing and his valuation fell far short of my expectations. He asked me how much I thought the F&F was worth, I said about £70.000, he estimated £35.000 which came as a shock to me, but after a short discussion he upped his valuation to £40.000 which was at least a little better. It only came out on the final removal day that it was actually Robinson's that were paying for the F&F and not Ash as we assumed, so in fact the valuer was working for Robinson's not Ash.

Conflict of interest would you say? We also had to wait several weeks to be paid which had not been pointed out to us at any stage of the removal process.

Unknown to me on the Sunday, our final trading day a host of friends, family and customers descended on us in the afternoon to give Grace and I a send off party. We received many, many bunches of flowers, champagne and other gifts to speed us on our way. Several staff's parents thanked us for bringing up their kids whilst they had been in our care, especially Leslie and Rob Lomas who actually cried whilst giving us their thanks. At the party I managed to give away lots of old spirits like cherry brandy, Benedictine and Advocatt, which I didn't think the stock taker would include in the stock take, everybody had a good time, and we had a memorable send off.

The removal men came and moved us on the Saturday, wrapping and packing up all the ornaments and struggling with the larger furniture down the small staircase. Thank goodness that Haley and Ben had come for the weekend to help with the move and enjoy our last few days at the pub. On Sunday Barry also came with his wife Rachael and at the end of trading after Sunday lunch they and Haley helped themselves to any food items that would otherwise be dumped in the bin. Staff also had a plethora of goodies which would only have been thrown in the bin.

Some of the big items of furniture like our wardrobes would have necessitated them being dismantled by Arigi Bianci who had fitted them some years prior and the settee and arm chair had entered the lounge by us having to take out the front window which I did not want to do again. So I asked Dave T. to come up with a price that was acceptable to both parties for Ash to keep them. I was distraught to leave all the bedroom furniture including a 6 piece fitted wardrobe, a matching dressing table, super king size bed, 2 large teak wardrobes, matching teak mirrored dressing table and the settee and arm chair, David came up with a figure of £600 which he thought I was lucky to get. Ash must not have believed his good fortune and snapped my hand off. Thinking about all the dismantling by professional workmen, the cost and all the upheaval, perhaps David was right in his assessment, but it hurt.

On departure day the stock taker arrived to count all the bottles, dip the barrels of beer and lager and assess how much food stock there was to hand over to Ash and Lesanne. Grace and I had both counted our stocks on cessation of trading the day prior, tallied up and come to a final amount. The stock taker was surprised when I informed him that we had already counted the stock and he asked me how much we had come to, I said I would tell him after he had finished. From experience I know that stock takers don't like doing food stocks so he asked Grace what final figure she had got for all the food and ancillaries, he accepted her figure without actually checking anything and when he'd counted the wet stock he gave us slightly more than my assed figure, in all about £10.000, happy days.

The only remaining task was to read the electric, gas and water meters which was left to the Robinson's DM Wayne Roach who said he'd pass on the figures to the relevant Co.'s. After we had departed Ash and Lesanne had obviously decided to put their own stamp on their new venture, the King is dead, long live the King and many of the items that were still insitue that they'd paid for as part of the F&F were dumped, they'd decided to erase all recognition of our time at the Egerton which had for the past 23 years proved a very profitable business, thereby throwing the bath out with the bath water.

There were so many bunches of flowers that we gave them to the Laurels care home on Canal Rd. for the residents to enjoy. This property had been the house where John Seddon was brought up until some of its land was compulsorily purchased by the council to build the Daven housing estate which stretched all the way from Canal Rd. to Park Lne.

That's what happens in life, it moves on and you've got to move with it.

After finalising all the stocktaking and paperwork that we needed to sign we set out on our new venture, but first a trip to DV8 for a quick one or two.

After six months of retirement
I am now proud and happy.

Printed in Great Britain
by Amazon

81957868R00078